THE WILD BUNCH

A Western Story

DANE COOLIDGE

SAGEBRUSH
Large Print Westerns

Copyright © Golden West Literary Agency, 2003

First published in Great Britain by ISIS Publishing Ltd.
First published in the United States by Five Star

Published in Large Print 2012 by ISIS Publishing Ltd.,
7 Centremead, Osney Mead, Oxford OX2 0ES
by arrangement with
Golden West Literary Agency

British Library Cataloguing in Publication Data
Coolidge, Dane, 1873–1940.
The wild bunch.
1. Western stories.
2. Large type books.
I. Title
813.5'2–dc23

ISBN 978–0–7531–8997–9 (pb)

Printed and bound in Great Britain by
T. J. International Ltd., Padstow, Cornwall

CHAPTER
ONE

It was June when the summer rains begin, and, as the first great thunder caps mounted majestically along its rim, the tawny San Augustine Plains lay quivering in the heat. The white bed of the sink, now dry and glistening with alkali, became a lake once more in mirage. A circle of blue mountains, half lost behind the horizon, reached up gaunt phantom fingers to the sky, but the storm cloud to the west sucked all the moisture to itself, spreading out to cover the peaks behind Show Low. It rose higher into the heavens, gleaming like silver in the sun, and, as its base turned black, a slender trailer of rain reached down and touched the earth. There was a flash, a lightning stab, a zigzag of flickering light, and then long after came the rumble of distant thunder and the solemn reverberation of the hills. A wind sprang up, rushing straight from the east into the swelling bosom of the cloud, and the cattle raised their heads and lowed. The burnished dome of the cloud rose higher till it cut off the sun and wind. There was a silence, a tense waiting, and out on Rustlers' Flat a lone cowboy turned his back and took the storm.

It swept down from the hills in a wall of falling water that roared like wind in the pines, and a cloud of dust

1

rose up in its path, where the heavy drops struck into the dirt. The sky was ripped open by a jagged streak of lightning and the horse cringed back on his haunches. At the crash of thunder he jumped and fought for his head, trying to break away and run for the hills, but the man on his back reined him around in dizzy circles and stopped him with his tail to the storm. So they stood, the horse trembling — and the man trembling, too, for it brought up old fears in his breast. As the earth seemed to rock beneath a second terrific crash, he gave the plunging broncho his head. Across the broad flat they went like the wind, and up a gulch and on through the rain, but, as they galloped over the ridge into Center-Fire Cañon, the cowboy pulled up with a jerk. There was a shod horse track in the mud not half an hour old and it was heading for the Figure 4 pasture.

Abner Meadows leaned forward and scanned the tracks closely, then paused and glanced warily about. There was a Wild Bunch in the hills, robbing trains and stealing horses and hiding in the lava beds to the north, and this was no Figure 4 horse. He knew, for he had shod every one for two years — and broken most of them, too — and their tracks were as familiar to his practiced eye as a baby's little bonnet to its mother. This horse was long and rangy, with exceptionally small hoofs, and he had been ridden at a swinging gallop — but where, and with what purpose? Meadows's hand slipped down to where his gun should have hung and he looked at the tracks again.

"Well, here goes nothing," he said at last, and spurred along the trail.

The Figure 4 Ranch lay in a narrow, sheltered valley that opened out on the plains at Show Low, and the rich green *vegas* that lined the watercourse had been fenced to make a thousand-acre pasture. Twice already within a month this pasture had been entered and the top horses of the remuda taken, and in their places other animals had been left which showed marks of quirt and spur, and then, mysteriously, the stolen horses had been returned and the other animals taken away. Only now it was the top horses that were ridden down and quirt cut and the mounts of the outlaws were fat. No one had seen the horse thieves when they came or when they went, and no one had ridden in pursuit. The times were troublous and men prospered best who minded their own affairs, but everyone knew it was Butch Brennan's gang and that they passed that way to the railroad.

The storm that had driven Abner Meadows to the hills passed by as suddenly as it had come. As the sun burst out, his spirits rose, also, and he followed the trail at a lope. The tracks grew fresher, although still half full of water. They were heading now not for the Figure 4 pasture, but for the mouth of a boxed-in cañon. Up that, as Meadows knew, there were caves in the sandstone that offered a shelter from the rain. As he approached the entrance, he reined in to a walk and his hand sought the holster in his chaps. It was empty, of course, but old instincts are strong, and he rode with his hand beneath the flap. In the freshly formed mud not a sound was made as his horse swung around the point. Then, before he knew it, he came upon his man, crouched down like a rabbit in a cave.

He was a dark, handsome man, with a high Texas hat and a long-handled pistol in his belt. His eyes, big and startled, leaped from Meadows's face to the hand inside his chaps. It was there, and not in belts that dangled and flopped, that most cowboys carried their guns. As Meadows returned his stare, he saw in a moment the cause of the fugitive's panic. On the smooth rock before him, laid out in orderly piles, each held down by a pebble or stick, was more paper money than one comes by honestly, spread out in the sun to dry. So complete was his surprise that the robber's left hand still held to a great sheaf of bills, and his right, that should have been handy to his gun, was stretched out to lay down a fresh stack. He had frozen like a rabbit or any wild animal that knows the cold terror of being hunted, and now, as he watched, only his eyes seemed to move, although his hand was drawing back toward its belt. It would have been safer by far for Abner Meadows if he had come upon a grizzly over its kill, for at a single false move this wild Texas fighter would shoot him before he could wink. But now the man was frightened and, believing himself covered, his desire was to placate and stall.

"Good evening," he said, slowly laying down the bills, while his lips drew back in a smile.

Meadows nodded grimly. "How-do," he returned with another glance at the money. "I see you've made a good haul."

4

"Damned right," agreed the bandit, picking up a bunch of twenties. "How'd ye like a little stake for yourself?"

"Nope," answered Meadows, "don't let me deprive you. I was just coming by when I cut your tracks, and I thought it might be one of the boys."

"Oh," observed the robber, and his tense face relaxed as he sensed the ring of truth. "Riding for Starbuck?" he inquired, going on with his work like a man who resumes a game of solitaire, and Meadows slumped down easily in his saddle.

"Breaking bronchos," he replied, and, as the talk went on, he withdrew his pistol hand from his chaps.

"Nice horse you got there," spoke up the outlaw at last, looking at the broncho with a quick, appraising eye. Then he rose slowly to his feet. His hands, which all along had been so carefully outstretched, dropped naturally down to his sides. As Meadows made no move, the right one crept back toward the rag-wrapped butt of the long pistol. Meadows saw the wolf look blaze up suddenly in his eyes, and then he was facing a gun.

"Put 'em up, dad-burn ye!" shrilled the outlaw violently, "up high, or I'll blow you to hell!" He stepped up closer, jabbed the pistol into Meadows's ribs, and reached inside his chaps. "Where's your gun?" he demanded, feeling fretfully about, and then he broke into a curse. "You ain't *got* none!" he repeated. "Well, by the holy, jumping Judas, why the devil didn't you say so before? Git down offen that horse and let me search them boots . . . how come you don't pack a gun?"

5

"Don't need one," answered Meadows, and the bandit grinned cynically as he stepped over and gathered up his money. He stuffed the half dry bills into the slack of his wet shift, and then he broke into a laugh.

"Like hell you don't!" he said at last. "Do you know how much reward I've got on me? Well, it's nigh onto fifty thousand dollars!"

"I haven't lost any reward," returned the cowboy shortly, and the outlaw chuckled to himself.

"All right, pardner," he said, "let it go at that. And now, if you don't mind, we'll just trade horses for a spell . . . my mare is plumb rode down."

"You're the boss," returned Meadows, and, stripping off her saddle, he transferred it to the bandit's tired mount. It was a tall and golden-bright sorrel, with wonderfully muscled shoulders and chest, and the slenderest of slender legs. At first glance she looked like a Thoroughbred running horse, but the small, flint-like hoofs and flowing mane and tail spelled broom tail, without a doubt. It was one of the thousands of hardy mustangs that ranged on the far North Plains and that Butch Brennan and his gang, in the interval between robberies, took a wild delight in chasing.

"Take care of that horse," admonished the outlaw, "I'll be back to git her someday."

"All right," assented Meadows, "and, if you don't mind my suggesting it, be as easy on that colt as you can."

"That'll depend," observed the bandit, cinching his saddle up tighter, and then he tied a bulging mailbag on behind and hung a pair of Mexican saddlebags across the horse. These last were filled to the very top with something that was heavy as lead, and, as he balanced them up, he grabbed out a handful of silver dollars and threw them impatiently away.

"Well, so long," he said as he swung up into the saddle, but now that he was free to ride off when he pleased, he seemed in no hurry to go. "Say," he began, with an ingratiating smile, "have you been working for old Starbuck long? I need a young feller like you to kinder keep a lookout around here . . . how'd you like to make a little easy money? All you'd have to do would be to watch out for the officers and give me a change of horses . . . and I reckon we wouldn't quarrel about the pay."

He slapped his shirt and laughed indulgently, showing teeth that were long and thin and white, yet no wider than those of a squirrel. They gave him a curious, cat-like look, as though in another mood they might sink into the flesh and rip and crunch and rend. But Meadows, although he was loath to oppose the man, drew back and shook his head.

"Nope," he said, "little out of my line. Just as much obliged, but I'll work for what I get . . . Dave Starbuck is a pretty good boss."

"But he'll never know," urged the outlaw eagerly. "Ain't you worked for him now for two years? Well, slip me the horses and say nothing to nobody . . . come on, boy, it's the chance of your life."

"No!" returned Meadows suddenly meeting his eye, and the train robber bared his teeth in a sneer.

"Oho!" he said, "you think you're too good, hey? Don't want no truck with the Wild Bunch! Well, lemme tell you something, my young Christian friend, you want to be careful what you say. I might take a notion to pull out my pistol and . . ."

"That's all right," broke in Meadows, his eyes beginning to burn. "I told you, and that's enough!"

"O-o-o!" shrilled the robber. "Say, you're a hot-tempered boy, ain't ye? I'm going to quit riding you, right now. But, jest between friends, how come you to be out here without your gun in your chaps?"

"Got into trouble one time," answered the cowboy grimly, "by having a gun too handy. Anything else you'd like to pry into?"

"No, that's all," replied the outlaw with a cheerful grin. "So long . . . jest wanted to know."

He threw the spurs into the half-tamed broncho but, as the animal plunged forward, grabbed into one of his saddlebags. "Take that, you damned fool!" he called over his shoulder, and threw a handful of money at Meadows. It fell at his feet in a golden shower — seven twenties, fresh and gleaming from the mint — easy money, to take or to leave.

CHAPTER
TWO

The outlaw galloped away, grinning mockingly as he glanced back, and Abner Meadows looked down at the money. It was stolen, beyond a doubt, and the man who had left it was one of Butch Brennan's big gang. Twice already since spring they had robbed the train at Belen, and half of New Mexico was their stamping ground. There were badmen from Texas, and ex-rustlers from Montana, and outlaws from all over the West. Loud in their boasts that no Mexican could arrest them, they rode the Western ranges at will. They robbed trains and looted stores, held up stages and ran off cattle, shot up towns and killed officers of the law, and in a Mexican-governed territory, with Mexican sheriffs and deputies, there was no man to say them nay. For, with all their faults, they were clean-strain fighting men, and the native population was afraid of them.

The time had been, in the early days of the occupation, when all the officials were Americans. There was an American governor, appointed by Congress, and judges and officers of the law. But those days were past and the newly enfranchised Mexicans had asserted their right to rule. Voting three to one, they had overwhelmed the white minority and elected their own officials. In Papalote County, where the Figure 4 range lay, they had swept everything before them. Yet, while Celso Baca, their so-called fighting sheriff, sat idly in his office at Papalote, half the outlaws of the West swarmed into his domain and set up a law of their own. They rode from ranch to ranch over all the wild country that lay west of the San Augustine Plains, and then they rode north, over the Datils and the Sawtooth Range, to the plains and lava beds beyond. If any lonely rancher tried to betray them to the Mexicans, they treated him as a traitor to his kind.

The gold lay there in the mud, just as it had been taken from the safe when this bandit had held up the train. As Abner looked it over and thought what it might portend, he turned and rode hastily away. There would be officers on the trail, and not all Mexicans, either, for the express company had hired guards of its own. If he were caught with the money in his possession, the affair would be hard to explain. Yet, as he came out into the valley and found it still vacant, he halted and looked over his shoulder. The money was still lying there, fresh and gleaming by the trail, and the first cowpuncher that rode past would come back to the ranch with big tales of a treasure trove. He would show the shining twenties and the stray silver dollars that the reckless Texas robber had left, and, if Abner Meadows claimed to have seen the money first, they would whoop and laugh him to scorn. But if he gathered it up now and hid it in some hole — Meadows turned back and rode for the cave.

Yes, the money was still there, but, as he looked for a hiding place, something told him to keep it in his pocket. It was his, for he had found it, and, if he hid it near that spot, the chances were good that it would be found. There would be a pursuit, a hunt through the hills, and, since the fleeing outlaw had taken shelter there from the storm, the cave and the cañon would be searched. But down by the ranch, or up on Sawed-Off Mountain where he had his lookout point, no one would ever come and he could leave it hidden until Brennan and his gang were forgotten. A hundred and forty dollars, with the silver dollars to boot, was some money for a hard-working cowboy. Put with some more that he had saved, it would hasten the day when he could have a little ranch of his own, and if he had a home . . . He thrust it in his chaps and swung up onto the sorrel.

The mare was gaunt and worn, but spirited still. As he put her to a lope, he saw that few pursuers could hope to catch her even now. Although she was a broom tail from the North Plains, she was a Thoroughbred still, the descendant of some Morgan or Kentucky hunter that had escaped from the emigrant trains. When he pulled her to a walk and patted her neck, she gazed back with soft, luminous eyes. Yes, she was a beautiful horse, but she was the property of an outlaw — they got the best of everything.

A single trail led along the pasture fence that ran far east and then south without a gate, and, as he came to the southern corner, he kept on to the butte named Sawed-Off Mountain. This was no more than a round hill, shaved off flat on top, standing out on the point of the mesa. On the farther side it broke off in short benches to the treeless valley below. There in the midst of a huddle of corrals and adobe houses stood the store and saloon called Show Low, a mere nothing in itself, but the last outpost to the west of a shuffling and precarious civilization. There at least was food and drink, a stock of clothes, and mail once a week from Papalote, while beyond for a hundred miles to the Arizona line there was nothing but scattered ranch houses, tucked away among the hills. It was a town, and to make good its claim there was a schoolhouse on the bench beyond.

It was on this building, in fact, that Meadows's eyes were fixed, for Starbuck's flock of children made up half of the attendance and the schoolteacher lived at the ranch. Every afternoon, at four o'clock or later, she came galloping up the road, and it had come to be his habit when he was out riding bronchos to accompany her home from school. The bronchos must be taught to start and stop, and to turn at the touch of the reins, and where he rode them was nothing to the boss as long as they were broken.

To the boss' son, Lute, the matter was somewhat different, for he often watched for the schoolteacher himself, but since he did his waiting in Chris Woolf's saloon and store, his company was not always so welcome. Justina Edwards had a special reason for disliking both Woolf and his saloon, and so she rather favored the silent Abner Meadows who followed her with such worshipful eyes. But today all was changed,

12

for his eyes were narrow and furtive, and he hoped for once that she was gone. There was the money to be buried and the robber's mare to be turned out — but she had seen him as he rode out on the point and was galloping up the road to meet him. He glanced about hastily, threw the silver dollars down a dog hole, and rode moodily down the hill.

The air was sweet with the incense of wetted cedar and the fragrance of storm-lashed pines. On the *vegas* below the fat prairie dogs were running to sit by their holes as they passed, but when she dashed up with a radiant smile, Abner Meadows barely met the schoolteacher's eyes. They were too honest, too serious, too much given to questioning glances and unspoken feminine reproaches — and now he had one more thing to hide. The exact history of his past life had never been revealed to anyone since he had come to Figure 4 — all Starbuck knew, or wanted to know, was that he was a good man at gentling horses — and now, of course, here was this meeting with the outlaw that no one but the boss must know. He smiled a fleeting welcome, then dropped his eyes and rode silently along at her side.

An admiring artist, who she had met by accident at an alfresco bohemian spread, had confided to Justina over his second glass of wine that she looked like Botticelli's "Queen of Spring". Later on in the evening he amended his opinion to include also a "Mona Lisa" smile and was frankly desolated when, upon later inquiry, he discovered that she had gone to New Mexico. Not really gone, but returned, for this fair, demure maiden with her long lashes and peace-destroying smile had sprung by some magic from that land of untamed savages and swarthy, treacherous Mexicans. There her father had been a scout, living alone in the wilds with his wife and little daughter until death had stepped in and the daughter, left alone, had been sent to New York to be educated. So much the artist learned, with the additional fact that her scout father had been suddenly killed. There that story ended and another story began, only now no one likened her to spring.

She was the schoolteacher in a place that had once been her home and that her Indian-fighting father had owned and ruled as absolutely as any border baron, but now it was claimed by a clerk in the store who had won it at a turn of the cards. He was a dark, unctuous person, suspected of being half Mexican, and he had appeared from nowhere and gone to work for her father, who had soon placed him in charge of the store. That was the beginning of his downfall, for the shrewd Woolf had sensed his weakness and insisted upon installing a bar, and then, in the mad carousals that followed, he had won all his money and the store. But Edwards was a cattleman, and even in his madness he still held fast to his herds until, in a passion, he staked them against Woolf's winnings, the loser to walk off and leave everything. The game was seven-up and Woolf had won six points, catching the jack and holding high, when the old scout made his last stand.

"Show low!" he shouted, striking his fist on the table. "Show low, and the ranch is yours!" Chris Woolf had thrown down the deuce and christened the ranch Show Low.

Whether he had used any tricks in dealing the cards is something that will never be known, for he was surrounded by his own gang of men, but Edwards rose up and went out into the night, and the next morning was found shot through the heart. It was to such a tragedy as this that Justina had been summoned, and, when Woolf had shown her his bill of sale for the property, she had had no recourse but to go to work. The Starbucks took her in, delighted to get such a teacher, and for nearly a year she had ridden to and fro, glancing hatefully at the smiling Chris Woolf. But in spite of her troubles her beauty remained, demanding as of old its tribute of covert glances, pretty speeches, and avowals of love. The cowboys were her slaves — even Chris Woolf had made advances — but this lone, silent horsebreaker with his soft voice and gentle ways had so far resisted her wiles. He was a man of few words, yet if she read his eyes aright, he loved her more than all of them. There was something mysterious, like the veil over his past life, that he always seemed to draw between them, even as now when he rode on in silence.

"Well," she challenged, looking curiously at the strange mare and trying to rouse him from his reticence, "how's the man of mystery today?"

"Meaning me?" he inquired, with his slow, somber smile. "Rather damp . . . got caught in that storm."

"But the sun is out now," she went on rapturously. "Isn't the *vega* beautiful, now that the rain has come? Oh, I'd just like to ride and ride. Come on, let's go. But we'd better look out . . . there's some train robbers back in the hills!" She reined in closer, glancing furtively up the cañon, but, as he smiled indulgently, she pouted out her lips and met his glance defiantly. "Well, there are," she declared, "and Celso Baca and four deputy sheriffs are down at the store there, watching for them!"

"Honest?" he challenged, and, as she nodded her head, he looked back down the road.

"Yes, they are," she ran on, "and I saw one of them looking at you when you came out on the point of the mountain."

He drew in his lips and she smiled triumphantly, although not without a certain alarm.

"Oh, Ab," she exclaimed, "it isn't true, is it? You haven't thrown in with Butch Brennan!"

"Who was telling you that?" he demanded fiercely, touching the jaded mare with his spurs, and she considered before she spoke.

"Well . . . Lute," she said, "and all the boys. They don't say it . . . they just kind of wonder." She was riding close beside him, her horse fighting for his head as he sensed the challenge to a race, but she held him resolutely in. "Can't you see," she urged, "what a mistake you make by not telling us who you are? We all know there is something wrong and so . . . well, you see . . . what can we say when they claim you've gone wrong?"

"Say nothing," he retorted savagely. "What do you care where I came from as long as you know who I am? It's what a man *is* that counts."

16

"Oh, then you haven't thrown in with them?" she exclaimed with great relief, but at the same time she waited for his answer.

"No!" he burst out. "Of course I haven't! There's some people that talks too much."

"No, I didn't mean Lute," she broke in apologetically. "It wasn't he, any more than the rest. They were all saying last night that they wondered who you were, and that maybe you were an agent for Brennan. But Mister Starbuck broke in and told them to shut up . . . and then he went on and said lots of nice things about you, and that they'd better begin to worry about themselves."

"Well, they had," returned Meadows, and, as he looked back again, there was an angry glint in his eyes.

"And he said," she rushed on, trying to calm the rising storm, "that you were the best hand with horses he'd ever seen, and that he'd never even heard you swear, and that he liked to have you around, just to show his children that a cowboy didn't need to be tough."

She paused at last and glanced across at him hopefully, and the hard lines had disappeared from his face. Dave Starbuck was his friend, had been from the first, and his praise was sweet to his ears, but this talk of Brennan had reached him before, and somehow it always came from Lute.

"Well, come on," he said, as he sighted horsemen in the distance, "there are those Mexicans coming up the road. You see what I get from all this loose talk . . . they probably think they're going to arrest me."

He galloped in toward the ranch and Justina rode after him, but she refused to let her bay start a race. Meadows's last words had a sinister meaning that her ears had been quick to detect.

"But Ab," she appealed as he stopped at the ranch gate and turned to face the posse, "you surely don't intend to resist arrest?"

"Never mind," he said. "You go into the house. I'll attend to these gentlemen myself."

CHAPTER
THREE

The Figure 4 Ranch was a cluster of log buildings, half a mile up the valley from where the main road turned off over the mountains toward Arizona. A long, broad lane, made for driving herds of cattle, led up to the ranch house bars. As they turned into this raceway, the Mexican posse came spurring and lashing like madmen. They whirled in a half circle about the man at the gate, and, when they had covered him, Celso Baca dismounted and prepared to make the arrest.

"Uhn-huh!" he said as he walked in on Meadows who was watching him with narrowing eyes, "so we've ketched you, *Señor* Brennan, after all. Put them hands up a little beet higher."

"My name is not Brennan," answered Meadows quietly. "What do you think you're going to do?"

"Oh, yes, that's all right," wheezed the sheriff good-naturedly, and then he halted and drew back. Meadows's hands had come down and there was a look in his eyes that Baca had come to know. He was a big, strapping fellow — a light-complected Mexican like most of the office-holding class — but his experience in arresting cowboys had already convinced him that discretion is the better part of valor. So he halted abruptly and stood breathing hard — for the ride had got to his wind — while he beckoned his deputies in. Then as they spurred in closer, he heaved a great sigh and grinned at his man triumphantly.

In the meanwhile the commotion had brought Starbuck from the house, and he came with his gun in his hand. "What's the meaning of all this?" he inquired in his deep, rumbling voice, and even Celso Baca flinched. He was a big man himself, but not like Dave Starbuck who was a mountain of fighting strength, and instinctively the Mexican gave back. It was said of Starbuck that in his younger days, when he was mining in California, he had met a two-hundred-pound grizzly bear in the trail and, being without the butcher knife he ordinarily carried, had beaten him to death with his fists. However that might be, he had never neglected since to keep his trusty butcher knife in his boot. In addition to that he had now buckled on his pistol, besides having snatched up his rifle as he passed. He was a tall, raw-boned Yankee from the backwoods of Maine, with a gray beard as broad as a spade. As he glared at the deputies, they became suddenly less arrogant, for he was known to have a prejudice against their race. Yet Celso Baca had ridden too far to be easily robbed of his prey and he answered him back defiantly.

"Thees is nothing of your beezness, *Señor* Starbuck," he spat. "I have taken thees train robber for my preesoner. My men have chased him t'ree days!"

"Not him," returned Starbuck. "There must be some mistake . . . he's been right here at the ranch."

20

"Who . . . thees man here? Thees fellow, Butch Brennan? Not moch, we know him too well. We have chased that sorrel horse till we know her anywhere, and thees is the man who rode her."

He advanced upon Meadows with the sudden confidence that his words had roused in his breast, but once more he came to a halt. Dave Starbuck had climbed over the bars of the gate and was standing beside his broncho buster.

"Now, lookee here, Celso Baca," he said in warning tones, "don't drive a good citizen too far. I know you well, and the way you've been running things, letting these outlaws come in and steal my horses, but just because you can't get your hands on Butch Brennan is no excuse for arresting my horsebreaker. This boy is Ab Meadows . . . he's been working for me steady for nigh onto three years now . . . and he don't even carry a gun."

"Hain't he got no gun?" inquired Baca with sudden interest, and then he whipped out his handcuffs.

"No, but I have," answered Starbuck significantly, "and I'm here in the interests of justice. If this boy is a lawbreaker and you can prove it, I haven't got a word to say. But until that time comes, he's just like my son, and you nor nobody can touch him!"

"Well, he's riding that sorrel mare!" burst out Baca indignantly after addressing his deputies in Spanish. "And my men know that horse . . . they would know her anywhere . . . and they say they're certain she belongs to Butch Brennan."

"Where'd you get that horse?" demanded Starbuck of his horsebreaker, and Meadows answered promptly.

"That's easy," he said. "I met a fellow and he threw down on me and made me change horses. He's gone away on my bronc'."

"Good enough!" exclaimed Starbuck with a great sigh of relief. "You hear that? This man was held up. He met this danged outlaw and he made him trade horses. So that's all right, Mister Baca, quite a natural mistake, but you took a little too much for granted."

He laid his great hand on Meadows's shoulder and began to let down the bars, but at this the Mexican deputies, who had looked on uncomprehendingly, suddenly burst into a chorus of protests. Not understanding any English, they had improved the occasion to take another drink all around which, added to the liquor they had imbibed at Show Low, put their reason in total eclipse. All they knew was that this prisoner — the renowned Butch Brennan with forty-five thousand dollars on his head — was being led away by a single American while Baca looked on and swore. They surged forward in a body, yelling and brandishing their pistols. Baca, taking advantage of their pot-valiant impetuosity, plunged in and made a grab at Meadows. There was a struggle, the flash of handcuffs, then a sudden blow, and the sheriff staggered back, spitting blood.

"You keep your dirty hands off!" cried Meadows in fury, and Starbuck stepped before him with his gun.

"Now!" he roared, still holding his rifle on Baca. "Will you listen to reason, or not?"

"I am the sheriff!" screamed Baca, whipping out a silk handkerchief and pressing it against his bruised lips. "You have struck an officer of the law!"

"Yes, and I'll kill you," returned Meadows, "if you touch me again. I won't be arrested by no Mex!"

"You're drunk!" bellowed Starbuck, glaring accusingly at the posse. "Go on now, get out of here . . . all of you!" He made a threatening motion with the muzzle of his gun, but the Mexican deputies stood firm. They might be drunk, but they were not drunk enough for that — only they wanted their man alive. Most of the rewards on Butch Brennan called for his arrest and conviction, and how can you convict a dead man? So they stood their ground, their faces flushed and determined, while Baca poured out his anger on Dave Starbuck.

"Meester Starbuck," he cried, "I know what you have said about the eeneficiency of Mexican officials! You have said we are no good, setting the American people against us and making these damn' robbers bold, but now that I have thees outlaw in my power, I will not geev him up for no man. He must surely come with me!"

"Well and good," retorted Starbuck, "if you can show me some proof. But my wife and the children and the schoolteacher here have seen this man every day, and so I say he ain't the man you want, and I refuse to see him abused."

"Maybe he ain't Butch Brennan," conceded the sheriff grudgingly, "but he is a member of his gang. I was told at the store that you had a man in your employ who furnished these robbers fresh horses. So I arrest thees man as an accomplice of the gang. There is no use . . . he must go to Papalote."

"¡Seguro!" echoed the deputies, catching the drift of their leader's talk by the motions of his eloquent hands. "¡A Papalote! Adelante! Vamos!"

They curbed their plunging horses as Baca beckoned them to one side and whispered hurried orders into their ears, and then, with their leader well up in front, they turned back and surrounded the Americans.

"Meester Starbuck," began Baca with a suave, oratorical flourish, "you say you are a good ceetizen, no? Your belief is in the law. Only now, in thees case, you think we have mak' a mistake? But if I will show you the evidence that thees man is a robber, you will, of course, let him go? Very well, we will have thees man search him."

He made a motion to the largest deputy, who swung down promptly from his horse, but as he walked up to Meadows, the cowboy drew back and shook his head at him grimly.

"Now, you see?" clamored Baca, dancing up before Starbuck and waving his arms in the air, "you see . . . that man is a criminal! He is afraid to be searched . . . he knows we will find the evidence! Meester Starbuck, you are protecting a robber!"

Then it happened — what they had counted on — for as Meadows turned his head, the big deputy jumped on his back. He went to the ground, without striking a blow. As the Mexican grabbed his hands and snapped on the handcuffs, the whole posse piled on top of them.

"He is my preesoner!" screeched Baca, shaking a warning finger at Starbuck, but the man who had once wrestled a grizzly bear did not stop to count the odds. Striking the hand aside, he strode to the pile and caught the first man up bodily. Then, swinging him above his head, he hurled him at Baca who went down as if struck by a log. Man after man was caught from behind and flung upon the struggling mass. When it was all over, the Mexicans were in one pile and Abner Meadows was free. But as he stooped to lift him up, Starbuck halted in his tracks and stood staring at something on the ground. It was a twenty-dollar gold piece that had fallen from Meadows's chaps while he was engaged in his brief struggle with the Mexicans.

"What's this?" inquired Starbuck. As he picked up the new coin, all his strength and fury left him. His voice which had bellowed like a mountain bull's was now suddenly cracked and thin.

As the Mexicans, scrambling up, caught the gleam of the gold, they rushed to search their prisoner. With a grand, triumphant gesture, Baca snatched away the coin and held it before his deputies, and then amid shrill yells he went through Meadows's pockets and fetched out four more gleaming eagles. They turned him over hastily and found two more on the ground. When Starbuck saw these, he picked up his rifle and departed without a word.

Justina alone lingered, looking on with startled eyes, but when she saw his face as he rose up fighting, she, too, left Meadows to his fate. Like a pack of hounds that have driven a wolf into a steel trap and fall upon him, yelling and gnashing, the Mexican deputies swarmed and tumbled about Meadows as he fought for a last chance to escape. Although his hands had been shackled, he wrenched one of them free and struck out with the dangling handcuff. As they closed in on him, he laid open a deputy's head before he was crushed to the ground. There they bound him hand and foot, now thoroughly convinced that he was no less an outlaw than Butch Brennan. As to why he should be traveling without his gun, that was something to be explained later, although it had doubtless saved several of them their lives. Now that they had him, they made off at a gallop, leading his mare by a reata about her neck. Out across the tawny plains they loped, heading east toward Papalote Peak.

Riding and resting, they pushed on night and day until the next afternoon they sighted Papalote. With his feet tied together beneath the belly of a spare horse and his hands securely shackled to the horn, Abner Meadows had submitted like a man in a dream to the exultant taunts of his captors. But as they neared the outskirts of the town and the Mexicans made him remount Brennan's mare, he awoke at last to his position. Not only was he enmeshed in a net of circumstantial evidence that would make his conviction sure, but he was deserted by his friend and about to be exhibited as a man who had murdered and robbed. He was to be paraded through the streets as the brutal Butch Brennan, who had terrorized half of New

Mexico, and, if he escaped from the violence of the mob, he could expect no mercy from the court. The natural apathy between the two races had been heightened by a thousand lawless acts, and now an American, once he was brought to trial, was practically convicted in advance. He had struck too late and his one hope of freedom lay in some last desperate attempt to escape.

It was evening as they passed through a gap in the hills and came in sight of Papalote, and, as their identity was recognized, the entire male population came galloping out to meet them. But instead of coming to gape at Meadows, they had news of their own to tell. When Baca heard it, he slapped his fat leg and took a drink with the crowd. Then Meadows was marched through a sea of hateful faces that lined both sides of the street until at last they came to the plaza.

In the lead went the sheriff, bowing and smiling to his admirers, who cheered him to the echo, but as the procession was stopped and men scrutinized the prisoner, a violent altercation sprang up. An old, white-haired Mexican came bustling through the crowd and stared Meadows full in the face. Then he turned to the crowd, shouting and shaking his head, and Baca whirled upon him with a snarl. They came together in a fury, both talking at once and waving their hands at the prisoner. Meadows, seeing that the question of his identity had come up, protested again that he was not Butch Brennan. Other men joined in, some supporting the old man and the rest taking the side of the sheriff, until finally in a turmoil they adjourned to the courthouse, carrying Meadows along in their midst.

The Papalote courthouse was a modern brick building, erected from the proceeds of the first county bonds that the Mexican taxpayers had voted, and their admiration of its plaster front, which faced the plaza, was only equaled by their pride in the jail. It stood just behind the ornate courthouse, a two-story square of solid stone, and a great crowd of Mexicans gathered about its ponderous door as Baca and the disputants surged in. They came out, and returned, engaged in mysterious preparations. Then, when all was ready, Abner Meadows was led over and passed in through the massive outer gate. A second barred door swung back before him, and, as he entered the darkened interior, he was aware of a mass of men that jostled him as he was thrust into a cell. Before he could adjust his eyes to the gloom, a light was flashed on and he stood face to face with a stranger.

He was a cowpuncher by his hat, which was stuck far back on his head, half concealing a shock of red hair, but his principal feature was a tremendous hook nose, bowed in the middle like a cigar store Indian's. His face was rough and red, his jaws set like a steel trap, but the eyes that stared out from behind the hump-backed nose seemed to twinkle with saturnine humor. Yet he did not speak, and in the silence that followed Meadows sensed the crowd of Mexicans, watching. They had confronted him with this man to establish his identity, but he had no remembrance of ever having met him — and a face like that was not speedily forgotten, so stamped was it with decision and cunning. So they stood there and stared until the cowboy's mouth relaxed and he showed his broken teeth in a grin.

"Hello there, stranger," he said with a hoarse cackling laugh, "what the hell have they got *you* in for?"

"Resisting arrest," answered Meadows, and then he added: "These Mexicans think they've caught Butch Brennan."

"Butch Brennan!" repeated the cowboy, and then he laughed a mocking, derisive whoop that destroyed the last hope of Celso Baca. The Mexicans outside the cell suddenly burst into a tumult, scolding and arguing and hooting at the sheriff, until at last in a fury he drove them all out and came striding back to the cell.

"Don't you know thees man?" he demanded of Meadows, shaking a trembling finger at the cowboy, and Meadows shook his head.

"Do you know thees feller?" inquired the sheriff of the cowboy, and the latter squinted his eyes down doubtfully.

"Believe I do," he replied, "but I can't say for sure. Gimme a drink . . . mebbe it'll he'p refresh my memory."

"Here!" snapped Baca, whipping a flask from his hip pocket, and the cowboy drained it at one pull.

"Hah!" he smacked, blinking his eyes at the bite of it and turning again to Meadows. "By grab, he shore looks familiar. But what's doing, Baca . . . what's the trouble?"

"That man is Butch Brennan!" declared Baca in a passion. "I know it! You can't fool me!"

"Well, who's trying to fool you?" demanded the cowboy hectoringly. "Come through . . . we're all in the dark."

"You tell me who that is and I give you some more wheesky!" burst out Baca with tremulous eagerness. "I give you a quart bottle . . . . sure!"

"All right!" came back the cowboy. "His name is Ab Meadows and he works for Dave Starbuck, breaking broncs. Am I right? Then gimme the bottle!"

"You lie!" wailed the sheriff, and, striking his hands against the bars, he rushed off and left them alone.

"Glad to meet you, Meadows," went on the cowboy solemnly as the cell-room gate clanged and was locked. "I'm a well-known character in your part of the country. Reckon you've heard of me . . . Wild Horse Bill!"

"Wild Horse Bill!" repeated Meadows and looked again, for the little sawed-off runt was Butch Brennan's right-hand man and a famous hunter of mustangs as well. He was one of the Wild Bunch, as the cowboys called them, the local boys who had been tempted by Brennan's success to join this bandit gang, and as no broken horse, no matter how staid, once he has joined the wild herds on the plains, will ever again submit to restraint, so Bill from a horse hunter had been changed into an outlaw who in turn lured other men away.

He was the hero of the cow camps for his deeds of lawless daring and his coolness in the face of danger, but now, it appeared, the Mexicans who he flaunted had brought his career to a close. For before a Mexican jury, with Mexican witnesses to testify and a Mexican judge to pass sentence on his crimes, the most that he could hope for was to escape with his life by pleading guilty to murder. Under the laws of New Mexico a man so pleading could only be imprisoned for life, whereas if he mistakenly pleaded "not guilty", he paid the extreme penalty for his crime. All this flashed up in Meadows's mind as he returned the cowboy's stare, and then, with a sudden surge of compassion, he advanced and held out his hand.

"Glad to meet you, Bill," he said with a friendly smile, "but I'm sorry to find you here."

"Oh, that's all right," returned Bill with a good-natured grin. "It's my own fault for going to sleep. Butch told me when he left that they'd pick me up, and, shore enough, when I come to, I was pinched." He laughed reminiscently and, sitting down on the bed, favored Meadows with a knowing wink. "But, cheer up," he whispered, "are you game to take a chance? Well, I'll have you out of here in jig time!"

"I'm with you," responded Meadows, "and I'll go the limit, too . . . but how are you going to work it?"

"Jest foller my lead." Wild Horse Bill nodded confidently. "I've broke half the jails in New Mexico. The first thing to do is to raise so much hell that they won't notice if you make a little noise. Then, *psst* . . . I'll saw through the bars. After that . . . well, all I need is a couple of candles and we'll stick 'em up with a phony gun. Hey, *hombre!*" he shouted, beginning to rattle the barred gate. "*¡Carcelero!* Hey, *da me* some *velas!*"

The jailer, an old man with a patriarchal beard and a huge bunch of keys at his waist, came and looked solemnly through the cell-house door. Finally, as it grew dark, he came jingling back with their supper and a single candle.

"Huh! One candle, eh?" grumbled Bill, as the old man passed it in and shoved their food through the panel at the bottom. "Well, this shore is a fine, swell jail! I wouldn't stay in a dump like this if they'd give me a hundred dollars." He lit the candle and glanced scornfully about, then fell to eating his beans.

"¿Quiere velas?" he sneered. "¡Muy bien, da me dinero!" He slapped his empty hand as he demanded the money, and Wild Horse Bill cocked his head like a jaybird. Then he snapped his fingers in the air, reached into his ear, and handed the old man a dime. An astonished exclamation burst from the lips of the jailer. He gazed at the coin incredulously until, convinced that the money was good, he rushed off and returned with some candles. But with him came also three guards from outside who glared at Wild Horse Bill sourly.

"Heh, heh," chuckled Bill, "here's where we git frisked. I reckon they've come back to search my ears." He held out his head and pointed facetiously, but the guards only watched him suspiciously. "Hey, hombre!" exclaimed Bill, pouting out his lips at the jailer, "da me tabaco . . . "

"¡Da me dinero!" returned the old man, taking his cue from Bill's wink, and the guards stood waiting for the miracle. Bill felt dubiously in one ear, then felt in

32

the other, and snapped his fingers in the air, but when he held out his hand it was empty.

"¡No tengo dinero!" he shouted hoarsely. "¡Da me tabaco!" — and he reached out his hand. The guards only laughed uproariously.

"No, señor," one of them answered, shaking his finger before his nose.

They all went out. The native New Mexicans were a simple-minded people, much given to jokes and strange tales, and this trick of Wild Horse Bill's put the guards in good humor by adding to their stock of weird stories.

"How's that?" inquired Bill, jerking his head at Meadows. "Oh, I savvy these *hombres* fine. Git 'em to carrying on once and you can do most anything . . . now watch me git some tobacco. Need the can to make me a key." He sat back on the bunk and listened to them talking, then, raising his cracked voice, he began shouting a song, half Mexican, half ribald American.

No tengo tabaco, no tengo papel
No tengo dinero, *god damn it to hell.*
I have no tobacco, I have no paper,
I have no money . . .

It was a plaintive ditty, much affected by Mexican *vaqueros* when they were holding the herd at night, and those outside began to whoop. They were in a mellow mood on account of the whiskey that had been poured out to celebrate the capture of Butch Brennan, and soon the jailer came shuffling back with half a dozen packages of tobacco. He handed them in, still staring

33

and incredulous, and Bill thanked him and the donors effusively, after which he quieted down.

"Now, listen," he said, "and I'll tell you how we'll work it. I can pick that danged lock with a little doodad that I'll make, if I can jest saw a hand hole through the bars, but old Santa Claus is suspicious and he'll come back on the run if he hears my hacksaw at work. So what we got to do is to start singing some songs to drown out the noise of the saw, and I'll begin the evening's entertainment with a song of my own entitled 'A Little Too Small'."

He cleared his voice with the assurance of a concert singer and began on what was evidently his masterpiece:

I'm one of these jolly young fellows, you know,
Who always enjoys a good time.
I pay up my fares wherever I go
And I'm willing to spend my last dime.
But I've had one misfortune, though I'm not to blame
Because I don't stretch and go tall,
And I think it a pity, a god-damned shame
When they say . . . You're a little too small!
You're a little too small, young ma-a-an!
You never will answer at all, young man.
You're young yet, I know, and perhaps you will grow,
But at present you're a little too small!

"How's that?" he inquired and, chuckling hoarsely to himself, he plunged into the second verse:

34

One eve while out walking by chance I did meet
A lady, a schoolmate of mine,
I escorted her home and of course I took tea,
I asked her to lunch or to dine.
I asked her if I might be an escort someday,
Or at her home I might call.
She says . . . I'll ask Ma, but I really believe
She'll say you're a little too small.
You're a little too small, young ma-a-an.

A peremptory knocking on the solid outer door brought his song to a sudden halt, but after a short pause, in which he cursed under his breath, Wild Horse Bill went blithely on. He was a well-known cowboy singer, an *improvisador* who made songs to fit any occasion, and like all true artists he loved a good audience and abhorred the base soul who interrupts.

Now there was another young girl in that town
I loved her, I did, for my life.
One night like a fool on my knees I got down,
I asked her if she'd be my wife.
To this she consented, in my a-arms she fell.
We were to be wed in the fall.
I'm single till yet and the reason I'll tell . . .
'Twas because I was a little too small.

The knocking at the door became more peremptory than ever as Bill bawled out the rollicking chorus, but he had just warmed up to his theme and even the voice of the sheriff did not serve to cut him short.

35

"How's this, now?" he nudged and, throwing back his head, he sang on despite Baca and his guards:

Not long ago since, my old uncle died
And of course I came in for my share.
His words were to me as I stood by his side . . .
My boy, you're a young millionaire.
No ends to congrat-ulations next day
When the ladies upon me did call.
But I says . . . Excuse me, girls, for I really believe
You're a little too tall, young gir-ir-irls . . .

The *clatter* of feet as the sheriff and guards trooped in threatened to drown out the chorus entirely, but a song incomplete is like a life half lived, and Bill finished regardless of consequences.

You never would answer at all, young girls.
I'm young yet, I know, and perhaps I may grow
But at present you're a little too tall!

The chorus was ended and the song was sung, but when it was over and Bill had cleared his throat, Celso Baca was towering above him.

"You shut up!" he roared, glaring in suspiciously. "I know what you're trying to do . . . you're making that noise so you can break out of jail!"

"What, break out of *this* jail?" demanded Bill, laughing derisively. "Nothing doing . . . it can't be done. But say, where's that quart of whiskey?"

He looked through the steel gate as if expecting Baca to have it, but the big sheriff was not to be diverted.

"Never mind," Baca commanded, pointing his finger like a gun. "You onderstand me, now? Keep still!"

"Hey, didn't you promise me," came back Bill defiantly, "that you'd give me a quart bottle of whiskey? Well, come through, or I'll sing all night!"

"Oh, you weel, weel you?" snarled Baca. "Well, we'll see about that. And I'm gon' search you . . . right now."

"Well, search and be damned to you!" burst out Bill in a pet. "You must have talked with that sheriff from Las Cruces."

"Yes, and with lots of other sheriffs," answered Baca grimly. "I know every treeck that you play. So I weel search you right now, and, when I am t'ru, maybe you don' have no dime in one ear!"

He burst into a guffaw, accompanied by such guards as could follow the thread of his remarks, after which they searched him, finding nothing more dangerous than the tin-foil from several packs of tobacco.

"What's dat for?" demanded Baca after unrolling the ball carefully and turning it over and over. "You t'ink you break jail with dat?"

"Sure thing," retorted Bill. "With a buttonhook, or anything. But say, what about that whiskey?"

"You can't have it!" returned Baca, shoving him back into the cell and beckoning his guards to go. "You've drunk enough already."

"I'll sing all night, then!" declared Wild Horse Bill recklessly, and began to hum and croon.

"Don't crowd him too far," whispered Meadows in his ear as he saw Baca looking back through the door, but Bill only shrugged his shoulders and began on a topical song:

> O-oh, it's beefsteak when I'm hungry and
> whiskey when I'm dry,
> A pretty gal when I'm lonely,
> sweet heaven when I di-i-ie!

He chanted the chorus defiantly, accompanying the words with drunken hiccups, and then he turned to the door. "Don't you like that?" he hailed. "Well, see how this suits you."

> O-oh, it's the chink's when I'm hungry and
> the saloon when I'm dry
> To the dance hall when I'm drunk and
> to hell when I di-i-ie!

He laughed with maudlin abandon and plunged into another vagrant verse.

> Old whiskey, rye whiskey, everybody tells me
> You have killed all my relations, now,
> damn' you, try me!
> You have broke me, you have ruined me,
> you have been my downfall,
> But you old red devil, I love you for all!

He was proceeding to further and more daring flights when Baca began to roar for the guards. They came rushing at his call and the sheriff strode in, his face set in a purposeful frown. Behind him came the jailer, bearing handcuffs and leg irons, and at sight of them Bill became suddenly still.

"What's the matter, Sheriff?" he said with his cracked, nervous laugh. "You ain't going to put them on me?"

"Yes, I put 'em on both of you," answered Baca thickly. "I onderstand . . . you goin' try to escape."

"What, from this big, new jail?" protested Wild Horse Bill weakly, and then he put out his hands. "All right, Sheriff," he said, "put 'em on, if you want to, but this feller, he ain't done nothing wrong."

"I put 'em on you both!" replied Baca inexorably. "You can't fool me. I'm wise."

He fitted the handcuffs with meticulous care, snapping them close to Bill's slim wrists, while a guard did the same to Meadows. Then he took the heavy leg irons and shackled their feet together, chaining the whole to the frame of the bed.

"Now," he said, "sing as much as you like. I guess that will hold you . . . no?"

He stepped back and smiled as he gloated over his handiwork, and Wild Horse Bill hung his head. Then the Mexicans went out, leaving them alone in their cell to await the coming of dawn.

CHAPTER
FOUR

By the dim light of their candle the two prisoners sat together and Bill sighed and rattled his chains, then he raised his voice in the lugubrious ditty commonly known as "A Prisoner for Life".

> *Fare thee well, green fields, soft meadows, adieu!*
> *Rocks and mountains, I depart from you;*
> *I am doomed to this cell, I heave a deep sigh*
> *My heart sinks within me, in anguish I die.*

As he droned out the song, he was wrestling with his handcuffs, pushing his thumbs down and limbering up his joints. While Meadows looked on, Bill suddenly slipped out one hand with a look of comical surprise.

"Hoo," he piped, and, laying hold of his other hand, he changed to a livelier tune:

> *Come, boys and listen while you have a little time,*
> *And I'll give to you a little jail rhyme,*
> *And it's hard times, poor boys,*
> *And I say, it's hard times.*
> *Now this Pecos jail is no jail at all*
> *You ought to take a turn in Wichita Falls,*

And it's hard times, poor boys,
And I say it's hard times.
The judge and the jury you all know well.
For a five-dollar bill they will need you to tell,
And it's hard times, poor boys,
And I say, it's hard times.

He stopped again with the same pout of surprise and held up his slim hands, free. Then he stuck out his tongue and looked over the leg irons, grunting contemptuously as he kicked them about.

"Gimme that tobacco can," he said, and, while he worked it to pieces by twisting the joints to and fro, he went on with his cynical song.

The judge and the sheriff you know by name.
They come to this county with the ball and chain,
And it's hard times, poor boys,
And I say, it's hard times.

He paused to roll up a thin strip of tin and bite it into shape with his teeth. As he fitted it experimentally into the lock of the leg irons, he crooned yet another bold verse.

Now the judge and the jury they have got it made out
For ten dollars more they will turn you right out,
And it's hard times, poor boys,
And I say, it's hard times.

He winked cheerfully at Meadows, who was beginning to stare, and showed him a crudely formed key. This he thrust into the keyhole, working it delicately to and fro, until finally there was a *snap* and a *click*. He kicked the irons aside with the smug smirk of a magician who has allowed himself to be handcuffed and chained, and knelt down to set Meadows free. Within half an hour after Celso Baca had manacled them, their shackles were on the floor.

"What'd I tell you?" exulted Bill, picking up one of the spare candles and warming it over the burning one. "The jail ain't made that'll hold me."

"What . . . do you expect to get clear out?" demanded Meadows incredulously, and Wild Horse Bill nodded assuredly.

"Feeling lucky," he said. "Everything's coming my way. You wait till I make me a gun." He wrapped the melted candle about the shank of another one, which he bent down like the handle of a pistol, then alternately heating it and pinching it into shape, he molded it to the rude semblance of a six-shooter.

"Put 'em up!" he exclaimed, snapping his neckerchief up over his nose and throwing down on Meadows with the gun. Then he went to work with the point of his key to make every line of it perfect. First he carved out the cylinder, with the bullets in the chambers, and smoked the muzzle hole black, after which he picked up the despised ball of tinfoil and wrapped it around the barrel. This was the last magic touch, and, as he laid it smoothly on, warming the candle grease to make it hold, the clumsy phony gun was suddenly transformed into a nickel-plated, man-size six-shooter.

"You're a wonder, Bill!" cried Meadows. As he glanced at the gun, the fighting fire came back into his eyes. All day — for two days — he had been a mere automaton, patiently submitting to whatever seemed his fate, but now that he saw a real chance to escape, his mind leaped forward to meet it. Up to the last few moments he had regarded Wild Horse Bill as a rollicking, rattle-headed cowboy, but a man who could thus scheme to collect candles, tin, and tinfoil and then turn them to such uses of his own was not one to be despised. Wild Horse Bill had a head, there was method in his madness, and his object was to break out of jail.

"You just tell me what to do," burst out Meadows eagerly, "and you'll find me right up there trying. Now what next . . . going to hold up the jailer?"

"Him or somebody," returned Bill, laying the gun aside and beginning to fumble with the top of his boot, "but I aim to git out of here first." He ripped open the seam and, from a pocket down the boot leg, drew out a slender strip of steel. It was the blade of a hacksaw, sewed in there long ago in anticipation of some such need, and Bill smiled once more in his innocent way as he tested the edge on a rod. Then he blew out the guttering candle and, stepping up to the barred door, felt about in the inky darkness.

"Now make a noise," he said over his shoulder, "rattle them leg irons and knock on the floor. That old jailer is inside here, somewheres."

His voice was tense, and he plied his saw cautiously in time to Meadows's rhythmic blows, but at last, as no one appeared to disturb them, he broke into a lilting song.

Bill Jones was a preacher, a Sunday-school teacher
His daddy was a preacher, too.
Bill took a notion to sail o'er the ocean
To visit the people of Tim-Booker-Too.
The cannibals took him, they started to cook him,
But he escaped from the band and he cried . . .
This is no place for a minister's son,
A minister's son, a minister's son.
I want to stay, but my feet wants to run
So I'll have to say good bye.
Father awaits for his wandering one,
For his wandering son, for his wandering one.
Maybe you think I'm out for some fun
But I'm not . . . I'm a minister's son!

One bar was sawed through, Meadows was *clanking* his chains regularly and stamping out time for the chorus, when suddenly the singing stopped. Bill was standing by the door as if he had been frozen, staring out at the gate beyond, and in the silence that followed there was the grate of a key and the grind of heavy hinges.

"Git into your handcuffs," whispered Wild Horse Bill hoarsely, making a jump and plumping down on the bed.

44

As they slipped on their leg irons, a light flashed out, revealing the white-bearded jailer behind. He peered in through the door, his eyes big with suspicion, his bull's-eye searching every corner of the cell. They let him look his fill. Undoubtedly he had heard the noise of their sawing, perhaps he had been spying for some time, but now, when he looked in, they were both entirely shackled and sitting side-by-side on the bed.

"*¿Qué cosa?*" he murmured, craning his neck to look closer, and, as he saw the old man's gaze revert to his handcuffs, Wild Horse Bill suddenly held them out.

"*¡Mira!*" he exclaimed, and with a dexterous flip he shook them off onto the floor. Then he snapped his finger in the air, reached into his shirt, and pulled out the phony pistol. "You are my prisoner!" he cried, leveling it straight at his breast. "Open the door, before I shoot you."

For a moment the jailer stood swaying on his feet, staring down the black muzzle of the gun. Then, muttering a prayer, he searched out the right key and threw the cell door open.

"*Muchas gracias*," returned Bill, stepping briskly out and relieving the old man of his gun, "and I'll just trouble you for that bunch of keys." He took the keys and the bull's-eye lantern with which the jailer had stalked them, and then, as the old Mexican began to cross himself and beg, he shoved him roughly into the cell. "Shut up!" he said. "You ain't going to be hurt."

Slipping the phony gun to Meadows, he tiptoed over to the gate. But as they reached the outer door and stood listening for the guard, the frightened jailer began to call for help.

"*¡Socorro!*" he shouted. "*¡Los ladrónes!*"

"Let 'im yell," muttered Wild Horse Bill, stepping back from the door. "As fast as they come in, I'll hold 'em up and you take away their guns."

"All right," returned Meadows

While they stood expectantly, startled voices rose up from outside. Then the door was snatched open and a man stumbled in, feeling about in the inner darkness.

"Hey, there!" spoke up Bill, suddenly turning on the bull's-eye and flashing it full in his face. As the guard stood in bewilderment, Meadows snatched away his pistol and made him stand with his face to the wall. A second guard burst in, wild-eyed with alarm, his rifle held ready to fire, but a swift blow from Meadows sent him sprawling to the floor where he was speedily overpowered and disarmed. The stentorian voice of the jailer still clamored from the darkness, imploring mercy and help. From the deck above the common prisoners joined in with a babble of yells, but although Meadows stood waiting with his pistol poised to strike, no one answered their vociferous appeals.

"Take a look," suggested Bill, still with his light on the prisoners.

Meadows peered through the crack in the door. The night was dark and there was no sign of Baca's deputies except their blankets and a row of saddled horses.

"Come on," beckoned Meadows, and Bill stepped softly out, shutting and locking the door behind him. Then he threw the keys up on top of the roof and stood

46

looking, a pistol in each hand. But no one rose to meet them; the deputies' camp was deserted — and a whoop from the saloon across the plaza explained their probable whereabouts.

"Take a carbine," advised Bill, sorting over the guns that the Mexicans had left near their beds, and, after they had helped themselves to the best, they slipped over to where the horses stood tied. Bill picked out a big bay and began shortening up the stirrups, but Meadows hurried onto where a well-remembered head was reared against the sky. It was Brennan's chestnut mare, that beautiful creature which already he had begun to covet. As he stepped to her side, she nickered softly and thrust her nose against his breast. He tightened the cinches and swung into the saddle with a wild, surging sense of victory. Against almost insuperable odds they had escaped from chains and prison and were free as the passing wind — and all on account of Bill. He was a marvel of invention, a miracle of efficiency, a past master in the rough work of night fighting, but now he sat silently, gazing over across the plaza, his hook nose raised high like a hunting dog's.

"What's the matter?" inquired Meadows, riding over to join him. "Come on, let's get out of town."

"No, danged if I do!" exclaimed Bill explosively. "Not till I smoke up them yaller-bellied Mexicans!"

He threw the spurs into his horse and went dashing across the plaza, with Meadows close behind. As he sat his mount in front of the saloon, he let out a piercing yell. "A-ah, hah, hah, hah!" he whooped. "Come and git me, you *bastardos!*" Drawing his pistol, he fired through the doorway, over the heads of the staring Mexicans. There was a *crash* of glass, the smashing of fixtures, and the terrified squeals of fleeing men. When the boldest began to shoot back, Bill turned his horse on one hoof and went rollicking out of town.

Out across the broad plains and into the velvety night Wild Horse Bill and Meadows galloped on. When they drew rein, they could hear drumming hoofs as the Mexicans came thundering after them. Bill listened a minute, his chin thrust out, his lips skinned back vindictively, and then he grunted to himself.

"Huh!" he jeered. "You're brave now, ain't ye? You're goin' to chase me clean to Show Low. All right, Mexes, I'll jest give you the road and let you run your fool selves to death."

He turned off up a narrow swale and looked back with a scornful chuckle as the posse rode blindly on, then, putting his horse to a shuffling trot, he ambled away to the north. But when the day dawned and revealed them to their pursuers, the fugitives fled on at a gallop. Far ahead, over a roll of the yellow prairie, a windmill top stuck up from some swale. Farther on the Gallinas thrust up their rugged peaks, feather-edged with tall spruces and pines, but all about was the undulating grass land, clipped short by cattle and sheep, with Mexican *vaqueros* like dots to the south. At the first peep of light they had spied the two Americans, now well on their way to the mountains, and, from wherever they happened to be, they came whirling across the flats, riding furiously to overtake them.

"Let 'em come." Bill grinned, pulling his horse down to a walk. "I shore do love to tease 'em. After they've rode their horses plumb down, we'll give 'em a surprise and leave 'em." He began to hum a little tune as he trotted on toward the windmill, and then started singing.

> *I shore do love to tease 'em*
> *And after they've rode their horses down*
> *We'll give 'em a surprise and leave 'em.*

"Say, I could write a good song about breaking that jail."

"I expect you could," conceded Meadows, "but what's this surprise? Those Mexicans are beginning to get close."

"I'll show 'em," boasted Bill. "Now you jest watch how they act . . . one white man could lick a million of 'em."

He dropped off of his horse just over the brow of a low hill and snatched out his stolen rifle, then with lightning rapidity he emptied it at the Mexicans, who suddenly wheeled and stopped.

"You see?" he demanded. "They think we've made a stand, and every danged one of 'em is yaller. They're afraid to run up on me . . . I've downed too many of 'em . . . and I'll down some more of 'em yet." He refilled his magazine and, taking a rest over one knee, aimed long and carefully at the crowd. Then he fired once, and a horse went down, while the Mexicans scattered right and left. "That'll hold 'em," grumbled

Bill, "if they don't double 'round. Now let's round up this man's pasture and ketch out a couple of fresh horses."

He swung up on his big bay and galloped down toward the windmill, which was inside a barbed-wire enclosure. When he came to the fence, he threw his rope across it, making it fast to the bottom of a post. Then he remounted his horse and rode off on the jump. At the jerk, the post and three or four others leaped up and were laid flat on the ground.

"How's that?" inquired Bill. "That's what they call quick work. Now, the idee is to round up every horse in the pasture so the Mexicans can't change, too, and foller."

He dashed out in a circle that covered half the field, and, as Meadows swung into the opposite direction, the remuda fled before them to the fence corner. There they huddled in a confused mass, ducking and cringing before the ropes. Working fast but with soothing words to their mounts, Bill and Meadows made a hasty change. Saddles and bridles came off and were slipped on restive bronchos that flew back and fought the rope. They were just swinging up to go when there was a yell from behind and their pursuers came pouring over the hill.

"Jerk that fence down!" yelled Bill, snatching his rifle from its sling and dropping down to shoot at the Mexicans.

Meadows checked his plunging mount, dropped a loop over a fence post, and laid it flat with one jerk. Then as Bill suddenly mounted, they drove the horse herd through the gap and went scampering away across the plain. A stray bunch of Mexicans, which had swung around to the west, made a half-hearted attempt to head them off, but Bill was in his element, whooping and riding like a drunken Indian, and they swept by in a cloud of dust. It was like a stampede or the wild rush of mustangs that have been jumped and flee for the hills. As the herd galloped on, Brennan's chestnut mare took the lead with her head held high. She was a broom tail again, leading the remuda across the plains while some wild stallion drove the stragglers in her wake. As the herd settled down to a steady lope, Meadows rode over and fell in with Bill.

"Say," he said, "where did Brennan get that horse? Do you think a man could buy her?"

"Not for a million dollars," returned Wild Horse Bill emphatically, "and, if you did, you couldn't keep her. Butch has got a horse thief that will get that mare from anywhere . . . and, if he failed, Butch would steal her himself. She's his *chula* horse, the pet of the bunch . . . I gave her to Butch myself."

"What? That horse? You gave her away? I'd give every dollar I've got for her!"

"How many you got?" inquired Wild Horse Bill shrewdly. "I might ketch you another one, jest like her. She's a broom tail from over on the plains."

"Yes, I know it," answered Meadows still with his eye on the *chula* horse, "but you'd never get another one like her. She knew me when I caught her, last night."

"Yeah, I've heard about you," observed Bill, laughing indulgently. "They say you can make up to any horse.

51

But I'll tell you right now . . . don't you steal Butch's mare or he'll foller you to hell and then kill you. No, you let that *chula* alone and I'll fix you up . . . I'll ketch you another one, jest like her!"

"Will you sure?" demanded Meadows, and, as Bill nodded assent, he turned in his saddle and considered. The chase was over and the posse, disheartened, had dropped far behind on the plains, but some would follow on and the old carefree life could never be his again. He could never go back to the old Figure 4 for he was an outlaw now, like Wild Horse Bill. Yet somehow he clung to the hope, nothing more, that in some way he might still make his peace. He had committed no crime other than resisting arrest and breaking his way out of jail, and now that he could never ride with her again, he longed for one more glimpse of Justina. He was an outlaw, a fugitive, even suspected of being Butch Brennan with a reward of forty-five thousand on his head, but Dave Starbuck was a power in that Mexican-ruled land, and he never went back on a friend. Perhaps he could square the case somehow.

"Let's go through Show Low!" burst out Meadows impulsively, and Wild Horse Bill squinted down his nose.

"Show Low or any place," he said at last, "as long as they've got some whiskey."

"No, let's not stop, then," interposed Meadows hastily. "I just wanted to see Dave Starbuck."

"Oh." Bill grinned. "I thought it was the schoolteacher. Well, Chris Woolf is good enough for me."

"Say, how do you know all these things about me?" demanded Meadows, turning suddenly red. "I'll swear I've never seen you in Show Low."

"I've been there all the same," answered Wild Horse Bill, "and we've got a system for picking up the news."

"Oh, sure," nodded Meadows, "I know about that. Brennan tried to hire me to be his agent when I met him back in the hills."

"We've got our agent," returned Bill mysteriously. "You'd be surprised, if you knowed who it was. But, say, what's your plans . . . are you going to throw in with us or are you going to skip the country?"

"What do you mean?" inquired Meadows, but in his heart he knew, and he knew, also, that Bill was right. There was no place in that country for a man in his position except with Butch Brennan's gang. Yet, if he joined them, if he threw in with the Wild Bunch, it was the definite parting of the ways. He could never turn back and retrace his steps to the path of respectability. He would be outlawed for life, pursued, proscribed, his name posted throughout the land, and, as the depredations of Brennan's gang drove the express company to retaliation, they would put a reward on his head. They would organize a plan of ruthless extermination such as had wiped out the Daltons and the Youngers, and every man who belonged to the gang would be hunted like a sheep-killing dog. In the end, of course, they would get him. But to leave the country, to push on to Arizona was simple — except for one thing. He would never see Justina again.

"I don't know," he said to Bill. As they swung west toward Show Low, he still pondered the pros and cons. Even if Starbuck was still willing to help him, there was nothing that he could do, more than to hide him out in the hills. If Celso Baca discovered his whereabouts, he would spare no pains to take him. The sheriff would be out of his head with chagrin, now that he had lost both his prisoners and the reward, and the mountains behind Show Low would be thoroughly combed before Baca returned to town. He was behind them now in that cloud of dust that dwindled but followed doggedly on, and his rage would be limitless when he rode into Show Low and found himself balked of his prey — Dave Starbuck could not even approach him.

"I'll tell you," suggested Bill, who was beginning to nod, "we'll change horses at Show Low and ride on until dark, and then take a little snooze. No, danged if we will!" he burst out resentfully. "They ketched me that way before. Them Mexicans seem to know that I'll do something like that and they tag along behind me on a gamble. No, gimme a quart of red-eye to keep me awake and I'll whip till I git to Frog Tanks. Them Walking X boys will give me a tip if any Mexicans come wandering down the road."

"All right," agreed Meadows, "I'll go with you that far . . . but I don't like your friend, Brennan."

"Who, Butch? Why, what's the matter with him?"

"Oh, nothing much," said Meadows, "only I don't like his style . . . and he got me into this trouble. I met him up the cañon with his shirt full of money, and he made me get off and change horses. Then, when he was going, he grabbed a handful of gold twenties and threw them down in the mud. Well, of course, I picked them up, and, when the posse jumped me, they thought they had Brennan, sure."

"Oh, ho, ho!" shouted Wild Horse Bill, quirting his horse and cutting a circle. "That's just like old Butch. Every man that he meets he gets him into some jackpot, and then he rides off and laughs."

"That's right, he laughed," admitted Meadows. "I suppose he knew all the time that Baca or his posse would get me. But if I'd known what was coming, I'd have walked back to the ranch and left his money in the mud."

"Yes, but you didn't." Bill laughed. "That's the hell of it with Butch. He always knows jest what you'll do. He knowed you'd ride that mare, because he seen you liked her, and who'd ever go off and leave money? And then, when Baca found you, he quit chasing Butch and let him git away with the loot. Did he still have that mailbag on his saddle?"

"A big sack of mail and two saddlebags. I'll bet there was twenty thousand dollars."

"Make it forty," suggested Bill. "I was in on that deal and I had over twenty myself. Then I laid down and went to sleep, and, when I woke up, I was looking down a big Forty-Five. Them Mexicans had been trailing me, to see if I buried anything, and, when they come up on me, using that money bale for a piller, you ought to have heard 'em laugh. It made 'em so good-natured they wouldn't think of killing me . . . and, besides, you should have seen 'em hide that money in their boots. The express company won't get hardly any of it."

"How do you like that kind of life?" inquired Meadows politely, and Wild Horse Bill slapped his leg.

"Fine!" he declared. "The best in the world! There's one thing about Butch, he shore knows how to do it . . . we get a horse load of money, every time!"

"He struck me as having a cruel face," observed Meadows half to himself, and Wild Horse nodded soberly.

"Yes, he's cruel," he admitted, "and he's a vindictive cuss, too. He never forgets an injury. But it takes a man like that to hold down the kind of men that you come across in our business. They're shore hard games, and you've got to be a killer or the bastards won't respect you."

"Oh!" said Meadows.

Bill hurried on to picture the wild delights of the game, but when he had finished, Meadows drew in his lips and looked ahead at Show Low. It was a question in his mind, whether to go farther with Wild Horse Bill or to leave him and hide in the Datils. But one thing was certain — after what Bill had said, he could not go on to the lava beds. With a man like Brennan — cruel, heartless, overbearing — he would not be at peace for long, and then the hot temper that he strove to keep down would flare up and bring on a quarrel. A quarrel with Brennan could be settled in but one way, if half of what he heard was true. He was a natural-born killer and his rag-handled pistol had shot down a score of men.

"No, Bill," said Meadows at last, "I'm afraid I've got to quit you . . . that train robbing don't appeal to me."

"Suit yourself," responded Bill, but he lost his rakish air and seemed to ponder darkly. "Well, all right," he said, "if that's the way you feel, but dog-gone it, I'll be sorry to lose you. Butch and them boys are all right, but they're too damned quarrelsome. I git tired of hearing them yammer. But you and me, Ab . . . say we could throw in together and have a peach of a time, ketching wild horses and breaking them, and, if you're stuck on Butch's mare, I can git you another one, jest like her." He looked up hopefully, but Meadows's face was set — they were riding into Show Low.

"Let's corral these horses," suggested Meadows absently. "The owner will be along to get them."

"Yes," jeered Bill, "he'll be along . . . with a shotgun. Don't you look for no mercy now."

"I'm not," responded Meadows, but, as Bill headed for the saloon, his eyes sought the schoolhouse and Justina. Was it expecting too much, when he had meant no wrong, to look to her still for mercy? Her horse was under its tree and the hour was late — perhaps she would ride by and see him. He changed horses and waited, looking back at the dust cloud and listening to Bill's laugh from the store, and after a few minutes Justina came out and rode down the road at a trot. Her horse was fighting his head to run, but she held him resolutely in. When she came opposite the corral full of horses, she stopped and looked at Meadows. Perhaps it was from curbing her high-headed mount, but to Meadows she seemed a little grim as if along with the grace of Botticelli's "Queen of the Spring" there was a dash of the Indian fighter as well.

"How'd you get back here?" she asked at last, and he answered with a deprecating smile.

"Rode back. Couldn't leave the country without stopping to say good bye. I hope you don't still think I'm Butch Brennan."

"No, I don't," she answered, "but I'd take it as a favor if you'd just tell me who you are. It's all right to be loyal and to stand up for your friends, but for all I know you're nothing but a horse thief."

"Well, let it go at that," he replied, turning away with a bitter smile, but she spurred over and reined up beside him.

"No," she said, "I know you're not a thief . . . but why won't you tell me who you are? I'm your friend . . . or I'd like to be . . . but it stops right here, unless you're willing to trust me."

"Well, it stops here, anyhow," responded Meadows slowly, "because I've got to get out of the country. But before I go, I'd like to let you know that I'm not on the dodge for some crime. I'm hiding from my people on account of a certain matter I've been trying for some time to forget . . . you understand, it's something purely personal."

"Wouldn't she have you?" inquired Justina, squinting her eyes down shrewdly, and Meadows looked away.

"That is my business," he said, and Justina jabbed her horse that was champing at his bit to go.

"Very well," she answered quietly. "I've always liked you, Ab, and I'm sorry you couldn't trust me. But this is a free country, and that's your privilege . . . I'll never ask you again."

Their eyes met then and a long silence followed, interrupted by a shout from the saloon.

"Hey, Ab!" hailed Wild Horse Bill, clanking out with a bottle, and then he saw the schoolteacher.

"Who's that?" demanded Justina, as Bill started toward them — her voice was eloquent with disdain.

"That's Wild Horse Bill," answered Meadows quickly, "Brennan's pardner . . . he helped me out of jail."

"Oh," she said with another look at Bill, and, swinging her horse in his tracks, she went clattering up the road.

"What the hell?" murmured Bill, gazing drunkenly after her. "Have a drink, Ab? It'll do you good."

"No, Bill," returned Meadows, "I'm afraid it wouldn't help much. Come on, let's get out of town."

CHAPTER
FIVE

It is the little things, after all, that turn us from our purpose and change the course of our lives. As Meadows rode away with the renegade horse hunter, he accepted him in his heart as a pardner. Wild Horse Bill was a drunken and irresponsible creature, but he was the only man left that Meadows could call friend and he took him for better or worse. Certain it was that without his aid Meadows would still be in the Papalote jail, and from there, unless some miracle intervened, he would have passed on to the Territorial Prison. But he had escaped that fate, and now he gave to Bill the friendship which finer folks scorned. Bill, noting the change, gripped his hand and made much of him and swore to stay with him through fire.

They rode up the cañon past the Figure 4 gate, driving Brennan's *chula* mare before them, and night found them hidden in the Saw Tooth Mountains by a water hole that Wild Horse Bill knew. There they ate again of the scanty lunch that Bill had obtained from Chris Woolf, and, as he drank up his whiskey, Bill enlarged on the joys that only a horse hunter knows. He told of chasing herds for three days at a time, changing horses again and again, until at last the fiery stallions abandoned their remudas and left the fleet mares to be roped. Then he told of horse traps, cunningly built about the water and left with gates open for months, until at last the wary mustangs ventured back to the spring, only to find themselves shut in at last. But of brutal Butch Brennan and the robbing of trains he made no further mention, and, before they slept, they had made all their plans for a trip to the horse country together.

They saddled up at dawn and swung back to the trail that led on to the North Plains beyond. As the sun rose, striking the high cliffs of the Saw Tooths that gleamed white in the crystal-clear air, they passed down through wooded hills to Trinchero Lake, where the wild cattle watered at night. Then from the summit of a last ridge, crowned with yellow pines and spruces, they looked out at the immensity of the plains. Standing blue against the horizon, they beheld the volcanic cones that marked the grim land called the *malpais*. There men were said to enter and never return. Even the Indians avoided it with awe, but to outlaws like Butch Brennan it gave a haven of refuge, a safe retreat from the most savage pursuit.

Down a broad, winding valley the trail led on, and, as the ridges fell away and gave place to rolling plains, the row of craters rose up higher against the sky. Their huge shoulders loomed up treeless, gray with cinders and volcanic ash, but along their flanks, where the lava flow began, there was a mass of spike-like pines. Low on the plain, a great forest appeared, black treetops above a sea of yellow grass.

"What's that forest?" asked Meadows as he saw it bar their way, and Wild Horse Bill broke into a laugh.

"It's the *malpais*." He chuckled. "Every sucker that comes over here seems to think it's a park or something."

"Well, what is it?" demanded Meadows. "You don't mean to tell me that those trees are growing in the lava."

"That's right," answered Bill, "and, as far as you can see them, you can bet your bottom dollar they're in the *malpais*. Wherever that stops, there's nothing but grass, or cedars and piñon trees on the hills. I reckon the lava must ketch the water, and for the rest of it they jest live on air."

"Is there any water in there?" inquired Meadows incredulously, and Bill closed one eye mysteriously.

"Sure," he said, "if you know the way to it. There's two springs in five hundred square miles."

So that was the secret of Butch Brennan's immunity — he had discovered the hidden springs. Strange stories had come in about trails through the lava beds, and of water holes that the Apaches had found, but, except for the tales that friendly Indians told, the rest was mere myth and fable. What everybody knew was that in the early days the Apaches had made the lava beds their stronghold, and that no troops of soldiers had ever had the hardihood to follow them into the *malpais*. Trails there might have been, but nobody could find them, and in the thousands of caves and miniature craters the Indians had slipped away like snakes. Since the Apaches remained hidden there, it was reasonable to suppose that they had found a water hole somewhere.

"Is that where we're going?" asked Meadows at last, and Bill nodded his head impressively.

"I'll take you to a place," he said, "where no white man ever went before . . . not until me and Butch found the trail. It's a big piece of pasture land right in the middle of that lava . . . a *rincón* that the lava flowed around. After I've took you in, I bet you a thousand dollars you can't find your way back out."

"Is that so?" observed Meadows, and, as they rode on across the plains, he turned and looked back toward Show Low. The porphyry cliffs of the distant Saw Tooths gleamed white once more in the sun and the Datils loomed bastion-like beyond, and there, on the other side, lay all that he loved, or had loved, for the past three years. He was leaving it now to venture into a land where Dave Starbuck and his cowpunchers never came, a wild No Man's Land, ungoverned by any law since the soldiers had wiped out the Indians. It was a sort of back eddy in the Western rush of civilization, and Celso Baca and his deputies avoided the men who chose to make it their home. But it was Butch Brennan's stamping ground, a principality in itself, where every man owed him fealty — otherwise, he would ride in and burn his cabin to the ground and leave him as an object lesson to others. If Meadows rode in over this trail through the lava, which no man could retrace by himself, what then, if they did not agree?

"Say, I don't like this," he spoke out at last. "I don't want to go in on that trail. That's the same as joining Brennan's gang."

"Aw, that's all right." Bill laughed. "You can stop over at Frog Tanks . . . there's the house on that hill below. But Butch is a prince. You'll git to like him fine. Come on, I want to show you my bronchos."

"But suppose you get me in there and I don't get on with Butch . . . what's the chances of my ever getting out?"

"Danged slim," declared Bill, "to tell you the truth. We don't want no outsiders to know that trail."

"Well, drop me at Frog Tanks, then. I'm willing to take a chance, but there's such a thing as being a fool."

"Aw, I'll fix it up," burst out Wild Horse Bill at last. "Come on, and I'll tell you what I'll do. I've got another trail that even Butch don't know about that comes in from 'way over on yon side, and, if you have a falling out, I'll take you across myself and tell Butch you got lost and died. How's that, now . . . are you game to go on?"

"Well . . . yes," agreed Meadows, and, although he had his misgivings, he put them out of his mind. What would it matter, after all, if this man-killer Brennan should file one more notch on his gun? Was he so valuable to society that his death would entail any great loss — in fact, would anybody miss him? If he never came back, would they send out a search party, or would he be presently forgotten? Judging the rest of his friends by a young lady he knew, his death would not cause even a ripple. He was just one more black sheep, coming from no one knew where, and going where all black sheep go. He was way-billed to hell, and a little excitement might add a pleasing fillip to the plunge.

The Frog Tanks Ranch rose up before them, a huge, fort-like mud house on top of a round hill that overlooked the cattle-dotted plains. At the foot of the hill were the corrals and branding pens, with a windmill to pump up water for the troughs, and below, where the flood waters from two valleys converged, was the sinkhole known as Frog Tanks. It was dry and silent now and glistening with alkali, but shortly after the next flood had melted the dried mud, it would be vocal with thousands of frogs. In the brief heyday of their freedom, they floated about in shoals, raising their voices in a deafening chorus. Then as the water was dried up by sun and wind, they bored down and holed up beneath the crust. In Indian-fighting days the Frog Tank Ranch had been famous as a camping place for soldiers, but now that the Apaches had been put on reservations, it had fallen away from its early good name. With the soldiers had gone law and order as well, and, when the Mexicans took over the county government, the last semblance of authority disappeared. No officer of the law had ever crossed the mountains to protect the scattered citizens in their rights and now not only this ranch but every ranch north of the Datils looked to Brennan for peace and protection. If he or any of his men happened to ride that way, they were fed and given fresh mounts, and, if any posse of Mexicans had had the nerve to follow, they would have received a grudging welcome. For this show of loyalty the hardy citizens of the North Plains claimed immunity from the raids of the gang.

Meadows's reception at Frog Tanks was friendly because he was riding with Wild Horse Bill, but the hard-faced Walking X cowpunchers continued to look at him askance until they changed horses and galloped on toward the *malpais*. Before them, running free and as tirelessly as ever, Brennan's *chula* led the way across the plain. As they neared the Punta de Malpais, the farthest point south of the gigantic flow of lava, Meadows noticed that it turned into a well-beaten trail that led on around the forest to the west. Now that he looked at it more closely, this great earth blanket of lava seemed more like a forest than ever and the plain, flowing to meet it, like some ancient ocean that lapped up against its front. Point after point of brown and black rock was thrust out into the sea of yellow grass, and down to its very edge the barren lava was bristling with a heavy growth of pines. Water there might be, caught and stored from passing thunderstorms and the melting of winter snows, but still there was none or any promise of nurture beyond the matted needles of the pines. They seemed to live, as Bill said, on desert air and water sucked up from deep cracks, but they stood out, full-fed and verdant, tall yellow pines and black, with cedars and piñons interspersed.

Jagged islands of rock, thrust up through the plain floor, turned their trail this way and that, and the ground became encumbered with rough chunks of lava, fuzzed over with clinging lichens. The surface of the plain was carpeted everywhere with mossy fragments,

66

snatched and strewn by the wind, and, as they approached the lava wall, Meadows saw that half its harshness was concealed beneath a mass of green and gray. But the lava itself rang beneath their horses' hoofs like steel or bell-metal bronze, and the wall, where they mounted it, rose thirty feet above the plain which it had covered for so many square miles. It had made its last thrust and then the high front had tumbled down like a piece of shattered gingerbread, and now, although millions of years had passed since Mother Earth had baked her cake, it still looked but half cooled, half arrested in its movement, a huge engine of destruction, poised to crush.

The place where Bill turned in was marked by no monument, nor was there the least sign of a trail. As he headed out through the tree trunks, it became evident to Meadows that his guide was following no signs. He rambled on over the molten surface, seeking always the easiest way, around blow holes, down through earth cracks, across natural bridges, twisting and turning from left to right but traveling straight into the sun that hung low above the tops of the trees. Behind him followed the *chula*, setting her small hoofs delicately but with the sureness of a mountain horse, and, as she paced along, she nipped at the sweet grama grass that rose up in thin wisps from the crevices. No wild horses or deer ever entered that silent forest to crop those waving grain heads. It was quiet, too quiet, and, as Meadows followed on, he felt the spell of the *malpais*, a silence almost of death. The wind soughed in the treetops, dainty fly catchers perched on high, but here

67

were no other birds, no chipmunks, no squirrels, no movement except their own.

As he led on across the waste of heat-wracked lava, Wild Horse Bill seemed suddenly changed — he was anxious, aloof, intent on some search that kept his head swinging like a hunting dog's — until at last he swung off to the north. Meadows looked all about, but there was no blaze on the tree trunks, no monument of rocks to mark the way. He was traveling by direction alone. For half an hour he spurred out, apparently at haphazard, forcing his horse over crevasses and blow-outs and around the tree-filled sinkholes, and then he came out into a clear space among the trees where the lava was level and solid. He set off at a trot now, and, as Meadows fell in behind, he saw a white blaze on a tree, then a monument of stones, standing up slim and straight in a space of the forest ahead. Bill had reached his marked trail, but could any other man find his way to where they had cut it? And if he failed, could he ever retrace his steps where all ways looked the same? Meadows gave up all effort to remember their course — he was at the mercy of Brennan and Bill.

The sun swung low and sank from sight. A heavy gloom filled the dark aisles of the forest, and, as Bill dismounted, he craned his neck anxiously, went forward on foot — then stopped, and came stumbling back.

"You stay here," he said, and began to walk in careful circles seeking a monument that was not to be found. "Have to go back," he said, and retreated to the last one where he had halted and circled again. "Damn that Butch!" he burst out at last. "He's always knocked over my monuments. What the hell!" he cursed, groping about in the half darkness, and then he sat down and considered. "Well, we're lost," he declared, "so the first thing to do is to build a big monument right here. Then we'll make a fire and cut circles from that . . . old Butch has done knocked down my monuments."

"But what for?" questioned Meadows.

"Well, so nobody can follow him in," Bill muttered. "He's worth forty-five thousand dollars to somebody."

"They'll never follow him in over *this* trail," said Meadows, and Wild Horse Bill chuckled hoarsely.

"No," he grumbled, "damned right they won't . . . can't find it myself, half the time. Here, *chula*, old girl, take me back to camp and I'll give you a feed of corn."

He reached out impulsively and caught the mare by the tail, dragging his own horse along behind, and after a moment the *chula* paced off demurely, her head held low to the ground.

"You see?" said Bill, "she smells Butch's tracks, going in. She can follow a trail like a bloodhound."

Then without a hitch, without turning to right or left, the beautiful animal led on, until they encountered Bill's monuments again and broke out at last upon a plain. A half moon in the west revealed a rolling stretch of prairie, fenced in by a circle of lofty pines. As they mounted and rode on, a horse in the distance gave vent to a challenging whinny. The mare responded, swinging forward at a trot, and then in the darkness a square of light burst out, with a man in the doorway, looking.

"That's Butch." Bill laughed as the man ducked aside. "Damn him, I've a good mind to skeer 'im. Better not, though, by grab, or he'll pump me full of lead. Oh, Butch, this is Bill!"

A low cabin emerged from the slope of a hill, taking form about the broad square of light, and, as they rode up before it, a voice came from the darkness, excited, querulous, eager.

"Who's that with you?" it demanded, and Bill laughed again as he turned to face his chief.

"It's Ab Meadows," he said. "You've met him. We've brought back your *chula* horse."

"Good for you!" exclaimed Brennan, stepping out from behind the house. "I was afraid them damned Mexicans would git her."

"They did, too," returned Bill, "but Ab stole her back when we broke out of the Papalote jail."

"Well, git down, boys, git down!" burst out Brennan hospitably. "Come on in and I'll show you the loot. We made a clean-up, Bill . . . thirty-two thousand in cash, and I ain't looked at half the mail. Glad to see you, Meadows. So you throwed in with Bill, hey? Well, come in, boys. I'm shore glad to see you!"

"What'd I tell you?" muttered Bill as he led Meadows in. "You're as welcome as the flowers in May."

"Where's your money, Bill?" jeered Brennan as they ducked into the low cabin and flung their saddles on the racks, "I don't see that flour sack anywhere!"

"Well, that's all right," defended Bill. "Maybe they did git my money, but I shore raised hell with their jail.

70

They'll think a long time before they shut me up again in their fancy, burglar-proof hoosegow."

"Didn't I say you'd git caught?" demanded Brennan hectoringly. "Well, why can't you take some advice? Now I expect you've come back to git half of *my* money, having thrown your half to the dogs!"

"Naw, keep your danged money!" exclaimed Wild Horse Bill truculently. "You'd win it all back at poker. What I want is some grub and I want it right quick . . . come on, Ab, I'll cook up some supper."

He strode over to a big box, nailed against the log wall to serve the purpose of a cupboard, and, kicking up the fire in the broad, stone fireplace, he soon had a frying pan sizzling. Then, as they ate a hasty meal, he related with great gusto all the details of his capture and escape. Butch Brennan sat by, his broad hat flung back and a twinkle in his handsome dark eyes. At every fresh disaster he burst into the loud laugh that Meadows had learned to dislike. It was full-voiced and hearty, but behind all his merriment there was a trace of devilish malevolence, as if he reveled in the misfortunes of others.

"So you come back broke, eh?" observed Brennan at last, flashing Bill a teasing smile. "Well, what do you think of this?" He took down a canvas bag from the top of the cupboard and poured the contents on the ground — golden twenties, silver dollars, great sheafs of bills. "Pretty good, eh?" he mocked. "Well, that's what you lost when you laid down and took that little snooze."

"Oh, I know it," grumbled Bill, rolling himself a cigarette. "We ain't all as smart as you are, Butch."

"No, damned right, you ain't," agreed Brennan vaingloriously. "I claim I can out-think 'em all. I got brains, see . . . brains . . . I look 'way ahead. I can guess what the other fellow will do. But you, dog-gone ye, as long as you've got a smoke, you don't give a whoop what happens."

"Well, that's all right," replied the self-satisfied Bill. "I may git into a few jackpots, but I notice I always git out again . . . the jail ain't made that'll hold me."

"No, not me, either," came back Butch, "because I'll never git into one. When a Mex comes for me, he wants to come shooting because there's one thing . . . I'll never be took."

"Well, *I* won't, the next time," returned Wild Horse Bill grimly. "These Mexicans are gitting too gay. But the next bunch that jumps me is due for a killing . . . I'm going to rise up with a gun in both hands. And after that, by grab, I can lay down and sleep anywhere . . . there won't be no Mexicans on my trail."

"That's the talk!" praised Brennan. "You're gitting to be a joke. Put the fear of God in their hearts. And another thing, Bill, look out for these detectives. You never can tell who they'll be." He glanced across at Meadows and gathered up his treasure, stuffing it leisurely back into the bag, and then, reaching under a bunk against the wall, he brought out a bulging mail sack. "This is half yours, Bill," he said. "You can't say I don't whack up."

"Hell, no!" exclaimed Bill, suddenly brightening up and making a grab for the sack. "I never said nothing like that. Damned white of you, too, because I don't deserve nothing after gitting caught like I did." He opened the bag and dumped the contents on a blanket that served for a rug by the fire, and, as he pawed over the pile of registered mail, he began to chuckle to himself. "Miss Sadie Gruenhagen," he read from a package. "Well, Sadie, you'll never git this. Piece of jewelry, I'll bet. Let's open 'em up, Butch . . . or will we divide 'em first?"

"No, let's grab, one at a time," proposed Brennan eagerly. "Come on, Ab, it's just like Christmas."

He glanced over inquiringly, but Meadows shook his head — it was registered United States mail.

"Aw, come on," urged Bill as he sensed what was coming, but Brennan had risen from his knees.

"Better join us, Meadows," he suggested quietly, and Meadows took the hint. The showdown had come, over accepting a gift, and it would go hard with him if he happened to decline.

"Well, of course, if you insist," he answered half-heartedly, and took the smallest box from the pile. It, too, was addressed in a woman's name, but he did not open it up. Just the fact that it contained her name and address made the theft seem all the more real. Some person had sent this gift through the mail, but Brennan and Bill had stolen it, and now Abner Meadows had become *particeps criminis*, a party to the crime. If he opened the package and took out the present, it would be breaking the United States mail, and many a daring and experienced train robber had scrupulously avoided that. The express company was a corporation, doing business with the railroads and paying an indemnity for its losses, but the United States mail was the government itself, and it never forgave or forgot. Whether the theft was of one cent or of one million dollars, the crime and the punishment were the same, and the pursuit of the criminal never slackened.

"Open it up," prompted Bill, and, as Meadows met his eyes, Bill gave him a warning wink.

"Sure," chimed in Brennan, "let's see what you got . . . sometimes them little skits is valuable."

"Well, all right," murmured Meadows, "but you gentlemen got this stuff and I don't want to take it away from you."

"Aw, sho, sho!" protested Brennan. "This is just chicken feed for us . . . we give 'em away to the gals. Say, what you got there? It looks like a ring!"

"A ring!" whooped Bill. "It's a bunch of diamonds with an engagement ring attached!"

He reached out and grabbed it, only to have it snatched away as Brennan caught the sparkle of the stones. Not for nothing had he been a looter of strongboxes and express safes — he knew they were gems of the first water.

"What do you want for it?" he demanded, thrusting the ring under Meadows's nose, and Meadows waved it away.

"Keep it," he said, glad in his heart to be rid of it, and Brennan lashed out his pistol.

74

"Say, lookee here," he snarled, "I thought you was one of the gang! But if you're not . . ." He paused, and Wild Horse Bill broke in, for Meadows did not reply.

"He's all right, Butch," he pleaded. "I got him to come in . . . and you asked him to join yourself."

"Well, if I thought," raved Brennan, "he was one of them detectives . . ."

"Ah, no, no," burst out Bill, "he's a danged good kid, and a nervy feller, too. Give 'im a chance, Butch. What's biting you? If you go on like this, you'll run all our side-kickers off!"

"I'm talking to *you!*" said Brennan to Meadows. "Are you one of the gang, or not?"

"I'm one of the gang," answered Meadows quietly, "as long as you treat me white, but . . ."

"But nothing," cut in Brennan, "it's yes or no . . . damned quick! And don't you never think you'll leave here alive if you ever look cock-eyed at me."

"Well, yes, then," spoke up Meadows, but his lips had gone white and his eyes were fixed straight ahead.

"Bill," demanded Brennan, "what the devil do you mean, bringing outside men in here? Sooner or later you'll git a dick and we'll all wake up dead. Do you think this man is safe?"

"I'd trust him anywhere!" cried Wild Horse Bill vehemently. "But you've got to treat him right. He ain't no Texas cow thief, he's a scholar and a gentleman, and you don't want to git him wrong."

"Well, all right then," responded Brennan, suddenly putting up his gun and summoning his ready smile. "I trust there's no harm done. My mistake, Meadows, and

I hope there's no hard feeling . . . now what about this ring?"

"You can have it," answered Meadows. "It's no use to me . . . and I couldn't accept it, now."

"Yes, you could," corrected Brennan, thrusting it roughly into his hand. "We gave it to you . . . how much do you want for it?"

Meadows looked at it again, and, like Brennan's chestnut mare, the stolen ring appealed to him. It was a rare and priceless thing, such as only rich men have, and its gleam brought a flash of decision. Since the ring had been forced upon him, he would play a bold hand and demand its full value in exchange.

"I don't think I'll sell it," he answered coldly, but Brennan was not to be denied.

"Yes, you will," he said. "I want that for my gal. I'll give you anything I've got."

"All right," responded Meadows, "I'll take that sorrel mare, then. It's either that or nothing."

An ugly scowl contorted Brennan's dark face, and he glanced at Bill accusingly.

"Oho," he said, "so that's your little game . . . you've got your eye on the *chula*. Well, let me tell you something, Ab. I'll kill you for a horse thief just as quick as I will for a dick. You're no 'tec, I see that, but I want to warn you right now . . . don't you never lay a hand on that horse."

"All right," agreed Meadows, "and, since the matter is becoming complicated, allow me to make you a present of this ring."

He held it out, and Brennan took it — then he opened up his bag and counted out ten hundred dollar bills that he slapped into Meadows's hands.

"Yours truly," he said, "and now let's have a drink. I hope that is satisfactory?"

"Yes, indeed," returned Meadows, carefully folding the bills and putting them away in his shirt. "I seem to be lucky tonight!"

"Sure, you're lucky!" declared Brennan, running to get a bottle of whiskey and pouring out the drinks all around. "And that's nothing to what you'll get by and by. I like a lucky man . . . and a nervy man, too . . . and I see already that you're both. So here's to you, Ab. We'll give you a chance, pretty soon, to have a whack at something big."

They drank, and, as Brennan's black mood passed away, he became suddenly and aggressively sociable. The fire was replenished, a whole case of whiskey brought out, the ill-fated mail sack kicked aside, and, as the drink mellowed them up, Brennan and Bill began all over again on the story of their hold-up at Belen.

"Say," laughed Brennan, passing the bottle to Bill, "you know that feller that hollered . . . 'Hey, there!' By grab, he had me scared stiff. I knowed there was an express messenger hiding out around there somewhere, because I found his gun in the car, but jest as I was fixing to blow the safe, a big, yaller parrot walked out! He was a sassy old jasper, and, when he saw me light the fuse, he hollered . . . 'Yoo, hoo! I know you! How are you?' Well, I couldn't stop to argue, and, when I come back, there wasn't no parrot to talk to. I didn't even find a feather!" He took a drink and slapped his leg reminiscently. "Say," he said to Bill, "you should've seen that mail clerk after them eight sticks of dynamite went off! I tapped on the partition jest before I touched the match and I said . . . 'Say, you, mail clerk, you'd better be moving . . . I'm going to shoot this safe!' But he wouldn't come out, and, when I went back, he was buried ten deep under mail sacks. Eee-hoo! He was a fright, he was so badly scared he couldn't hardly shut his mouth, and, when he did git to talking, he says . . . 'I . . . I thought you was goin' to shoot it . . . with a gun!' A-ah, hah, hah, the pore, ignorant yap didn't know much about how we shoot safes! I reckon next time, when I tap on his door, he'll come like a bat out of hell. Well, being as I was in there and had blowed the partition down, I stuck my gun in the air and says . . . 'Gimme your registered!' And he opened up his safe and shelled out!"

"Well, maybe you think *I* didn't have some job!" boasted Bill when his chief paused for a drink. "There was that engineer and the fireman to watch every minute, and the whole train of cars, to boot. And every time some Jew drummer or peanut butcher would git foxy and stick out his head, I'd have to fan him with one gun while I held up the engine crew with the other. They was one old woman, right up in that front car, that struck out her head three times, and, the next time she did it, I filled her nighty so full of glass I reckon she's fishing for it yet. Gave her warning three times, and the next time she tried it, I smashed the

78

whole window right over her. Heh, heh, reckon she believes me now."

"Huh! That engine crew!" scoffed Brennan. "Why, I had them boys so scared the fireman couldn't hardly pass coal. You could have stood 'em on their heads and gone off for an hour and found 'em in the same position. I swung up on the steps, jest as they pulled out from the water tank, and the fireman started to kick me in the face. 'Git off of there!' he says, and I slipped out my gun and jabbed it up in his face. 'You must want to ride awful bad,' says the engineer, 'to pull a gun, like that.' 'You're whistling,' I says. 'I'm not only going to ride, but I'm going to take charge of this train. I'm no hobo, I'm a hold-up, and the first one of you that resists, I'll kill him before he can wink. Now go ahead till you see a light down the track.' Scared? Well, I wish you could've seen that fireman . . . I scared him from one fit into a thousand! A piece of white chalk would make a black mark on his face, and the engineer was almost as bad. He begged for his life like he thought I was going to kill 'im, and then Bill flashed up his light and put it out. 'Oh, my Lord,' he says, 'how'll I know where to stop? That man done put out his light!' 'You'd better blow your whistle a couple of times,' I says, 'and see if they won't answer.' That was my signal to Bill . . . two blasts from the whistle . . . and, when Bill heerd it, he knowed I was on board and the hold-up was coming off. So he turned on his lantern, and the engineer slowed down like he was stopping to enter a switch. I made him jump down and kicked the fireman down after him . . . the bastard had tried to

79

kick me . . . and, while Bill was holding them, I shot up the train and warned everyone to keep their heads in. Then I got the engineer to persuade the express messenger to open up his door, but by the time I got up there, he had jumped out the other side, so I had to blow the safe. If we'd had another man, and another spare horse to pack off the rest of the loot, we'd've cleaned up a hundred thousand dollars . . . wouldn't we, Bill?"

"And then some," chimed in Bill. "But you treat Meadows white and he'll go along next time and help us. Nothing to do, Ab, but hold the horses and help load the sacks. What d'ye say . . . are you game to take a chance?"

"I'll consider it," answered Meadows, "but where's the rest of your gang? I thought you had lots of men."

"Sure, we have," explained Brennan, "but it ain't every man we can trust . . . some fellers git too excited. And they's another thing, too. The fewer they is in on it, the more loot they is to divide. Bill and me have worked alone, but that ain't quite enough, because one man ought to stay with the horses, and, if any of them express guards should happen to put up a fight, we might find ourselves set afoot."

"And another thing," put in Bill, "we know you're good with horses, and it takes a man like that. All we ask of you is to stay there and wait for us, in case the guards should try to smoke us up."

"You'll get your full third," added Brennan reassuringly, "and then you can ride where you please. After we rack up the treasure, it's every man for himself until we git back to the hide-out. What d'ye say, would you like to come in on it?"

For a moment Meadows hesitated, but the question had been decided long before it was propounded by Brennan. When he had picked up Brennan's twenties, when he had thrown in with Wild Horse Bill and come in over the secret trail — he had made his answer then.

"Why, sure," he said, and Bill slapped him on the back, but Brennan only sat back and smiled.

CHAPTER
SIX

Those who live by crime are seldom deep philosophers — if they had stopped to inquire into the meaning and purpose of life, they would have sought some other road to happiness. For it has yet to be proven that the mere possession of wealth, no matter how innocently acquired, adds anything to the wild joy of living, and the consensus of opinion among Attic philosophers is quite the other way. It is currently assumed that, outside the pleasure of acquisition, there is no great virtue in riches, and, when they are acquired by fraud and violence, they are even reputed to carry a curse. Yet happiness is a condition of mind that eludes all analysis and cannot be attained by taking thought — hence we find Wild Horse Bill, from the depths of his depravity, expounding short cuts to the despondent Ab Meadows.

There was no denying that Bill was always happy, nor that Meadows was as uniformly sad, and over a last bottle of the bonded whiskey Bill was trying to point the way out. The evening was late, Butch Brennan had taken his gun and blankets and retired into the lava to sleep, but by the dying fire Bill was preaching the old doctrine that happiness must be reached out for, and

grabbed. Being in a drunken condition, he gave con-
crete instances, all proving that the train robber has the
best of it, and he ended up by a maudlin rendition of
that old outlaw song, "Bonnie Black Bess". Like all
outlaw songs, it gave his text the lie, picturing, in fact,
the regrettable end of bold Dick Turpin, who robbed
coaches in the days of Queen Anne. Yet it suggested
another moral to the mind of Ab Meadows, which
served Bill's purpose as well, for when Fortune, blind
goddess, fled Dick Turpin's abode, Black Bess had
been his one friend. Bill sang it with deep feeling, his
voice tremulous with emotion, and, as Meadows
listened to this ballad of a man and his horse, his heart
went out to the golden *chula*.

When Fortune, blind goddess, fled my abode,
Old friends proved unfaithful so I took to the road,
To plunder the wealthy, to relieve my distress,
I bought you to aid me, my Bonnie Black Bess.
No vile whip or spur did thy sides ever gall,
For none did you need, you would bound at my call,
For each act of kindness you would me caress;
Thou art never unfaithful, my Bonnie Black Bess.

When dark sable midnight her mantle had thrown
O'er the bright face of nature,
many times we have gone
To the famed Houndslow Heath,
though an unwelcome guest.
To the minions of fortune, my Bonnie Black Bess.

83

So gentle you have stood when the coaches
we would stop,
The money and jewels down to me they would drop,
We would ne'er rob a poor man or ever oppress
The widows and orphans, my Bonnie Black Bess.

When Argus-eyed justice did me hot pursue
From Yorktown to London like lightning you flew,
No tollgate could stop us,
high waters you would breast
In eight hours you made it, my Bonnie Black Bess.

Hark! The bloodhounds approaching,
but they never shall take
A dumb friend like you, so noble and great,
To save me, poor creature, you have done your best
Thou art worn out and weary,
my Bonnie Black Bess.

Now hate gathers o'er me, despair is my lot,
And the law doth pursue me for the many I've shot.
Some will pity, while they all must confess
It's through kindness I kill you,
my Bonnie Black Bess.

No one can ever say ingratitude dwelt
In the bosom of Turpin, a vice never felt,
We will both die together and soon be at rest.
There, there . . . I have shot you,
my Bonnie Black Bess.

In years after years when I am gone
This story will be handed from father to son,
I will die like a man and soon be at rest,
So fare ye well forever, my Bonnie Black Bess.

Bill finished it in tears, as many a cowboy has done before, for it is a song that touches them, and in the silence that followed he took a last drink and stumbled away to bed. But Meadows sat alone, gazing into the fire and plotting out his life anew, and, since destiny had denied him all else in the world, he set his torn heart on Brennan's *chula*. The fact that she was denied him, that his desire was known, and that Brennan had threatened him with death made her all the more precious in his sight. Since he was doomed to become a thief, why not steal something that he loved and flee — to Arizona, to Mexico? He felt no loyalty to Brennan and his gang, for he had joined them against his will, but now that he was there, he fixed his mind on her, the most beautiful horse he had known. Perhaps it was his love for smiling Justina, settling at last on another object, also beautiful, or his old love of beauty, that would not be downed, his desire for the best, or nothing. Whatever it was, it demanded an object wholly beautiful and greatly to be desired, something rare, unattainable, to take the place of lost dreams, something worthy, to fight for and die for. The golden *chula* was all of that — or so she seemed to Meadows.

Morning came, and with it Butch Brennan and his blankets and his rag-handled gun near at hand. He routed out Bill and greeted Meadows cordially, but the

85

same dark thought that had sent him to the lava still lingered and glittered in his eyes. He needed them in his business, but, when he was asleep, he preferred his privacy to their company. They were his business associates, a necessary evil in the industry of holding up trains, but outside of office hours he preferred to be alone, and especially when sleep lulled his senses. That was the message his narrowing eyes revealed as he came in from his hiding place in the *malpais*, but Meadows and Bill overlooked the implied insult and Brennan passed it off with a jest.

"I woke up one time," he explained to Meadows, "with a Mexican sombrero a-straddle of my brisket. Since then, for some reason, I prefer to sleep alone . . . my nerves ain't what they were."

"What'd you do to the Mex?" inquired Bill, cackling hoarsely as he anticipated the *bon mot* of his chief, and Brennan chuckled grimly.

"Oh, nothing," he said. "I jest put two buttonholes where he only had one before . . . One time," he went on reminiscently, "when me and Sam Minehan got into a racket up north and a posse of six Mexicans took after us, we rode all day and night and were camped for our breakfast when Sam saw the *paisanos* coming. 'They're coming, Butch,' he says, 'now what'll we do?' 'Shoot it out,' I says, 'ain't you good for three Mexicans? Well, take them three on your side.' We set there by the fire, me with my guns under a newspaper that I held in my lap like I was reading, and the Mexicans rode clean up, not ten feet away, before they jerked out their guns and threw down on us. Well, I started shooting and knocked two out of the saddle before they knew what was happening, but Sam was kind of nervous and only got one and the rest of them dropped off and took cover. It was nip and tuck then, and, while I was shooting, Sam hollered into my ear. 'Look out fer that big feller, he's shore going to git ye!' And he pointed to a sand hill right close. Well, I'd felt them bullets pass me, and, when he rose up again, I bored him through and through, and the rest of the cowardly bastards made a run for their horses and went off and left him kicking. I went up to him then, and, of course, he began to beg, the way these Mexicans will. 'Oh, don't keel me,' he says. 'I got a wife and seeks babies. I'm a good man . . . I never hurt nobody. I take care of seek peoples' . . . and all that kind of stuff, until you'd think he was a regular angel. 'Well, hell,' I says, 'if you're as good as all that, you'll go to heaven, anyway.' And then I give him what he shore had coming to him . . . I hate these damned Mexicans like pisen."

"Here, too," chimed in Bill who was grinning at the tale, "and old Ab don't love 'em none too well. When I come through Show Low, Chris Woolf up and told me that he tried to whip five of 'em handcuffed!"

"Is that right?" exclaimed Brennan, suddenly warming up to Meadows. "Well, you shore are a fighting fool. Give you two six-shooters and you'd shore make a hand . . . what was the occasion of this fight you put up?"

"It wasn't much," answered Meadows deprecatingly. "Baca and his posse rode up to arrest me, and I put up the best fight I could."

"Shore did!" praised Bill. "Chris said one of them Mexicans had his head laid wide open by a handcuff, and the sheriff was chopped up like dog meat. Oh, he's a fighting man, Butch. You want to be good to him and you'll never live to regret it."

"What d'ye mean?" demanded Brennan, whirling savagely on Bill, and Bill gave a deprecating laugh.

"Heh, heh," he said, "that does sound kind of funny . . . what I mean is, you'll never regret it."

"Well, say what you mean!" answered Brennan vindictively. "And what's biting you . . . ain't I always been good to him?"

"Shore, shore!" protested Bill. "But jest keep right on being so, and you'll find he's a danged handy man."

"Huh!" grunted Brennan, and took his hand from his gun where it had leaped at the first hint of trouble. "You're an awful loose talker, Bill." He got up then and went out the door, and Wild Horse Bill winked a caution at Meadows.

"Don't say nothing," he whispered, "he'll be listening outside . . . he's shore feeling ugly this morning." Then in a louder voice he laughed good-naturedly. "That's Butch," he said, "worse'n a nigger about luck . . . always listening for every little word. But he's all right, Ab, and, say, on robbing trains, he simply can't be beat!"

"So I hear," responded Meadows, and Bill rushed on in praise of his chief, but all the time there was a worried look in his eyes and he hurried his preparations for breakfast. Then, as he banged on a tin pan, Brennan came stalking in and ate as if nothing had happened, but it was Bill who told all the sprightly tales while Meadows looked on in silence. It was a mystery to him how happy-go-lucky Bill could put up with such a tyrant as Brennan, and that a man so unreasonable should be the head of a great organization seemed totally beyond belief. Yet that such was the fact was quickly demonstrated, for, as they were standing by the door, there was a whoop from the pine forest and a messenger came galloping across the flat. He was a wild, bearded Texan with startled blue eyes that seemed haunted by some ever-present fear. After a glance at Meadows, he beckoned Brennan aside and began to speak in his ear.

"That's Ben Cady," whispered Bill. "He's the horse thief I told you about . . . always looks like he'd just seen a ghost. Come on, let's go out to the corral."

The log cabin of the outlaws was in a cove of the broad *rincón*, not a hundred yards from the wall of lava that enclosed the whole pasture like a fence. Where the cove pinched in, it formed a natural pocket that served as a corral for their stock. A fence of heavy poles extended across the entrance to this pocket, making a pen for holding their horses, but the bars were down and the trail, passing through, led up over broken slabs of lava.

"This goes to water," explained Bill, and took the lead across the *malpais* until they came to a sinkhole, no different from any other, yet cupping a basin of water. A rank growth of bushes and horse-trodden sedge marked the margin of the hole, but for all the

89

years that the Indians had used it, there was no sign to indicate its presence — no monument, no rock pointers, no blaze on the pines, only the dim, uncertain trail and a flock of piñon jays that rose up with strange cries from its edge.

"I found this," bragged Bill. "Come in here by my lonesome, and, believe me, it took a little nerve. Did you notice old Cady? Well, that's the way I used to look when I'd been lost in the lava a spell. I'm the first human being to come into this *rincón* since the Apaches was here in the 'Eighties, and it shore had me scared up, boy. It's all right when you got company, but you come in by yourself, and it's shore going to give you the willies. But now, say, about Butch, he's jumpy as a cat on account of the excitement of that hold-up, so don't oppose him, understand, and, if he wants anything you've got, jest politely make him a present of it. He's a kid, that way . . . anything that *you* like *he* likes, but if you leave him have it, he'll soon git over it and, like as not, give it back. But don't talk up to him or he's liable to pull his gun and blow a big hole plumb through you."

"All right," agreed Meadows, "but is your conscience quite clear about capping me in on this game? I thought from what you said that he'd at least be reasonable, but, Bill, that man is crazy!"

"Don't you think it," burst out Bill, laughing heartily at the thought, "he's jest like a kid, I tell ye. Jest a big, spoiled boy that's been having his own way until nothing on earth will stop him."

90

"Well, I'll stop him," said Meadows, "if he crowds me too far."

"They ain't a ranch this side of the Saw Tooths that ain't got members of our gang, and lots of them boys over around the San Augustine Plains, too. Butch is framing up something big that I can't put you onto . . . something that'll call for a big bunch of men . . . and this Cady that he's talking to now goes back and forth with the news. Oh, I tell you, Ab, you didn't make no mistake when you throwed your feet under our table, and before we git through, they'll be some of these smart Mexicans hunting their holes like a passel of prairie dogs. But say, look . . . Cady's rounding up the horses!"

He pointed across the flat where, from the rolling prairie beyond, Cady was driving in a herd of forty horses. As they trotted toward the corral, Brennan's mare took the lead, head up and tail in the air.

"Ain't she grand!" Bill sighed. "I shore hated to part with her. But Butch, he was crazy to have her. Seems like everything I git, he wants."

"You're easy, Bill," said Meadows. "Why don't you stand up to him a little? A man has got *some* rights!"

"You don't know him," grumbled Bill. "He's got us all buffaloed. Come on, let's see what they're up to."

He started back to the corral where Butch had roped out the *chula*.

"Going out," snapped Brennan. "May not be back for a week. You boys stay here . . . understand?"

"You bet ye," responded Wild Horse Bill, and they looked on in silence until the chief and his messenger had departed.

"Saved again," observed Bill. "He shore gits on my nerves. Now, come on and we'll ride a few bronc's."

CHAPTER
SEVEN

With the departure of Butch Brennan a great peace seemed to be settling over the hidden *rincón* of the outlaws. Wild Horse Bill whooped with joy as he began forefooting bronchos. Meadows joined in on the work with a vim, and, as they were taming a wild one, a huge flock of piñon jays came flying in to water. They perched on the tall pines, craning their necks at the horsebreakers and sifting through the branches like a wind. Their clamorous cries, that had once seemed so strident, appeared to take on a new note of rejoicing. The sun swung up higher above the tops of the trees, fleecy clouds scudded by and were lost in the immensity that shut in their little world, and, safe at last from all danger and pursuit, Meadows sighed and reached out to grab happiness.

That was the only way, according to Bill, that happiness could ever be attained: it must be clutched at the moment, or it is lost forever, like a snowball left on a stove. So they lived each day as if it were a separate entity — with no past to embitter it with unpleasant memories and no future with its useless forebodings. As Meadows caught the spirit of his light-hearted companion, he began to see life through his eyes. Each morning was the beginning of another day, each night put his failures behind him, and, since no good end is served by vain repining, he forgot that he was an outcast and an outlaw. Life is ours to be lived, and our little mead of joy is the sum total of all our glad days. Whether that gladness comes from breaking wild bronchos or from breaking safes and jails was all one, according to Bill. Meadows might have had his doubts, but he kept them to himself, and Bill illustrated with the story of his life.

"I've been fighting," he said, "ever since I was four years old, and I never whipped anybody yet . . . but that's no excuse for not trying. I'll try anything once and there's one thing I *know* . . . the Mexican don't live that I'm skeered of."

All his life had been spent in the wild regions of New Mexico, catching horses, trapping wolves, punching cows, until the spirit to overcome had become the passion of his life and he sought out new worlds to conquer. Butch Brennan had happened by and led him on to greater dangers, holding up trains and robbing the express, and now, still unsatisfied, he looked forward to the time when they would wage open war against the Mexicans. This was the "big move" of Brennan's that he had hinted at so mysteriously that would need such a large body of men. Its purpose, according to Bill, was to break up Mexican domination and make New Mexico "a white man's country". A big contract, to be sure, but not too big, if the whole state of Texas was called in, and the way the Texans were coming west, it would not be long till they had a fighting majority. This was life as Bill saw it, a kind of modern Valhalla, where men fought every day and were restored overnight to carry on the battle again. In all that he did, he showed a true craftsman's pride in the perfect performance of his task. He described in great detail the proper manner of drawing a pistol, and at Meadows's request he gave him daily instructions in the technique of drawing and shooting. With Bill it was one movement, too swift to be seen, and he always shot from the hip. At each sudden swoop there came a look into his eye that bade all enemies beware. It was a source of wonder to Meadows and taught him a new respect for this doughty little man, but just as the solitude had made them blood brothers, Butch Brennan came riding in. He was more grim than ever, like a savage lone wolf returning from some far chase and kill, and a restless eagerness to be up and away showed in every swift move that he made.

"Git ready, boys," he said as soon as he had eaten. As Bill went dancing off, Brennan turned to Meadows with a quick imperious gesture. "Take two pack horses," he directed, "we're liable to need 'em." Meadows knew they were to rob another train.

They left the *rincón* along toward evening, closing the trail against the horses with brush and ropes. Darkness had fallen when they broke out of the *malpais* and took the trail to the east. Spurting on in advance, Brennan rounded the Punta de Malpais and rode north and east all night, and so on for three days until Meadows saw in the distance the smoke of a passing train. Where they were he did not know, nor what were

Brennan's plans, but, as they drew closer to the railroad, Brennan opened his sealed lips and held a guarded conference with Bill. Then Bill fell back and informed Meadows in an undertone that the train came through about midnight. That was all he dared to say for Brennan's nerves were on edge, and Brennan turned and scowled at them irritably.

It had not been pleasant, following glumly after Brennan over the roughest ground in New Mexico, but Meadows had stood up to it stoically. It was necessary, of course, to avoid all roads and trails, not to pass a single man or house, but Butch had made the trip as joyless as possible by forbidding them to sing or even talk. If Bill had had his way, he would have taken the main trail and left the rest of it to luck, but in this he was just the opposite of his chief who never took a chance on anything. It was that which made him such a merciless killer — when in doubt he shot first and asked afterward — and which made him a hard man to take. Now, as he rode along in the lead, looking out all the country ahead, he was nervous in the way that big cats are nervous when they stalk some wary prey.

Brennan knew that the express company, aroused by his last robbery, had hired manhunters and put them on his trail, but he also knew that they sought him in far places, where he had craftily let himself be seen. This blow would be a surprise, coming so soon after the last one, and upon that depended its success. Yet, a single Mexican, seeing them ride past his brush house, might rush in and tip their hand. Then they would be met at the train with a volley of rifle shots, mounted men would follow hot on their trail, and the treasure, if they got it, would have to be abandoned to save their own skins from stray bullets. So with infinite caution Brennan edged in on the railroad, spying out the country with his powerful field glass, and not a word would he speak or allow spoken until he stood beside the track.

The spot he had chosen was on the edge of a rocky mesa, where the railroad, crossing the river, mounted up on a long trestle until it passed through a deep cut to the high ground. If the engine were stopped at just the right place, the express car, with its treasure, would be out on the mesa, while the passenger coaches, with their troublesome occupants, would be left on the trestle below. There even an armed guard could do little or nothing since there was no way of getting off the train. Brennan pointed this out briefly, spoke a few words to Bill, and left them just at dusk. To him again fell the difficult and dangerous task of holding up the engine crew, and, as he started up the track toward a distant town, Bill shook his head and sighed.

"Poor old Butch," he said, "he shore takes it hard . . . but, believe me, he comes home with the bacon."

With this bit of philosophy, which he had been saving for three days, he led the way up a nearby wash. Now that Butch was gone, he threw off all restraint, talking and laughing and humming low songs. He was happy again, after days of suppression, happy once more to be his old self. As the hours dragged by, he managed to communicate to Meadows a part of his reckless abandon. It was easy, he assured him — all they had to

97

do was to carry out their part and keep calm — but, if the guards put up a fight, he abjured Meadows by all things holy not to go off and leave them afoot. That was the one unpardonable crime on the part of the horse holder, a crime that, with Butch, would be held to merit death and with him the end of their friendship. Butch would hold up the engineer and blow the big safe, and Bill would take care of the passengers. All that Meadows had to do was to *stay right there* until they came back with a barrelful of money.

The night wore on, Bill slipped out to look, and at last he came back running and lit up his bull's-eye lantern, for the train was pulling into the town. The headlight stood glaring while the engine took water, and, as it whistled to start, Bill flipped up his black neckerchief and hung it over the hook of his nose. Then he crouched and drew his pistols, flashing one at a time and then both guns at once. As he practiced on his draw, he chuckled to himself in nervous anticipation of the fight.

"Well, so long, Ab," he said, and, picking up his lantern, he went down to flag the train. It came toiling up the grade, puffing and thundering and sending up sparks. As it rumbled out over the trestle, the engineer whistled twice, the signal that Brennan was aboard. Meadows rose up quietly and stood by the five horses in his charge, tied bit to bit with short straps. As the engine ground to a stop, he could see dark forms drop off and start back along the train. Then Bill's pistols began to bark, spitting their fire against the night. In the flashes Meadows could see him, standing at the

98

edge of the cut and raking the train with his bullets. He paused to reload and in the silence that followed Brennan called on the express messenger to open up.

There was a longer silence then, with muffled parleys back and forth. At last the great door rolled smoothly back and revealed the dimly lighted interior. A man stepped into view, reaching down a reluctant hand, and the next moment Brennan was in the car. His tall agile form stood silhouetted in the doorway as he peered suspiciously inside. Then, with the messenger going before him as a shield, he disappeared in the space behind. A long wait followed, longer than Meadows had ever known, but broken at intervals by shrill cursings from Bill and the *bang* of his heavy .45. It was a slow and tedious business, preparing to blow the through safe, and the inquisitive passengers could hardly be restrained in their efforts to get off the train.

Brennan dropped to the ground and threw in his sack of dynamite and shouted a warning to Bill who came hurrying. With him, like automatons, came the engineer and fireman, and two other prisoners as well. They all scuttled away from the train. Then it came, a blinding flash followed by a roar and a bump, and the roof of the express car suddenly vomited up light as it was breached by the force of the explosion. That was all that Meadows saw for at the first jet of flames his horses all flew back at once. They jerked him from his feet as if he were a feather, but he held on resolutely, planting his high heels and dragging back until he brought them at last to a halt. He was soothing them down when Wild Horse Bill rushed up and unfastened the first of the pack horses. These animals were supplied with heavy canvas grub sacks into which their plunder could be hastily thrown without danger of its falling off. While Meadows held its head, Bill loaded the snorting horse with four heavy bags of coin.

"Back in a minute," he gasped, and dashed off toward the train where Brennan was fretfully holding the prisoners. Then a lantern flashed out, somebody gave Brennan a boost, and he leaped into the car. His bull's-eye flitted about and he plunged into the wreckage, to return with a single light sack. It was small, compared to the others, but it had come from the through safe with its time lock and massive steel doors, and Meadows knew from the way he held it that Brennan had made a big haul. He leaped down quickly, turned his lantern on the prisoners, and gave them a few sharp orders. Then the darkened train pulled slowly past while Brennan and Bill crouched and watched it. But no furtive guards dropped off the train, there was no one who had the hardihood to shoot, and, as they came running with their plunder, Bill and Brennan were talking and Bill was laughing hoarsely.

"Heh, heh," he burst out as Meadows helped him catch a horse to pack the remaining sacks, "did you hear what Butch told the messenger? He said, if the company didn't put some steps on them express cars, he was going to quit holding 'em up!"

"It was the same damned crew!" chimed in Brennan in high spirits, "the same bunch we held up last, and the conductor and all of 'em, they knowed us on sight and called us Shorty and Slim. I call that downright friendly, myself. Cinch them packs on tight, boys, while you've got a good chance, and then we'll hit the wind!"

They hung the heavy sacks high up on the packsaddles, balanced them against each other with thongs, and then they threw the lighter sacks on top and lashed them fast with a diamond hitch.

"Good enough!" pronounced Brennan and started off through the night, heading south, as was his custom, for the Datils. Ab and Bill followed behind, each leading a pack horse that traveled at a swinging trot, and, now that the first burst of his enthusiasm had passed, Butch Brennan retired into himself. He was thinking as he rode, hatching out some new scheme or mapping out his line of retreat, and his mare glided on as if the trail were a speedway and she a grain-fed mount. Bill and Meadows had to spur and use their quirts to keep up with Brennan's heartbreaking pace, and, as day dawned at last, Bill called for a halt and a redistribution of the load.

"That's all right for you, Butch," he said, cantering ahead to the *chula*, "but we're both dragging packs and them bags are working loose so I'm going to stop, right here."

"Going to take a little snooze?" inquired Brennan facetiously, and Bill rumbled dourly in his throat.

"Never you mind," he replied, "but if a third of this stuff is yours, you might as well help us pack it."

"Why, sure," returned Brennan, "want to divvy up now? If you're game, I'll tell you what I'll do. I'll give you two for one to git paper money for my coin and you boys can ramble by yourselves."

"Suits me," answered Bill, and, as Meadows agreed, they spread out their treasure on the ground. There were four bags of silver dollars, almost too heavy to pack, besides some smaller bags of gold, but the real money, of course, was in the sack of currency that Brennan had taken from the through safe. They set it all before them, and, while their horses nipped the grass, they divided it into three even piles. Then Brennan exchanged his silver and even his gold twenties, two for one for their paper currency.

"Quick work, boys," he said, nodding at their great heap of coin. "You'll be rich if you git that to the *rincón*. But take a tip from me and don't stop to pick no flowers. I've warned you . . . and now I'm going to drift."

He gathered up his currency and counted it over hastily. Then, filling his shirt with the larger denominations, he tied the sack on the back of his saddle.

"Not so bad," he observed, "twenty-one thousand, six hundred. Well, so long, boys. Don't break into jail." And he rode away.

"Not so bad, hey?" repeated Bill, scooping up the golden twenties and adding them to his store. "Well, what's the matter with this? I can't see where we lose anything, because we already had this silver, and the gold don't make much more. And we'd have to pack it anyway . . . Butch would never turn a hand . . . so I figure we're all to the good."

"Fair enough," agreed Meadows, "unless Brennan wants to ditch us. He may know something he didn't stop to tell."

102

"F'r instance?" suggested Bill, binding his money bags tightly with the smile of a self-satisfied miser.

Meadows glanced back down the trail. "Well, I don't know why it was, but he bet us two to one we'd get caught. Come on, let's hit for the hills."

"That's the truth!" burst out Bill, leaping up to repack. "We ought to knowed it, by the way he laughed. Damn his heart, he's trying to ditch us . . . ain't he a crooked son-of-a-bitch? But we'll fool 'im . . . you follow my dust!"

The way of their flight led up a broad cañon that twisted and turned like a broken-backed snake, and, as his horse began to lag, Bill burned him with his quirt, driving the pack animals before him on the run. They passed the high point of Wiley's Mesa and broke out onto the rolling ground beyond, and they crossed over into the valleys to the south that drain downward to form Red Lakes. There was no trail now, only narrow winding paths where the cattle had gone down to water, and Bill headed through the hills in a last burst of speed that brought him out suddenly at a ranch.

"We'll change horses," he said, riding straight to the corral. Without so much as a glance at the scared woman by the house, he caught out four horses from the pasture. They changed and packed hastily, leaving their own horses in the corral. As Bill lashed on the money bags, he dumped out a hatful of dollars to pay for the damage done. His rage against Brennan and his determination to escape had transformed him into almost a madman. His face was drawn, his eyes grim, and the old, cheerful smile had given place to a set grin, as rigid and implacable as a mask. He rode with quirt and spur, swinging a rope end at the pack animals that popped like a pistol shot behind them, and all the time he kept looking back for the posse that Brennan thought would catch them.

They swung down at last into the sandy bed of the Alamosa, which drains the north slopes of the Saw Tooths and Datils, and flows east to the Río Grande. It was seventy miles from where they had left the railroad, and fifty miles more to the *rincón*. As they toiled up the river bottom with its rank growth of shady cottonwoods, Wild Horse Bill began to nod. It had come back upon him again, the intense and fatal drowsiness that had betrayed him once before to his enemies, but he shook it off fiercely and lashed the horses to a gallop, following the well-worn trail up the stream. Across sandy flats and up over rocky points, he drove them on mercilessly until they began to bush up, seeking shelter from his rope in the brush. Then he slowed down and allowed them to trot, and once more his chin fell on his breast.

"Damn it, Ab," he complained, "I jest can't keep awake . . . haze 'em along, and haze me along, too."

A high, wooded ridge rose up at their left, leading on to the far peaks of the Datils, and far to the west the gleaming cliffs of the Saw Tooths caught the glory of the setting sun. All night and all day they had ridden without rest, and most of the day before. Meadows swayed and nodded, too, then pulled himself together and lashed the plodding horses to a lope. Bill rode like a dead man, swaying drunkenly in the saddle, one thin hand holding tightly to the horn, but each time he awoke, it was to spur on in a fury, shaking his head to fight off the sleep. A stone house rose before them on the point of a hill, looking vacant and roofless but with children running about. As they passed by below, a woman came out and ducked back inside the door.

"Bunch of Navajos," grunted Bill.

As Meadows looked around, he made out their camps among the willows. It was nothing but a clear space with some fire stones in the middle and some blankets and tin cans strewn about, but as they rode on through the brush, Meadows saw something else which had escaped Bill's drowsy gaze — a pair of snaky eyes, staring out from behind a log. They belonged to a Navajo, probably a member of the hunting party who had stayed in to guard the camp, and he was letting no detail escape him. The Navajos were peaceful, not making any trouble more than to shoot a little game out of season, but this buck had a look in his beady black eyes that augured no good to the fugitives. If their pursuers were close behind, he would take up their trail and lead the posse straight to their camp.

"Let's take to the hills, Bill," suggested Meadows at last. "You can't keep awake, and, if we follow this main trail, those Navajos are likely to find us."

But Wild Horse Bill was obdurate. "Not much! They don't ketch me again. I'm going to ride, by grab, until I git to the lava beds. Old Butch, he knowed what he was doing."

"Suit yourself," answered Meadows, and, tired as he was, he was glad to abide by Bill's decision. Butch

Brennan must have known something to make him give two for one to get rid of the weight even of gold, and, as long as flagging horseflesh could stand the strain, it was best to keep on up the trail. The old stone house, once the home of a cowman who had been murdered by marauding Apaches, was the last good camping place on the river. The farther they went now, the farther they left behind them the possibility of treachery and pursuit. Except for Brennan's warning they would have camped at Red Lakes, or at the IM Ranch, farther down the river, but now they were under the huge bulk of the Datils and well on their way to the lava beds.

The night fell dark, and, as they passed over a low point, the pack slipped and brought one animal to a halt. Wild Horse Bill dropped down and tried to boost it back, then loosed the ropes and tried again.

"Oh, hell," he burst out, throwing the load to the ground and flying into a pet. "Come on . . . I'm going to camp."

"Right here?" exclaimed Meadows. "Well, let's get out of the trail . . . some posse might ride right over us."

"I don't care if they do," declared Wild Horse Bill recklessly. "I'm dead on my feet for sleep. Let 'em come, if they're looking for trouble!"

"All right," soothed Meadows, "but come on over to that cottonwood . . . it's out of the road a little."

He gathered up the treasure that had been thrown into the dirt and led the tired pack animal to the cottonwood. It stood on the brink of the vine-tangled riverbank, the first tree of a great grove that stretched up and down the stream and across to the opposite bench. The river at this spot ran close to a high mesa, being diverted just enough by a point up above to leave a little corner of low ground, and the tall lone cottonwood was about equally distant from it and a point down the stream. A low, flat-topped hill rose up on the right and the river bottom lay to the left, so that they were camped in a hole, surrounded on three sides by higher ground and with the riverbed not fifty feet away — the last place in the world that Meadows would have stopped if Bill had not gone out of his head.

But he was a monomaniac now with one fixed idea, to lie down right there and sleep. Under the shelter of the broad tree they threw their packs off hurriedly, and, as Bill unsaddled to get at his blankets, Meadows caught the feeding horses and hobbled them. Then he, too, spread his saddle blankets and dropped down beside Bill.

When Meadows woke up, it was day. The dawn had passed unnoticed and the top of the flat hill was illuminated by the first rays of the sun. Meadows sat up with a start and felt for his six-shooter, then reached over and woke up Wild Horse Bill.

"What's the matter?" complained Bill, coming to life with a jerk and staring wildly about. "What the hell is biting you, anyway?"

"I heard something," answered Meadows with his eyes on the flat hill. "There's somebody up there, sure."

"Don't see nothing," grumbled Bill, suddenly beginning to take interest. "Say, where have them horses gone?" He buckled on his gun.

Meadows got up slowly and stood looking at the hill. It rose before him in a series of rocky benches, dotted at intervals with a few low trees, and yet, barren as it appeared, something left over from his dreams gave him warning that it sheltered an enemy. What it was that he had heard, what had roused him from his sleep, he could not even vaguely recall, but a premonition of danger had snatched him from his blankets and sent his hand to his gun.

"There they are!" exclaimed Bill after peering up the trail. On the edge of the flat, Meadows saw the outline of a horse, half concealed in the brush and trees. "Come on," said Bill, and, picking up a rope, he started off across the open flat. Meadows hurried after him, still vaguely oppressed, still listening over his shoulder for some sound. As they drew near their horses, he started and looked back, for a voice had spoken from the hill.

"Halt!" it said, and, as he dropped to a crouch, two Mexicans rose up on the hillside. They were big, powerful men, each with a star on his breast, and each with a rifle raised and aimed.

"Halt!" commanded one again, but the other man opened fire, and Bill cursed as the bullet almost struck him.

"Give 'em hell!" he hissed, and they pulled their guns together. The big Mexican on Meadows's side had held his fire, and, as Meadows threw down on him, he shot. Bill's gun spoke out twice before Meadows pulled the trigger, but when he shot, the Mexican fell.

"Got 'em both!" shrilled Bill, turning to look for more, and then he lurched to one side and fell. A gush of blood stained his red hair still redder, running down on both sides of his neck. As Meadows stooped to lift him, there was a volley from the hillside and the dirt leaped up into his face. He whirled then and ran, heading for the cutbank of the river which here was very close, but hardly had he taken shelter behind the bank when he was knocked in a heap from behind.

He came to in a moment to find his leg bleeding from a bullet that had pierced it through and through, and, as he lay hidden in the low willows, a murderous fury came over him — he reached for his pistol and waited. Whoever had shot him was across the stream, concealed in the heavy brush. As he watched the bank, he saw a bush move as if something had struck its base. Time was nothing to him now. He raised his gun up slowly and waited with his finger on the trigger. The bush moved again and an Indian's head craned up — it was the same snaky-eyed Navajo he had seen the day before, peering out from the brush as they had passed. Meadows glanced along the sights, held squarely between his eyes, and shot him without a tremor.

It was the Navajos, then, who were firing from the hill and who had sent poor Bill to his death! Meadows settled down patiently, ready to meet all comers. As he waited, a kind of grim peace crept over him, for Bill had not died unavenged. Where the Mexicans had sprung from, how many there were of them, or what they were trying to do were things he could only guess at, but the rifle shooting had ceased, and, if they were closing in, they would not find him unprepared. He wriggled swiftly through the thick undergrowth to the shelter of a cottonwood that had been undermined and had fallen into the streambed. With it on one side and the cutbank on the other, he lay quietly, listening intently for every sound. A long wait followed, in which he bound up his bleeding leg. Then he heard a hoarse voice, calling.

"Hey! Ab! Oh, Ab!" it cried, and then it broke and grew shrill.

Meadows leaped up from his hiding place. It was Wild Horse Bill, and he was calling for help. Meadows scrambled up and looked over the bank. Bill lay where he had fallen, but, as Meadows answered, he raised his voice to a shout.

"Come and help me," he pleaded, "I'm blind . . . I can't see! Oh, Gawd, Ab, don't leave me out here!"

Meadows's heart almost stopped, first with joy that Bill was alive, then with pity to hear him call. As he struggled over the edge, trying in vain to get some foothold, the Indians on the hilltop opened fire. He toppled and clutched a bush while the bullets rained about him as the Navajos pumped their repeaters, then his wounded leg gave way, and he fell to the bottom, carrying the bush and a shower of dirt with him. But the bullets had gone wild and in the silence that followed he heard Bill sobbing and cursing by turns.

"Oh, Bill!" he called, and, when Wild Horse Bill answered him, he shouted: "Crawl over here!"

"I can't!" wailed Bill. "I can't see nothing!"

110

"You can *hear* me!" encouraged Meadows, and, as he kept on calling, the dirt spilled down from the top of the bank and he saw Bill's bloody head.

"He'p me down," moaned Bill, rolling up his sightless eyes. "The dirty damned dogs are trying to kill me. He'p me down, for Gawd's sake, and then take my gun and go and kill me a Mexican."

"I'll do it," promised Ab. Struggling back up the bank, he eased him down to the ground. Then, limping to the water, he brought some in his hat and washed poor Bill's face and neck. The bullet had passed through from side to side, just under the base of the skull, and, as the water cooled his wound, Bill closed his staring eyes and dropped off into a doze. Or was it death? Meadows watched him a long time, lying closely by his side and scanning the banks of the stream, and then he remembered his promise.

"Give me your gun, Bill," he said, trying to pull it loose from its scabbard, and Bill opened his eyes with a jerk.

"Where you going?" he complained, and then he sat up with a sudden yelp of joy.

"I can see!" he quavered. "By grab, Ab, I can see! Hey, gimme that gun back . . . what you think you're trying to do? Well, I'll kill that Mexican myself!" He rose up carefully and felt of his neck, and the old grin crept back over his face. "They jest creased me!" He laughed. "Like you shoot wild horses when you can't ketch 'em no other way! Jest shot me through the neck cords, but, hell, they never teched me. Come on, let's get out of this dump!"

CHAPTER
EIGHT

There is nothing like a large and man-size hate to put strength into crippled limbs, and, as Meadows limped off down the shallow stream bed of the Alamosa, he barely noticed his leg. It dragged and held him back, but it did not kill his spirit or weaken his passion for revenge. As for Wild Horse Bill, now that his sight had come back, his one desire was to meet up with some Mexican. If it came to a fight, that wound through his neck would be paid for dearly by somebody, but their retreat was undiscovered, and, when they were far down the river, Bill put up his gun with a sigh.

"The yaller-bellied bastards!" he burst out vengefully. "I'd like to take on about twenty of 'em. And that bunch of dirty Navajos . . . I'll shore make them hard to ketch if I ever git out of this alive. What's the dope . . . can you travel on that leg?"

"I've got to," answered Meadows. "Wait till I cut me a crutch and I'll keep on as long as I can."

"Where to?" inquired Bill. "You ain't thinking of Show Low? You'll never make it, Ab."

"It's our only chance," returned Meadows gloomily. "I've got friends over there . . . or I used to have."

He hobbled out into the willows and cut a forked pole that he whittled down and padded with his vest, and then he set his face to the huge rampart of the Datils which loomed up across their way. Over that wall of yellow sandstone and earthquake-shattered porphyry, and far down on the other side, lived the only man he could count on to protect him — Dave Starbuck, at the Figure 4 Ranch. There would be a big reward and a systematic search, for two Mexican officers had been killed, but all the money in the world could not bribe Dave Starbuck, once he took a man in as a friend. But, loyal as he was to all his friends, there was one thing that Starbuck would not stand for and that was defiance of the law. The question was — would he harbor an outlaw?

Meadows thought it all over as he swung along up an old trail that led over the far summit of the Datils, and sometimes his heart rose as he remembered their former friendship, and then it fell as he remembered his misdeeds. Not only had he broken jail and killed a Mexican officer, but without justification or any shadow of an excuse he had been guilty of robbing a train. Right there was where he stuck, for Starbuck could be charitable, but he had his own standards of right and wrong. In his own turbulent life there had been many deeds that would now put him beyond the pale of the law, but down beneath it all he had a New England conscience which drew the line at crime. Crime was low and self-seeking, without the urge of high passions or the excuse of some fancied wrong — it was cowardly, in fact, which is why Starbuck hated it, although he had never dissected his emotions.

In the days when Dave Starbuck had come to New Mexico, every man carried his life in his hands, and courage had become his religion. If a man was brave, if he stood up to adversity and took no thought of the odds, that man was Starbuck's friend and could call on him for anything, even for protection against the officers of the law. But if he was cowardly, like Butch Brennan, always seeking some advantage and never taking a chance, Starbuck hated and despised him and made no concealment of his scorn. Now Meadows himself, although sorely against his will, was numbered with the outlaws in the Wild Bunch. For long hours he brooded while his leg swelled and throbbed and his head whirled with hunger and fatigue, and then he turned to Bill, who was following along behind him, and laid the problem before him.

"Hoo . . . easy!" expounded Bill, sinking down in the shade and flinching as he felt of his neck, "don't tell him you robbed the train. You didn't rob no train . . . that was me and Butch . . . all you did was hold the horses."

"Well, what about this money that I've got in my shirt . . . did I come by it honestly, or not?"

"Hide it in the rocks," suggested the ever-practical Bill, and Meadows saw that his advice was good. His hunger and weariness had destroyed his own caution — instead of plotting to escape, he let his mind ramble on, splitting hairs over the ethics of the case. But Bill was always practical, no matter how he suffered or how dark the prospect seemed. Picking up a fruit can that had been left on the trail, Meadows stuffed his paper money inside it. Then, spying a pack rat's nest, he clambered up the ledge and buried it in the mass of sticks. The rats would steal it anyhow, if he hid it in their neighborhood, so it was safest, after all, to leave it in their custody but protected from their teeth by the can. Knowing the practices of the piratical trade rats, Meadows claimed as his toll, in exchange for the money, the last of their store of pine nuts.

In the fall of the year, when the frost cracks the pine cones and the rich seeds fall to the ground, the rats work for weeks picking out the biggest and soundest and storing them away in their caves. Now, although the winter was passed and there were new cones on the pines, this provident pack rat had a hatful or more of nuts buried deeply at the back of his ledge.

"This is a bad business, Bill," observed Meadows, smiling wanly as he came down with the rat's precious store, "a man gets so low he'll rob rats."

"Aw, forget it," grumbled Bill, who hunger had rendered desperate, "if I could ketch him, I'd eat the damned rat." He scooped up a handful of nuts from the hat and began to crack them with marvelous skill, turning the shells on edge and making them pop open with one carefully graduated bite.

"Gee, I'm thirsty," Meadows moaned. "Waded right down that river and never once thought to take a drink. How far is it to Dog Springs?"

"Six miles," responded Bill. "Don't make much difference nohow, them Indians will be on our trail. Yep,

115

somebody will git us, shore . . . we're worth too much money. But we'll fight it out together, hey, Ab?"

He nodded encouragingly and pressed on up the steep trail, looking back every minute for the pursuit, but the sun rose high and sank, and, when they came to Dog Springs, the trail behind them was bare. They hid that night in the rocks above the springs, where they could cover the trail with their six-shooters, and, as morning dawned, they started on again, still watching for the expected pursuit. The path led on beneath spruces and yellow pines, then down through the bull pines to the piñons and cedars and the rocky cañons below, but no one rode up on them or disputed the trail. They seemed lost in a wilderness of high peaks. Yet somewhere behind them was an armed posse of Mexicans and Indians, and farther back on the trail would come more, and Bill's head alone was worth thirty thousand dollars, to say nothing of the cash on his person. Bill was always practical. He clung to his money on the off chance that he might still escape, but when at last his vigilance was rewarded, he only grunted grimly.

"There they come," he said, and Meadows, looking back, saw a dim bit of motion on the trail. It was a string of mounted men, creeping slowly over the summit, far away, yet clear in the thin air.

"Look like Indians," he suggested, and Bill squinted again, then blinked his eyes in assent.

"That's right," he observed. "Can't see like I used to. It looks like they're dragging a pack."

"Let's give them the trail," proposed Meadows. "That outfit isn't looking for trouble."

"Well, mebbe not," agreed Wild Horse Bill, and they climbed up among the high rocks.

The pack train had vanished, but at last it appeared again, winding slowly down the near slope. As it drew near their shelter, Meadows recognized the four pack horses as the ones they had lost the day before. The two packsaddles were loaded with their hard-earned treasure, but the burdens flung across their former mounts were the bodies of the Mexicans they had killed.

"Let 'em go," murmured Meadows, and Bill assented although he still gazed wistfully at the treasure. There on those two pack animals was a king's ransom in money, for which they had already nearly given up their lives, but if they tried to regain it, the surviving Indians would surround them and a Mexican posse would do the rest. The Navajos rode on dumbly, hunched down in their saddles, for they were fearful in the presence of death, and the fugitives were content to let them pass, since they could not gain back their mounts. They had played the game, and lost, and it would be time for an attack when they were healed of their wounds and armed. But now they were weak and their hurts were sore and the courage had oozed out of their hearts. After the Indians had passed out of sight, they limped down and turned off on a side trail.

The sun was sinking low when, with their strength almost spent, they toiled up the slope of the last interminable hill and saw the Figure 4 pasture below them. It was still far away, a vivid ribbon of green shut in by cedar-crowned ridges, and, as he gazed, Meadows saw spots of red and white and yellow, moving about on the sun-struck *vega*. They were his horses, his pets, that he had tamed and cared for as gently as if they had been children, and he knew them, every one, by the color of their sleek hides and the way that they moved about. He knew them by that instinct which comes from hunting horses and from watching them feed from afar, and, as he started down the hill, a tear splashed before him for the days that were gone forever. But the time for repining and repentance was past, and he dragged his aching leg recklessly.

The trail wound down the slope and into a broad cañon where Figure 4 cattle were browsing, and, as this cañon joined another one that came down from the summit, they crossed a mountain stream. This was the source of the water that flowed past Starbuck's house and filled the big tank for his stock, and in order to protect it Starbuck had winked at a practice that had ultimately given him title to the ground. Certain men in his employ had from time to time taken up claims along the creek, and, after they had proved up on their quarter sections of land, they had sold their useless homesteads to the boss. But the headwaters of the creek were still open for settlement, and, as they passed around a point, they came upon a cabin, fresh and new but standing deserted.

"Hello!" exclaimed Bill after a lengthy stare. "It looks like somebody lives here!"

"Nope . . . come on," answered Meadows shortly, "just leave that house alone."

His voice rose up fretfully, but Wild Horse Bill was interested and he tried the door, which was locked. Then he turned and looked at some tracks on the ground and glanced accusingly at Meadows.

"Oho!" he said, "so it's the schoolmarm's, eh? Looks like she'd been up here today."

"Yes, it's hers," confessed Meadows, "but don't bother it, Bill. Come on, let's go down to the ranch."

"What, with that leg of yourn?" inquired Wild Horse Bill pointedly. "Say, mebbe she's got some grub!" He tried the door again, then reached into his pocket and brought out a thin-edged key. "Keno!" he observed as the door opened before him, and stepped boldly into the house.

It was a one-roomed log cabin with a fireplace at one end and a table and bed at the other. Over the window — sure sign of a woman — was a curtain of dainty cloth. Meadows stood outside, dangling weakly on his crutch, and then Bill raised a shout.

"Here's some bread!" he clamored, taking a hasty bite and holding out half of the loaf. "Come on, you damned fool, don't stand there and starve . . . if she was here, she'd cook you a meal!"

"Well, I hope so," answered Meadows, and sank down on the steps where he devoured the last of her bread. This was no time for nice questions of yours and mine, nor yet of right and wrong. He was famished and Bill was famished, and her house had just happened to be the first. He had known all along that they would pass her little cabin, where she came every weekend to work, but the memory of their parting still rankled in his breast and he had determined to pass it by. But Bill was more human — and her bread was good. He was glad now that Bill had used his key.

"Here's a big jar of peaches!" burst out Wild Horse Bill. "And, oh, gee, boys, a whole lot of stuff! Say, we'll camp right here, Ab, and, if she happens to come back . . . well, that'll be up to you!"

"No, we won't!" came back Meadows, but after he had eaten, he sprawled out on the floor and lay still. Nothing mattered to him now as long as he could rest and favor his aching leg.

When Meadows awoke, he was lying in her bed and Bill was bathing his wound. Then he slept again, and it was noon the next day when he roused up and looked around. Bill was lying by the fireplace, rolled tightly in a blanket just as he had dropped off to sleep long before, and not even the thunder of galloping hoofs could break the profundity of his dreams. Meadows reached under his pillow and found his pistol, carefully placed there by the practical Bill, but as the sound died away, he drowsed off into oblivion, and, when he woke up, it was dark. There was a fire in the fireplace and Bill sat before it, eating peaches from a two-quart jar.

"Git up," he invited, rolling his eyes toward the bed, "git up and have something to eat. Say, my neck is stiff as a post."

Meadows rose up slowly and with much groaning put his stiffened limb to the ground, then he reached

120

for his crutch and limped painfully to the fire, every muscle in his body protesting.

"Think you can travel?" queried Bill. "Gitting kind of warm around here . . . bunch of Mexicans rode by a while ago."

"No, Bill, I can't do it," answered Meadows despondently. "There's something the matter with my leg."

"Don't I know it?" agreed Bill. "You used it too hard, dragging it up over that Dog Springs trail. It's starting to go bad on you, inside."

"I had some dope," mused Meadows at last, "that I used to use for doctoring cuts . . . it's right down there at the ranch."

"Yes, and a bunch of crazy cowpunchers and about forty dogs. They'd run you down like a rabbit!"

"Better stay here, then," responded Meadows. "It's the only chance I've got. But don't let me keep you, Bill."

"Oh, that's all right," said Bill, and lapsed into silence squinting thoughtfully into the fire. He was a hard man to look at, with a week's growth of beard and his stiff neck wrapped up in a rag, but he had a quality which more than made up for it — he never went back on a friend. Meadows laid off the bandage and bathed his throbbing wound, and then they sat there together, waiting whatever fate had in store for them, content with whatever might befall. At last, as they listened, they heard the drumming of hoofs and Bill kicked out the fire.

"Here goes nothing," he said, and stood back in the darkness, his pistol pointing at the door.

CHAPTER
NINE

When a cowboy turns his horse off the brow of some hill in pursuit of a flying steer, his curse and his prayer, his one comment on it all is the old cynical saying: "Here goes nothing." Here goes his life, if he is killed — his worthless cowboy's life that he never has held very dear — or a leg if he is crippled, or a big patch of skin, or maybe his pet saddle horse. But what are they, after all, in the immensity of time and space and the general futility of it all, and a few years more or less mean little to a man who regards life itself as a joke. And so Wild Horse Bill, rising up to shoot it out, uttered his protest against a world gone wrong.

As for Meadows, he sat silently, listening intently to the hoof beats that were thundering along up the trail. There were two horses, at least, and they were coming at a lope, racing up to their very door, and then a man's voice spoke out.

"What'd I tell you!" he challenged, and, as he burst into a laugh, Meadows muttered under his breath. That laugh was Lute Starbuck's, the other Starbuck boy that he never could learn to like, but the voice that answered belonged to Justina — she had come back to stay at her cabin.

"That's all right," she was saying, "I could beat you if I wanted to. But I told you not to come."

"Well, I told you not to go," he came back teasingly. "Come on, let's ride back to the house!"

"No, I won't," she answered flatly, and in the silence that followed Meadows heard her drop off and tie her horse. "You can go back now," she said, and a moment later her key turned softly in the lock.

"Oh, I don't know," he replied, suddenly changing his tone. "It's a wonder you wouldn't invite a fellow in."

"If I'd invited you to come," she responded evenly, "I might consider inviting you in. But this is not the time of night for young ladies to receive visitors, as you know very well, Lute Starbuck."

"Aw, who's going to know?" he went on coaxingly. "What's the matter, Justina? Don't you like me?"

"Never you mind," she returned, "and, if you know what's good for you, you'll get back on that horse and go!"

Her voice rose as she spoke, then suddenly the door was jerked open, and she whisked in and locked it behind her. There was a long minute of silence, in which Bill and Meadows held their breaths, and she spoke again through the door.

"Lute Starbuck!" she warned. "I've stood enough from you. Now you do what I tell you and leave me alone, or I'll report your conduct to your father."

"I didn't mean anything," he protested, laughing, but as she made no reply, he took another tack. "You ought not to stay here," he argued. "Those outlaws are around here, somewhere. That man, Brennan, is a bad one, and

Wild Horse Bill is capable of doing anything. But, of course, if you think that tall fellow was Meadows . . ."

"Now you mind your own business," answered Justina peremptorily, "and kindly go away from my door. If you knew what it was to act like a gentleman, you wouldn't need to be told."

"Yes, a gentleman," he jeered, "like Ab Meadows, eh? Well, your gentleman has gone and joined Butch Brennan . . . I always knowed he was a crook!"

There was a clump of dainty boots as she strode across the room and fumbled in the top of her trunk, and then she stepped back and flung open the door while a pistol gleamed in her hand.

"Now, you git!" she said, her voice trembling with rage, and the hush that followed was broken by a scramble and the clatter of hoofs down the trail. "The fool!" she burst out, shutting the door and turning the key, and then she felt about for her lamp. In the corner Wild Horse Bill nudged Meadows in the ribs and rose up quietly in the darkness, but when the light flared up, he stood there alone, with his hands held up for peace. Justina put on the chimney and glanced swiftly about, alarmed by the change in her room, and then she caught sight of Bill. The man who had compared her to the "Mona Lisa" little dreamed of the Spartan courage behind her smile for, when she saw Bill, she barely flinched.

"Who are you?" she demanded, and the anger roused by Lute flared out in her level eyes. "Oh, yes, you're that Wild Horse Bill." She spoke the name slightingly,

124

and Bill dropped his hands for her tone had cut to the quick.

"Shore," he said, and straightened up defiantly, but she had caught a glimpse of Meadows. He was sitting in the shadow with his wounded leg thrust out, and she had to look twice before she knew him.

"Oh, I see," she said, glanced again at them both, and then at the disordered room. "So you moved in, did you?" she observed at last, but her voice was far away — she was thinking of something else.

"Yes, we moved in," replied Meadows apologetically. "I'm afraid we've left it a wreck."

She looked about again — at her tumbled bed, her looted food box, and the dirt and rags on the floor — and took no pains to conceal her disapproval.

"Yes, you did," she agreed, and then Wild Horse Bill spoke up with his twisted, broken-toothed smile.

"Mighty sorry," he explained, "but we hadn't et for two days and Ab got shot through the leg. He can't travel, that's all, or we'd be up and gone. Mighty sorry to make you all this trouble."

"Oh, don't mention it," she said with a sardonic bow, and then she stood gazing at Meadows. "And so you've come to this!" she exclaimed reproachfully. "Were you there when they robbed that train?"

"Oh, no, miss . . . ," burst out Bill, but Meadows cut him short.

"Yes," he answered, "I was there."

"And perhaps," she went on, "you killed that poor Navajo . . . or one of the Mexican officers."

"Yes," he admitted, "I killed them both. It was that Indian who shot me through the leg."

"Oh," she murmured, and turned her face away, whereupon Bill butted in once more.

"He never killed them officers . . . I killed 'em myself . . . and that Indian slipped up behind him. I'll be going now, Miss Edwards, if it'll make it any pleasanter, but Ab shore needs some medicine."

"No, you stay here," she ordered, "and you don't need to lie . . . we all know just what you've done. It's a question with me whether I ought to give you up or make myself a party to a crime."

"Well, suit yourself," said Bill, but there was a challenge in his voice which hinted that he personally did not care.

"Let me talk to him alone," she spoke up at last, and Bill slipped like a weasel out the door.

She stood thinking for a minute, then moved about the room, picking up bandages, clearing the table, starting a fire.

"I can't understand it!" she cried out at last as he met her eyes with a wan smile. "Oh, how could you do it, Ab?"

"That's easy," he replied. "I couldn't help doing it, Justina."

"Yes, you could!" she declared, sitting down by the fire and preparing to argue the question. "You didn't need to kill that poor Indian."

"Yes, I did," returned Ab, "or he'd have killed me. I shot him in self-defense. And it's been like that from the beginning. It all dates back to that first time, when

I met Butch Brennan in the hills." He told her briefly of his first meeting with Brennan and of all that had followed hard upon it, and then of the jail break and the trip to the lava beds, the hold-up and the battle with the posse. "And all that," he ended, "came from a stroke of lightning. Don't you know, I believe our lives are laid out for us?"

"In what way?" she asked, awed by the hush in his voice. "I don't know what you mean."

"No, of course not," he went on, "and I don't know why I'm telling it, except that . . . well, you understand. A posse may come along any time. But Bill is out there now, watching for them, and, if they come, you must leave me, because I'll never be taken alive."

"But why?" she protested, breaking in on his story in her anxiety to put him right. "Why won't you surrender? It's the law!"

"Yes, I know," he conceded, "but I'm not built that way. And I'd rather be shot than hung!"

"Oh, Ab!" she cried, and threw out her hands, but he shook his head and went on.

"No," he said, "I'll never have it said that Ab Meadows surrendered to a Mexican. The Meadows have been soldiers for too many generations to make that easy to do. But I was speaking about the lightning."

"Yes," she nodded, and he gazed into the fire before he went on with his story.

"If that stroke of lightning hadn't come when it did and scared my bronc into the hills, I'd never have cut Brennan's trail. And if I hadn't cut his trail, I wouldn't have followed it up, and come back with his horse and all. And if I hadn't had his money and been riding his horse, I wouldn't have been arrested by those Mexicans . . . and so on, and so on. Don't you see how that lightning has changed my whole life? Well, here's the rest of my story. I was up in Colorado, and the times were bad there just the same as they're bad around here, but I guess I'm too proud to steal. I was then, anyhow, but I had a cowboy friend that did quite a business in wet horses. He stole them, you understand, and the time came at last when I decided to throw in with the gang. Ed had rounded up some horses and we were driving them out of the country, although I'll confess my heart wasn't in it, when we ran into a mountain storm. The lightning was striking everywhere, and somehow I got the feeling that it came straight from God's own hand, but I'd promised to stick and I wouldn't go back on Ed, so we hazed them along over the pass. They were darting here and there and trying to turn back on us, and we were yelling and cursing behind them, when there was a smash all around us that knocked our horses flat and killed every bronc' in the herd. My mouth was wide open, calling down a curse on everything, when the lightning came out of the sky, and since that time I've never sworn an oath, nor taken a stolen dollar . . . until now."

He sighed and shifted his leg, which was giving him pain, and she reached over and touched his hand.

"But back of all that," she suggested gently, "wasn't there something else that started you wrong? The lightning couldn't have saved you, and this last stroke couldn't have ruined you, if there hadn't been something behind it. The trouble has been, you don't care."

"Yes, that's right," he agreed, "and perhaps it's for the best. I have a hunch it will soon be over."

"Is your wound dangerous?" she asked.

He nodded his head. "And the worst of it is, I can't ride."

"But perhaps . . . ," she began, and then paused and puckered her brows in thought. "I might ride down to the ranch," she suggested at last, "and get you the carbolic you need."

She rose up quickly, and stepped to the door, only to close it and come flying back.

"He's gone!" she cried. "He's stolen my horse! Oh, that Wild Horse Bill . . . he's taken Nipper!"

"Go out and look around," he suggested quietly.

She did and came back with a smooth, white board.

"Look at that," she said and pointed to a sign, scrawled with a coal by the light of the stars:

I'll be back
Bill

"What will we do?" she asked, and a strange look came into his eyes as he contemplated this last blow to his hopes.

"We might sit and talk," he said.

In the last night before death, when his whole life rises before him and mocks him with its waste and shame, the desire of a condemned criminal, if his nerve is weak, is to confess and be shriven of his sins. But if his nature is more hardy and he has that within him which steels him against all natural ills, then he craves only the companionship of some kindred spirit until he crosses the Bridge of Sighs. So Meadows, left alone by the slippery Wild Horse Bill and deprived of his last chance to escape, turned to the woman he had worshiped and adored from afar and asked the boon of her company. The circumstances were unusual but Justina understood, and they sat by the fireplace together.

"Do you remember," he began, "how you used to ask me who I was, and I would never tell you? Well, I'll tell you now . . . but you'll be disappointed. I'm just what you always thought I was . . . another black sheep, come West. No, I'm not an escaped criminal . . . and my folks are not rich enough to make me a remittance man . . . I'm just a man with a genius for mistakes and a temper that sometimes gets away from me. My first mistake, of course, was falling in love with a woman who never made any mistakes herself. She thought it all out carefully and married the other man . . . that's why I came out West. I was afraid, if I stayed, I might kill somebody."

"I know," she nodded, "my father was like that. He had times when he just saw red. That's why the Apaches were so dreadfully afraid of him . . . he'd fight the whole tribe with one hand. But I think Mister Starbuck has a better idea . . . he believes that those old days are past and gone and that now we should abide by the law. You know, when I came back and found that Father had been killed . . ."

130

"Killed!" exclaimed Meadows. "I thought he committed suicide!"

"I know they all say that," she went on steadily, "but he didn't . . . that wasn't his way. He might drink and fight and gamble away all his property, but he wouldn't commit suicide . . . that's cowardly. And when I came back and saw the man who had ruined him actually glorifying in what he had done . . . naming the town Show Low and boasting of how he had won it by causing the death of my father . . . why, something came over me, and, before I knew it, I was asking Mister Starbuck for a gun. So you see, I can understand."

"Yes," responded Meadows, and looked at her again as she sat, brooding and silent, by the fire. There was nothing effeminate or coquettish about her now — her gray eyes were glowing, her smiling lips set, her penciled brows drawn down in a frown. The soft lines and demure graces had fallen away from her and left a grim Indian fighter's daughter.

"But I'm still here," she went on, "and I won't forget. Chris Woolf can't understand why I keep coming to the store when I could get my mail with the Starbucks', but by rights that store is mine, and I'll go into it when I choose, no matter if it is a saloon. At first he was afraid of me . . . I could see it in his eyes and his guilty, hangdog stare . . . and then, the poor fool, he thought I was in love with him and wanted to marry him to get back my property. Oh, how I hate that man, with his fat, greasy face and that piggish look in his eyes, but I

131

must be patient a while longer, until I get certain evidence, and then he'll understand."

She glanced at him meaningfully, and Meadows heaved a sigh, for her life was still before her. No matter what its tragedy, it was hers to be lived, but his was forfeit for his crimes. She was more beautiful than ever with the color in her cheeks and the fine flash of anger in her eyes, more like a woman and less like a child that goes through life without a thought of its purpose. She had revealed her soul, even as he had revealed his own, and somehow they seemed nearer each other.

"Justina," he said, "I'm afraid I've misjudged you. You won't mind if I tell you, now, but I've never taken you very seriously before. I've wondered, of course, but it never occurred to me that you had anything like this in your mind."

"No, I've noticed it," she observed. "You've always treated me like a child. And I might have helped you . . . once."

"You helped me, anyhow," he answered, "and I didn't want to ruin your life. You had troubles enough without shouldering any of mine, but I loved you, just the same. I can say it now, because it won't make any difference, and I'm sure you'll understand. What we commonly take for granted or leave unsaid comes out at a time like this, and, when I am gone, I hope you'll remember that they *all* meant I was in love with you . . . everything unsaid. I used to dream about you . . . we must all dream of someone, and you are very different from her . . . and, even when I picked up those

132

accursed twenties of Butch Brennan's, I was thinking of buying a home. I had some more money saved up."

"But you never would admit it," she said with a wan smile. "You're the only one that never made love."

"Yes" — he smiled back — "it was a great game, wasn't it? But I had learned already that love is too precious to be bandied to and fro . . . and the home was only a dream. I knew I could never win you, or even have a home, but a man learns to cling to his dreams. If I had told you I loved you, the dream would be gone and no one left much the happier. You see, I'm losing my nerve."

"Yes," she murmured absently, "they say the best riders are those that have never been thrown. But do you know what I'm going to say? I wish you had told me before."

"And I wish . . . ," he began, and then he shook his head. "But wishing time is past, I'm afraid."

"No, it isn't!" she replied, putting her hand trustingly in his. "It's never too late to try. And I think a great deal of you, Ab."

"Yes, I know you do," he answered gently, "and that's why I'll never make that wish. It's getting late, Justina, and perhaps it would be better . . ."

"No . . . wish!" she insisted, moving closer to his side and gazing up into his eyes. "Did it have something to do with me?"

"Yes," he responded, and then he gave in, for her eyes were smiling now. "I wish that I hadn't killed a couple of men and got this hole through my leg. And I wish Celso Baca and about forty Mexicans weren't

133

coming out hot foot to catch me . . . also that the express company didn't have a posse on my trail. I wish I was back where I was a month ago, breaking bronc's for old man Starbuck and seeing the schoolma'am home."

"Is that all?" she asked, and, when he nodded, she shook her head reproachfully.

"That's enough," he sighed, "if I were back there again . . ."

"But Ab," she broke in, "you were back there . . . once! What difference if you were back there again? Didn't I used to smile, and beg and wheedle, to get you to tell me who you were, and what was making you so sad? But you wouldn't even tell me. I might have helped you, but you treated me just like a child. And now, when I offer to help you again, you refuse even to *wish!* You mustn't think, just because I act foolish and let all the cowboys make love to me, that I'm only a scatterbrained fool. I have troubles, too, as bad or worse than yours were, and that is my way to forget. I had to do something or I'd go out of my head, and so I got up dances and went out riding with the boys and did all those ill-considered things. But *you* wouldn't help me, and, oh, don't you see, a woman can suffer, too!"

"Yes, I suppose she can," he answered. "I'd have been glad to help you, Justina."

"But you didn't!" she reminded him. "You always slipped away from me. And even when Lute began to pay me attention, you wouldn't even admit you were jealous!"

134

"I was, though," he broke in, "but I wouldn't show it to him. I don't like him, Justina, and never did, but I put up with him on account of his father, and, when I saw you and him together, and considered what it meant to the old man . . ."

"You were just faint-hearted!" she burst out resentfully. "You don't *deserve* to have anything!"

"No, and I haven't *got* anything," he answered bitterly. "So I guess you must be right."

"No, now Ab . . . ," she began, and then she stopped. "Oh, how can I make you understand? You're not honest with yourself, that's the point . . . you're whipped before you start! You just wait around until some Mexicans try to arrest you before you put up a real fight, but if you'd decided what you wanted and fought that hard to get it, you wouldn't be where you are now. You're not cowardly, I won't say that, but you've lost your nerve! There, I heard you say it yourself. You're like a man that's been thrown from a bad horse and is afraid to mount even a gentle one, but just because you had a little trouble back home is no reason for never trying *anything*. You've just been a drifter, without any purpose in life, and this is what it's brought you to, but if you'd be honest with yourself . . . and honest with me . . . Will you try it, Ab? I'll help you."

She took his hand again — he never would take hers — and pressed it while she waited for his answer, but at the end he heaved a great sigh.

"Well, I'll be honest with *you*," he said at length, "and I'll tell you . . . there isn't a chance. I'm older than you are . . . only twenty-eight, at that . . . but I know what I'm up against. I have killed a deputy sheriff in the performance of his duty, and that's something that can never be squared. If I'm taken in New Mexico, or extradited from any other country, these Mexicans will hang me, sure. And that's a death that I don't like to contemplate. So I'm going to fight till I'm killed. Can you suggest any other way out?"

He paused and smiled cheerlessly into the startled gray eyes, which were beginning to fill with tears, and continued with his pitiless logic.

"So much for the Mexicans . . . if I had two good legs, I wouldn't be scared of a thousand of them . . . but now comes this express company that we robbed. All I did, to be sure, was to hold the horses while the other two held up the train, but that makes me just as guilty in the eyes of the law as if I had blown that safe. The express company has lost over a hundred thousand dollars by waiting on these incompetent Mexican officers, and they'll be in here with their own manhunters soon. And when *they* come, Butch Brennan and all his gang will go, and they won't all go to heaven, either. I know that kind of detectives, I've seen them in action, and they hunt down a man the way a wolfer tracks a wolf . . . and give him about as much chance. They hunt train robbers for the reward just as wolfers hunt for the bounty, and there'll be ten thousand dollars on my head. They'd follow me anywhere for that. And then, to top it off, this leg of mine is bad, and I expect, sooner or later, it will kill me."

"Oh, Ab," she moaned, and buried her head against his breast, and then she sat up suddenly.

"Now, listen," she said, "all this trouble has come about because you always have said . . . 'What's the use?' You've imagined all along that the whole world is against you and that you didn't have a chance to win, but if you'd only been brave enough to put up a fight, you could have had . . . oh, you could have had *anything!* Now I'll tell you what to do . . . I'll walk down to the ranch and bring back that bottle of medicine . . . and then you can hide right here until your leg is well and I'll help you out of the country. And after that . . . well, it all depends on whether you ever say . . . 'What's the use?'"

She rose up with decision, threw some wood on the fire, and stepped out into the night. As Meadows lay, listening for her footsteps to return, he pondered on what she had said. Had not this woman, this seeming child, put her finger on the very spot, the weak place which had ruined his life? Was there not a chance of his mending the broken span yet? She was right about other things, was she not right about that? And she was with him, heart and soul. Other women he had known had appealed to him by their beauty or attracted him by some quality of mind, but this was the first who had lifted him up and put new faith into his heart. She had come as a friend, with the bold courage of a man and the sympathy and sweetness of a woman, and, after he had laid his ruined life before her, she had marked out a way to mend it. First, his wound must be healed, and she had gone off through the night to bring back

137

the medicine to cure it. Then he must flee both his enemies and his friends, and she had promised to speed him on his way. But was he worth it? He frowned and put the demon of doubt behind him — he must never think in circles again.

As the will to live, after all medicines have failed, sometimes snatches a man back from death's door, so joy and hope and something to live for have also achieved their victories. Death is a surrender of the spirit, a giving up of the ghost, which sometimes flits away in sleep, but when a man lays hold with avid fingers and clutches life to his breast, it takes something more than a bullet hole or two to pry those fingers loose. Abner Meadows had blinked at death, almost beckoned it to come, but when Justina returned with the powerful antiseptic that he had used to heal cuts on his horses, the very touch of her hands seemed to restore his wound and drive out the foul forces of corruption.

CHAPTER
TEN

A day and night had passed since Justina had returned and taken him under her care, but now Sunday had passed and Monday had come, and with it the call of school. She had slipped off and left him, locking him up in her cabin, the better to protect him from pursuit, and half the day had lapsed before he sensed the midday heat and the brightness of the great outdoors. But was it that alone which had roused him from his dreams? As he lay there listening, he heard a cautious step and the scrape of a key in the door. Fate had found him then, after all, and the first of the manhunters had come to the end of the trail. He reached for his pistol and sat waiting, steady-eyed, and the door swung slowly open. A head peered in and jerked quickly back, and then a voice spoke up — the hoarse, eager voice of Wild Horse Bill.

"Ah, Ab!" he called, and, as Meadows responded, he came stumbling in through the door. "Where are you?" quavered Bill, staring blindly into the darkness and crouching with one hand on his gun, and then, with a laugh and a whoop of joy, he came running over to the bed. "Well, damn your old heart," he burst out profanely, "how the hell are you gitting along? Say, that schoolma'am is all right, even if she don't like the color of my hair ... what'd she say when I stole her pet horse?"

He laughed hilariously and slapped Ab on the back, then turned and went to the door.

"All right, boys!" he shouted, and, as Meadows hobbled over, he saw a cavalcade coming down the trail. There were fifteen or twenty cowboys, every man of them armed, and at the head of the band rode Butch Brennan on the *chula*, while Justina's horse was led along behind them. They came on at a sharp trot, and, when Ab appeared, they gave voice to a high, joyous yell.

"What'd I tell ye?" Bill laughed. "Didn't I say I'd come back? Well, here I am, by grab, and I brought the bunch with me. The whole danged caboodle from the lava *malpais!*" He hopped off the doorstep and began exchanging witticisms with the grim-visaged riders, and they, after a first hard look at Meadows, crowded about to shake his hand. In the lead came Butch Brennan, in rare good humor, and, as he presented his followers, he made a sort of speech, disguised as a running introduction.

"Meet Curly Harris, Meadows, one of my old-time sidekickers that we called in to he'p us out. And believe me, Ab, if them Mexicans had took you prisoner, we shore would have took you back. This is Hank McElvey that you met at Frog Tanks ... Bill found the whole bunch of us there ... and we were all keyed up to go plumb into Papalote and get you out of jail. Shake hands with Willie Johnson, he's from over by Quemado

140

and right there when it comes to fighting greasers. Just as good at fighting booze, as far as that goes . . . and that reminds me, boys, the drinks are on me. Come on, let's go down to Show Low!"

"Yes!" yelled the cowboys rushing to swing up on their mounts and, regardless of the proximity of Mexican posses, they went whooping and romping down the trail. Some of the older hands remained behind until Ab was safely mounted, but as he rode off down the cañon with Bill at his side, the lure of the drinks drew them on. One after the other they pulled ahead, glancing back apologetically before they leaned forward in the saddle and went racing after the bunch, until at last only Bill and Meadows were left to tag along behind.

"Big doings!" Wild Horse Bill grinned, licking his lips in anticipation. "Butch is going to buy out the bar. This is the beginning of what I told you about, and after the big drunk the whole works will march on Papalote. We're going to take the town, boy, and everything in it, and make this a white man's country. And if Celso Baca and his bunch of rawhides come along and try to stop us, they's going to be the damnedest killing that's ever been seen in these parts. Say, spur up a little, can't ye. I want to be in on this . . . Butch is going to buy the whole town."

Meadows spurred up a little, although his leg ached in protest and his conscience called for a halt, but the change in his fortune was so sudden and complete that he could not refrain from exulting. He had escaped, after all, although not as they had planned when Justina had laid out his life for him. His rescue had come from the source least expected — from cowardly Butch Brennan and his gang. Never before had Brennan showed the slightest interest in the fate of his partners in crime, but now, when the country was aroused to a furor and Mexican posses were everywhere, now, out from his hiding place and from the far North Plains, he had come galloping to save the life of one man. Instead of dying, with his back to the wall and all organized society against him, Meadows found himself a hero, surrounded by fearless men, ready and eager to fight his battles. He was saved, to begin his life anew — but not as Justina had planned.

She had pictured weeks of hiding, a flight to other lands and years of patient waiting, but this had come by magic and the big days to follow might bring even greater rewards. Butch Brennan was in the saddle, surrounded by desperate men and with the dream of an empire in his mind, and fewer men than his had overthrown governments along the banks of the Rio Grande. It was the old conflict all over again, of the Texan against the Mexican, the white blood against the dark, and in a struggle like that there was but one place for a Meadows, for his grandfather had fought at Buena Vista. Whether right or wrong, he was committed to the cause of these man-killing, Mexican-hating Texans, and, if they fought as their fathers had fought before them, they would be bandits and outlaws no more. For a rebellion, when successful, turns rebels into patriots, and outlaws, when they band themselves together and beat down the forces that oppress them, go down to posterity as heroes.

The store at Show Low was an enormous affair, built when labor and mud bricks were cheap, and it sheltered under one roof hotel, warehouse, and saloon, besides the corrals and stables outside. A long, board verandah, with a horse rack in front and a series of seats in the shade, extended the whole length of the house, and at one end was the store and saloon combined, opening into the hotel parlor and the rooms. Behind was a patio where Mexican servants washed and cooked and did the work of the house, while Chris Woolf and his barkeeper were always at the door when a band of cowboys came by. But they were inside and busy when Bill and Meadows rode in, and Brennan was making a speech.

"Take anything you want, boys," he shouted above the racket, "and it won't cost ary one of you a cent! I've bought this hyer store and everything in it, as long as my money holds out. He'p yourselves to a new hat and a new pair of boots, and the drinks and cartridges are free. This treat is on me, boys, but the express company pays for it, so drink hearty . . . and here comes Bill!"

Wild Horse Bill swaggered in, a cheerful grin on his red face as he received the plaudits of the crowd, and behind him followed Meadows, limping painfully on one leg and seeking the nearest chair. But if he stayed out of the revelry and retired quickly to the parlor where he could stretch himself out on the couch, it was not so easy to escape the attentions of his new-made but riotous young friends. Some were boys that he

143

knew, and others he had heard of before they had joined the Wild Bunch, and, as Bill came racking in with an assortment of medicines, they came trooping along behind. Butch Brennan might be the brains, but Wild Horse Bill was the heart and soul of this band of cowboys gone wrong. As they gathered about his couch and looked at his wound, Meadows felt their hearty friendship. They were a good bunch of boys, and he had met over half of them on the roundups of the Figure 4, not vicious at bottom, but just easily led and carried away by the contagion. Because, with two shots, he had killed his two men, he was counted nothing short of a hero.

In the bar the old-timers, Brennan's own personal following, herded together as they talked over their plans, but wherever Bill went, the local boys trailed after him, and his friends were theirs, to a man. He was in fine spirits now, talking and laughing and composing songs to the tune of "The Old Chisholm Trail". The hotel parlor was first riotous, and then calm again as he surged back and forth from the bar. Meadows caught it at last, that wild, unreasoning enthusiasm which had tempted these boys to join the gang, and he was just beginning to enter into the spirit of the occasion when Brennan passed through with a woman.

She was a tall, dark creature and strikingly handsome, but with a strained, unhealthy brightness in her rolling black eyes and a discontented droop to her lips. It was the woman of mystery that Show Low had been gossiping about ever since she had appeared at the hotel, and that was six months before. At first, it was

144

whispered that she came as Woolf's mistress and then, as she openly flouted his attentions, that she was engaged on some secret mission. What that was no one knew, although they were all free to guess, and not a few had whispered that she was an agent of Brennan, who had passed through there repeatedly of late. There were others, however, who, noting her influence over Woolf and the abject fear which she evoked in him, ventured the shrewd suspicion that she was a woman detective in the employ of the long-suffering express company. But whoever she was, hers was a striking personality that drew men about her like flies, and, when she so chose, she could wring the innermost secrets from the lips of the most close-mouthed cowpuncher. She came and went, sometimes taking long rides, and then remaining in seclusion for days, but now she was laughing, and, as she passed by Meadows, she smiled from the corner of her eye. Then she went on with Brennan into her rooms beyond, and Wild Horse Bill scowled a warning.

"Look out, boy," he whispered as soon as they were alone, "that's Rose, Butch Brennan's woman. Don't you look at her like that, because if Butch ever sees you . . ."

"Aw, shut up!" broke in Meadows. "You must think I'm a kid. I never even looked at her!"

"Yes, you did," warned Bill, "and take a tip from me . . . she's got her eye on you."

He added some further unsolicited advice that made Meadows's ears begin to burn, but when Rose Sheridan happened to pass by again, he looked discreetly away. Bill had spoken as a friend, and one who knew whereof he spoke, and the gist of his remarks was that Rose was a she-devil, to be placated but left strictly alone. Otherwise, through the wiles of which she was mistress, she would dazzle his fool soul with a smile — and try to arrange it so that Brennan would be looking on and kill him, just to show how much he loved her. This was Bill's version of the woman — and his burning words more than hinted that he, too, had not wholly escaped — but when she appeared suddenly and turned aside to speak to him, Bill responded with a Judas glad smile.

"Yes, howdy-do, Miss Sheridan," he broke out nervously, "yeah, meet my friend here, Meadows. He ain't feeling very good. Will I git you a drink, Ab? Reckon the boys have hoorawed him too much."

He scurried off for the drink, but, instead of leaving him in quiet, Rose Sheridan sat down by Meadows's couch. She was keyed up and excited, and her eyes, when she was talking, roved restlessly to and fro, and her power of fascination, if such she possessed, was not centered at the moment upon Meadows. He answered her quietly, keeping his own eyes upon the door through which Brennan might enter from the bar. As he lay there watching, he heard a commotion in the store, and then a sudden lull. The loud and wrangling voices were all hushed but one, which ran on drunkenly until brought to a stop, and then a woman's voice spoke out clearly through the silence — the voice of Justina Edwards.

146

If he had forgotten her for a time, he remembered her now, and the thought of her disapproval made him cringe, but she was talking to Wild Horse Bill and his hoarse, cackling laugh gave evidence that he was badly at a disadvantage.

"Yes, I'll tell you, Miss Edwards," he burst out apologetically, "I'm shore mighty sorry about that horse. Wouldn't have taken him for nothing, only Ab was so bad, and I knowed them Mexicans would ketch him."

"Well, you are no friend of Ab Meadows," she answered resentfully, "or you wouldn't teach him to fight and steal. And now, if you're through with him, I'll take my horse back . . . I hope you haven't ruined him."

The silence fell again, and then her high-heeled boots came *clacking* across the store, and Meadows shrank back fearfully as she passed by the door and dropped two letters into the box. She turned and started out, but something seemed to tell her of those staring, watchful eyes for she glanced in swiftly — and stopped. Then her head went up haughtily and she looked straight ahead as Rose Sheridan rose to meet her. Yet her eyes stole back once more as she was turning away and in that glance Meadows read the death of all his hopes and the end of yesterday's dreams.

CHAPTER
ELEVEN

It was a belief among the Mexicans that the malevolence of the Gila monster is concentrated in the glance of its eye and that, at a single *coup d'œil*, it can strike down birds in full flight. Else how, they argued, could the baleful reptile catch them, since he is slow and a creature of the sand, yet often he is found with a dove in his jaws, and a dove is a creature of the air. So much for the *paisano* logic and the belief in the supernatural that explains away the mysteries of their life, but if a stroke of the eye could by any chance produce death, Justina would have perished in an instant. She had rebuffed the first advance that Rose Sheridan had ever made, and the response was a glare of hate.

"Do you know that woman?" Rose demanded of Meadows, and he saw that she was wild with rage. It shone from her eyes like the black hate of a sorceress who merely meditates the swiftest way to kill, and, when he nodded, she burst out in a frenzy, yet talking half to herself. "I'll show her," she hissed. "I could have made her *rich* if she'd treated me like a lady! But just because I'm staying with Woolf . . . well, I guess she could *speak* to me, anyway!"

148

She stopped and bit her lip. Then, as Brennan appeared, she rushed to clutch him by the arm. They passed out together, she talking beneath her breath, he listening with an indulgent smile, and Meadows returned to his thoughts. Then Wild Horse Bill came in, chapped and grinning after his call down, and they agreed between them that women were the devil and the best thing to do was to keep away from them. That was easy for both of them for, as the drinking went on, even the Mexican women deserted the kitchen, and night and day the town of Show Low resounded to cursing and revelry. On the flat before the store, matched horse races were pulled off on which the owners bet all the money they had, and, as whiskey barrels were emptied, they were rolled across the open and made the target for lightning-quick gun practice. The whiskey was free and the ammunition was free, but the man who could hit the bunghole every time it rolled into view was considered to have won the drinks. No one worried about the pay, unless it was Woolf, and he did not dare open his mouth.

As they waited day by day and no Mexican posse arrived, the fighting ardor of the outlaws knew no bounds. They made their boast that they would go through Papalote like the cowboys from hell that they were, and then they would ride on to Albuquerque and Santa Fé and drive all the Mexicans before them. They would take the Territory and make it over again until they were lords of all they surveyed, and no bunch of rawhides, or express company detectives, either, could make them submit to a Mexican government. It was

149

the white men against the Mexicans, and what true son of Texas would ever consent to be governed by a passel of yellow bellies?

But not even the iron constitution of a cowpuncher can stand free whiskey forever, and, as several fell ill and broils and rackets increased, Butch Brennan began to shut down the lid. First he called off all drinking except over the bar, and that only at stated intervals. Then he sobered up Wild Horse Bill by the simple expedient of locking him in a room. When Bill finally dug out, there being no lock to pick but only a padlock and chain, he was sober enough to listen to reason, and reason dictated a speedy retreat. The word had come that the manhunters of the express company would shortly descend upon them in force, and that, of course, would cloud the racial issue and lead to some desperate killing. These manhunters were white men, not a few of them former outlaws who had turned against their associates for pay, and, whatever their moral deficiencies might be, there was none of them lacking in nerve. It was high time to move, lest their white man's revolution should be shattered against the rock of white man's force and Bill set himself resolutely to the difficult task of reconciling the embroiled factions of their band.

Nearly a week had gone by since they had ridden into Show Low and sent their proud defiance to Celso Baca, and now, although they were divided into numerous cliques, they numbered more men than ever. The news of their raid had spread like wildfire and half the cowboys on the ranches had thrown up their jobs to

150

be in on the historic drunk. In new boots and hats and all the regalia that a cowpuncher loves so well, they swarmed about the store like satiated burglars, still picking out shirts and new silk handkerchiefs and making more grief for Chris Woolf. As his bookkeeping had mounted up, Chris had begun to be anxious, and at last he had made a statement to Brennan for the total damage up to date. But here he suddenly found himself a fox among wolves, for Brennan turned against him with so wicked a snarl that he fled from his presence in a panic.

It is one thing to charge for your whiskey by the glass when you shove it across the bar to a lone cowpuncher, but Brennan's men were wolves, and they ran in a pack, and a saddle-colored storekeeper was nothing to them. The presentation of the bill had brought up the question as to whether Chris Woolf was a white man, and, if the payment of his claim was dependent upon their decision, the chances of collection were slim. An olive-brown complexion and a ready flow of Spanish had been one of Woolf's greatest assets, when it came to the Mexican trade, but now with this wild gang of Texans on his hands, it bade fair to leave him a bankrupt. But all that was up to Butch Brennan, who had a fortune in bills in his shirt, so Woolf worked and sweated and scaled down his estimate while he prayed for the departure of his guests. They had overstayed their welcome by several days, and now they were waiting for the dance.

Unfortunately for the schoolteacher, as well as for Chris Woolf, a dance had been announced two weeks before to take place on Saturday night, and the changeling cowboys who had ridden in to drink with Brennan were sobering up to dance with Justina. The experience of the past year had demonstrated conclusively that Justina would not tolerate a drunken man, and now, as Saturday dawned, all those who were going to the dance swore off religiously. The others caroused on, regardless of everything but the lessening flow of free whiskey. Some were Brennan's old-timers, who still herded by themselves, and others were local boys who had joined Brennan's gang and knew that they would not be welcome for Justina had announced that the dance was "respectable" and no outlaws and horse thieves need attend. So it stood at evening, when Brennan appeared with Rose.

She was pale now with anger and the gleam in her set eyes showed how deeply she still felt Justina's slight. When Brennan announced that he would attend the dance that night, her lips parted in a slow bitter smile.

"I've got this country licked," he continued with a swagger, "and these people might as well learn to like it, if they expect to keep out of trouble. I'm going to that dance . . . and I'll say right hyer, they ain't no man got a prettier gal . . . and, if I ain't received as the equal of the best of them, they won't be no dance, that's all. So sober up, boys, and put on your prettiest and we'll swing 'em around in style."

There was a whoop from the boys who had kept on with their drinking and a murmur of disapproval from the rest. Justina was a favorite with all the Show Low cowboys and they had hoped for a quiet dance. Yet, if the whole country were licked, Justina was not. As she rode back and forth, she took no pains to conceal her scorn for their wild debauch. She had set her face firmly against whiskey, and even Lute Starbuck, if he came from Woolf's saloon, was not good enough to ride with her. She stood for prohibition against the world, and her recent experiences had not softened her grudge against Woolf and his saloon.

Within it was housed the man she had sheltered and tried passionately to set right with the world, and beside him she had seen hovering that sinister woman who had haunted the place for months. Who she was she did not know, and she did not care, but certainly, after the way she had conducted herself with Woolf, no lady could afford her acquaintance. Besides that, out of spite, she had tried her wiles on Lute, thinking thereby to bring Justina to terms, and Lute, out of bravado, was half boastful of his conquest, as if she could possibly care. No, the actions of this woman and of all her admirers were of less than no importance to Justina. She stood on her dignity as the first lady of Show Low in refusing to recognize Rose Sheridan. She had gone into the store because she regarded it as her property — and because she had found Nipper tied outside to the rack and heard Wild Horse Bill laughing inside — but for any woman who would so far demean herself as to live in Chris Woolf's disreputable hotel she had nothing but pity and certainly no desire to take her to her bosom as a friend. So she had cut her cold when the opportunity had offered, and now it was war to the knife.

When Brennan had come out with Rose on his arm and announced that he was going to the dance, Meadows had divined on the instant that a woman's war was on with no quarter asked or given. Justina was not the kind to compromise with evil, and Rose was certainly far removed from the type that sobs out their grief in private. She was the feminine counterpart of bold Butch Brennan, a man who never forgot an injury or allowed his hate to grow cold. Hers was the same handsome beauty, the flashing dark eyes, and the lithe, feline method of approach and combined with her charm was the subtle capacity to rouse up a world-consuming hate. She could love and she could hate, and she could summon up love or hate. As she prepared for the dance, she had a smile for Brennan that made his eyes snap and gleam. Then they set off together, after the dance was well started, while their admirers came trooping along.

Behind them followed the curious, the shamefaced and the drunken, with the intention of looking on from outside, and behind them all limped Ab Meadows, the apostate, vaguely worried for Justina and her dance. The schoolhouse was not far, just up on the low bench that rose on the edge of town, and those who went to dance made the trip on foot while the roisterers dashed by on the lope. As a precaution against surprise Brennan was accompanied by an armed guard, and he wore his heavy gun and belt, but this was to be a battle of women and wits and he cloaked the rag handle with his coat. It was his social coming out, his first bid for equality and recognition as a power in the land, and

154

many a greater rascal than he had been received without question — but not by Justina Edwards.

The dance was at its height, with the musicians stamping time and gay young couples whirling to and fro, but the news of their coming had gone before them and every eye was turned to the door. The crowd of idle onlookers made way before the bandit and then surged back to stare. Brennan, with a flourish, saluted his fair partner and joined in on the end of the waltz. Another dance was called and they entered with the rest, but Justina Edwards, who was dancing with Lute Starbuck, never turned her pretty head. She waltzed on demurely, a vision in white, and not by so much as a glance over her shoulder did she recognize the existence of her rival. Young admirers crowded about her at the end of the dance, each striving for the honor of her hand, but, as an encore was called, she floated off with Lute while Rose whispered savagely in Brennan's ear.

The encore ended abruptly. As the couples broke up, Butch Brennan strode forward and, bowing low to Justina, requested the pleasure of a dance. This was intended as a showdown, to call her hand and compel her to recognize his presence, but Justina merely glanced at him and, declining politely, went on with her conversation with Lute. But Brennan was too good a bandit to be so easily discouraged, especially with Rose looking on, and with another gallant bow he requested an introduction to some of the young ladies present. Now, as hostess of the occasion, it was Justina's duty, of course, to present him, if she considered it proper, and if not, to state that fact. The showdown had come and she met it calmly while the whole room hung on her words.

"No," she replied, "you were not invited to come here, and I must ask you to leave the floor."

"Indeed?" said Brennan with exaggerated politeness. "Then allow me to make myself known. I am Mister Brennan, that you may have heard of, and . . ."

"Yes, I've heard a great deal of you," answered Justina tartly, "but nothing that was to your credit. We will have the next dance" — she turned and motioned for the music — "and I will ask you not to dance, Mister Brennan."

She stood there facing him until the music struck up, then turned to look for Lute, but just when she was planning to dance off with him bravely, she found herself left in the lurch. Her partner was gone, and, as she glanced about angrily, she saw him dancing with Rose. He was hanging his head, as he had full right to do, but Rose was smiling and whispering softly in his ear while she glanced coquettishly at Butch. A laugh went up from the half-drunken cowboys and was swelled with high whoops from outside, but although she had lost the first trick in the game, Justina still held a few trumps. As custodian of the schoolhouse and chaperon of the dance, she had absolute authority on the floor and she motioned the musicians to stop. They kept on fatuously, pretending not to see her, and she rushed across the room.

"Stop the music!" she commanded, and, as the dance broke up in confusion, she stepped out on the platform. That was her place of authority when school was in session and it served its purpose still. "That will be all for tonight," she announced in a clear voice. "The company will please clear the floor!"

"No! No!" yelled Brennan's cowboys, and, as the others joined in, Brennan took the situation in hand.

"Go on and play, boys," he said, winking amiably at the musicians, and then Justina put down her foot.

"You get out of here!" she ordered, pointing her finger in his face. "You're drunk, and I won't have you around!"

"Oh, I don't know," responded Brennan. "Who's going to put me out? I came over here with my boys to have a little dance and I . . ."

"I'll put you out myself," she answered defiantly. "Unless," she added, looking expectantly about the room, "some gentleman will do it for me?"

She paused and a silence fell upon the gaping company, for they all knew what she meant. It was up to the honor of every cowboy present who ever expected to claim her as a friend to step forth and do her bidding, but no man raised a hand. Butch Brennan had turned, and now he laughed mockingly as Justina stabbed each faint heart with her eyes. But no man moved, until there was a commotion near the door and Ab Meadows came limping forward. He advanced toward the platform, carefully avoiding Justina's eyes, but when he found himself confronted by Brennan, he met his startled glance fearlessly. It was not bravado, it was just a lack of fear, a smiling confidence that disarmed all opposition, and his voice, when he spoke, was almost apologetic, although it had a certain ring of mastery.

"Well, Brennan," he said, "I guess we're all included in this, and, since the lady has said she doesn't care for our society . . ."

He paused and smiled again, with a fleeting glance at Justina, and then Brennan's keen face relaxed. He laughed, almost jovially, and with a nod to the schoolteacher strode briskly across the floor. There he spoke to Rose, who stood talking with Lute, and they all went out together. The rest of the gang followed, bewildered by the change, and soon the room was empty — except for Justina and the musicians, who were putting up their instruments. Then a grinning head appeared and Wild Horse Bill stumped in, holding up a bundle of bills.

"Hey . . . you!" he called, beckoning enticingly to the fiddlers, and the queen was left alone with her victory.

The battle was won and lost and neither the victors nor the vanquished had escaped without a few wounds. Justina had carried her point and ejected Brennan, but he had departed with all her musicians — and her recreant escort Lute had deserted her for the hard-eyed Rose. Brennan had been ejected, not by some true-hearted champion, but by the man she had flouted, Ab Meadows. No, it hardly could be said that Brennan had been ejected — Meadows had simply requested him, as a fellow outlaw and miscreant, to comply with the lady's wishes — and the dance, when all was over, was as thoroughly broken up as if it had ended in a gun play. Perhaps, after all, the battle was a draw and hers but a moral victory. For while she had had her own way and carried her point, she was left with a pang in her heart — Ab's limp had seemed so pathetic.

Back in Woolf's store, although there was music and dancing and Rose Sheridan had stolen Lute Starbuck from the schoolteacher, the soul of Rose was deeply stirred and she poured out her wrath on Butch Brennan.

"No!" she spat back as he asked her for a dance, "I'm not dancing with a man that's a coward. Ain't you ashamed, Butch Brennan, to let Ab Meadows put you out, and him with a limp in one leg?"

"I didn't put him out," broke in Meadows with a laugh. "I didn't even ask him to go. We all left together and . . ."

"Ah, *you're* afraid of *him* now," she cried provocatively, pointing a scornful finger at Ab. "You know very well that you can't put Butch out and get away with it afterward." She waited expectantly, looking from Brennan to Meadows with a taunting, maddening smile, but neither man spoke and she gave her arm to Lute, who led her into the thick of the dance.

"Feeling on the prod tonight," observed Brennan impersonally, but Meadows held his tongue. Let him talk as he would, he knew that Butch Brennan was like clay in the hands of Rose Sheridan, and on her third finger, like a spray of white fire, gleamed the diamond ring that he had sold to the chief. It had appeared there suddenly this very same evening, when she had come out dressed for the dance, and, whether it was a present or the sign of their engagement, it showed where Brennan's heart was fixed. He was in love with Rose in his false, selfish way, and she, in her own equally false and selfish way, had pledged him whatever faith she owned. Now, although the words seemed to invite some response, Meadows smiled inscrutably and said nothing, for death lay very near when Brennan's pride was touched, and Rose had called him a coward. But nothing more was said, and, as Meadows turned away, he saw Brennan's eyes fixed on Lute.

In the lower types of mind, love and jealousy are inseparable, and whoever intervenes in the savage game of hate and passion will find himself the loser. So it was with Butch and Rose, and in their reckless hide-and-seek other men were mere buffers and pawns. Wild Horse Bill had spoken truly when he said that Rose's desire was always to embroil others with the chief, and, if by any chance Brennan should kill some brainless fool, she would count it as a token of his love. Her game was known to the wise ones of the gang and they refused to play into her hand. Only swelled-up boys like Lute still responded to her wiles — at least, when Brennan was about. The others danced together in wild bear hugs and caperings, giving the lady free passage down the floor, and, except for the space which always opened out before her, no one would guess that they were aware of her presence. But Butch knew and they all knew that Rose was in a tantrum and that she was carrying the game too far. Brennan stood it for a while and then his brow clouded and he ordered the fiddlers to stop. He took a drink standing, inviting no

160

one to join in with him, and then he gave the word to saddle up. Before he rode off, he spoke a word in Rose's ear that left her silent and distrait.

In the brief settlement that followed, Chris Woolf came out the loser by something like a thousand dollars in stock, and his face went pasty white as he watched Brennan put up his roll. Of that great sheaf of bills he had stripped off only a few, and, when he handed them over, he looked Woolf in the eye as if waiting for something he might say. But Woolf knew so well what Brennan was waiting for — and what would result from it — that he did not say a word. The old, killing look had come back into Brennan's eyes and all he wanted was an excuse to shoot. Chris Woolf was half Mexican, and there was in his safe what would make royal loot for the gang, so he accepted his money in staring, breathless silence and ducked back into his private room. But Brennan knew him well, and the second day out he beckoned Wild Horse Bill to one side.

They were well over the Datils and the end of their carouse had left them morose and cold. Bill was feeling flabby, but when Brennan began to speak, he straightened up suddenly in his saddle.

"Shore!" he nodded, and, as Brennan talked on, Bill turned and beckoned to Meadows. "Say," he burst out hoarsely, "d'ye want to go back to Show Low? Aw, come on . . . Butch wants us to go. Hey, come over here!" And he led him to one side. "We can go by that rat's nest," he whispered behind his hand, "And pick up that money you cached . . . damned Injuns are liable to find it."

"Well . . . ," began Meadows, and Bill turned back to Brennan.

"All right, Butch," he said, "and, if I don't come back in three days . . ."

"I'll know you're drunk," ended Brennan.

"No, you won't," retorted Bill. "You'll know I've been took and I want you to come a-running."

"Hop to it." Brennan nodded, and, as the cowboys trailed along, Bill and Meadows turned back to the south.

"Old Butch has got a hunch," confided Bill as they rode off, "that danged Jew is framing something up. Trying to sell us to the express company, or run off with his gal, or throw in with them Papalote Mexicans. Shore will be up to something, after what we done to him, and we're to hide out and watch. And then, oh, my! If he tries the double-cross, Butch will come back and bust him wide open. That'll be lesson number one for these back-country Mexicans . . . it'll learn 'em to stand without hitching."

"But suppose," suggested Ab, "we run into a posse of white men, out hunting for Brennan and his gang . . . ?"

"Nothing to it," broke in Bill. "We'll keep off the main trails and come out at Show Low after dark. Then we can hide out on Sawed-Off Mountain and see who comes and goes . . . and then we'll ride down and buy a drink." Bill cleared his dry throat and began a little song that he had picked up in some railroad saloon:

162

Then give us a drink, bartender, bartender,
For we love you, as . . . you . . . know!
And surely you will o-blige us, o-blige us,
With another drink . . . or . . . so!

That brought something else in his mind and he began on "Fort Worth Frankie", and that led to something worse, until at last he drifted off into the byways of balladry, the *index expurgatorius* of song. But all the time his eyes were on the ridges and seeking out a passageway through the hills, and at dawn the next day they were safe on Sawed-Off Mountain, with the store and schoolhouse just below them.

There were strange horses in the corral, but that was not surprising as strangers were always coming through. Far from being crowded with Mexican deputies or American detectives, the town seemed practically deserted. Mexican servants came and went, the town children raced down to school, and others came riding from distant cañons. Only the strange horses and a well-developed hunch kept Wild Horse Bill from riding straight to the store. He was silent now, thinking of his morning drink and the canned goods on Woolf's half-stripped shelves, but reckless as he was, he waited and watched patiently until the sun was several hours high. Some instinct of danger held him back from the quiet store, perhaps just because it was so quiet. When at last he rode back from the point and took the trail down to the flat, he grumbled uneasily to himself. But Meadows was concerned with quite a different problem and he stopped when they came to the road.

"Bill," he said, "let's not go to that store. I know you . . . you're going to get drunk."

"*Whoo*," mocked Bill, "won't do nothing of the kind. Jest want to git a bottle and I'm gone. No telling who might come along."

"No, and there's no telling who might be there. Those horses might belong to a bunch of detectives . . ."

"T'ell with 'em," burst out Bill. "I'm going to git that drink if the whole damned store is full of 'em. I been honin' for it so long I can't pucker my lips to whistle . . . I'm just perishing or I wouldn't go down."

"You stay here," offered Ab, "and I'll go and get it for you . . ."

"Aw, what d'ye think I am!" demanded Bill indignantly, and set off down the road at a lope. Meadows galloped along behind him, but, just as he caught up, Bill let out a couple of playful yelps and leaned far over the horn. His horse hit the wind as if he had been lifted from the ground, and Bill reined him up short at the store. Meadows rode in behind him and they dropped off together, just as Woolf came hurrying out.

"Hello!" hailed Bill, stepping in bluffly despite Woolf's efforts to delay him, and there in the corner he spied two Americans sitting over some papers at a table. Bill thrust out his chin and squinted at them a moment, then went clanking over to the bar.

164

"Gimme a drink!" he shouted, slapping his hand on the counter. "Come up, gentlemen!" he invited. "Come up and have a drink . . . and gimme a bottle, Chris!"

He leaned one elbow on the bar and, with his hip hunched up, stood calmly regarding the strangers. They were not cowmen, he knew that, nor were they regular manhunters, but something somewhere between — more like deputy sheriffs or deputy marshals, or perhaps express company detectives. Which is why Bill stood with his elbow on the bar and his hip hunched away from the front rail. But Chris Woolf, from going white and shrinking away from them, was now suddenly all cordiality and effusiveness, and the scared, troubled look that had come into his eyes had given away to a gleam of wolfish cunning.

"Yes, come up, gentlemen," he chimed in, "and meet my friends. I guess you've heard of Wild Horse Bill."

At the mention of the name the officers looked blank, then rose up and advanced to the bar. They had pistols on their hips, but their badges, if they had any, were concealed beneath their coats. They glanced at Woolf as they drank.

"Glad to see you, Bill," beamed Woolf. "Have one on the house. Won't you join us, Meadows . . . have a drink!"

"No, thank you," answered Meadows, and, as they took the drink together, he noticed that the officers were looking at him. They were officers, for a certainty, and he and Bill had run into a man trap, only they had taken the trappers by surprise. Their reckless gallop down the road, like a pair of carefree cowpunchers, had completely deceived even Woolf, and now Bill, the devil, was trying to bluff it out by pretending to become very drunk. Or was it the real thing? — for Woolf was setting out the drinks with a most lavish and flattering hospitality. Meadows stood by the doorway, where he could look out at their horses and watch what was happening inside. As Bill rushed on from drink to drink, Ab scowled and shook his head.

"Hey, Bill," he called, "get that bottle and come out!"

Bill cackled hoarsely. "Nothing . . . doing," he returned, speaking slowly like a drunken man, although Meadows knew he could not be drunk yet. "Come in, Ab, and meet my friends!"

He turned to the officers, who were beginning to call for thin ones, and insisted upon their taking one more drink. Then he lurched over to the haberdashery department and called for a pair of suspenders. Woolf hastened over to wait on him. The two officers exchanged glances and withdrew to their table for a conference. Meadows stepped outside the door. The atmosphere inside seemed surcharged with electricity, with the terrible tension that comes when men's lives depend upon the turn of a hand, yet through it all Bill was calm. He was too calm, in fact, as he had formerly been too drunk. Woolf, for one, seemed to know it.

Chris Woolf had taken his life in his hands when he mentioned Bill's name — if these men, indeed, were officers — and, as he spread out the suspenders, the sweat ran down his cheeks and fell from his quaking jowls. He was scared, and with good reason, for if a shooting occurred, he would find himself in the midst of it. But the nerve of the officers had cracked in the pinch and they hesitated to attempt the arrest. Perhaps the whiskey that Bill had forced on them had not served to sharpen their wits, for as Bill pawed over the suspenders, one of them drew out a paper and wrote certain words in the blanks. Then he walked down to Bill, who did not even look up, and stood waiting with his hand on his gun.

"Say," he said at last, "are you Wild Horse Bill?"

"My card!" replied Bill, flicking a cartridge from his belt and holding it under his nose. "I'm Money Gitter, Number Forty-Five."

The officer glanced at Woolf, who beckoned him on nervously, and cleared his throat again.

"I've got a warrant for you," he announced, holding out the paper, and Bill raised his hooked nose and stared.

"Well, read it to me!" he snapped, and turned back to the suspenders, laying out a red pair and a pink. The officer hesitated a moment and glanced at his partner, who was equally lacking in nerve, and then automatically, as if impelled by some power whose influence he could not resist, he let his eyes drop to the warrant. In that same fraction of a second Bill's hand went to his gun and his drunkenness fell away like a mask. He covered the two officers, and Chris Woolf, too, and his thin lips drew back in a sneer.

"I'll take these," he said, snatching the red suspenders, and backed out the door.

CHAPTER
TWELVE

It was a disastrous moment for avaricious Chris Woolf when the thought of the reward on Wild Horse Bill's head made him forget the gang behind him! Thirty thousand dollars cash — and revenge on Butch Brennan — but the officers had bungled it, and now the stern-eyed Nemesis was hovering above Show Low. Bill went whipping up the cañon, yelling back curses and threats, and, when he returned, Butch Brennan was with him and the leaders of the hard-riding gang. They came the second night, before Woolf was expecting them, and then began that Lesson Number One that Brennan had been saving for some Mexican. Woolf was not only a Mexican but a traitor as well, and, when Brennan stalked in, he dropped down on his knees and began to beg for his life.

"Git up there!" commanded Brennan, giving him a lightning kick as the gang filed in behind.

As Woolf rose up whimpering, he struck him to the floor with the weight of his rag-handled gun. Then he beat him about the store like a man abusing a hound, and Woolf bellowed and cringed and cried out for mercy while Wild Horse Bill looked on and laughed. It had been a long ride for Bill — to Frog Tanks and back in half a day and a night and a day — but he had never stopped until the store was surrounded and Woolf was caught in the net. No one knew better than Woolf what his fate would be if he lingered too long in Show Low, but he had waited to collect certain outstanding debts and now retribution had overtaken him.

"*Don't* kick me, Bill," he pleaded as Bill came forward and clouted him in the ribs. "Ain't I always been your friend? Them fellers was detectives, but I didn't know it . . ."

"No you didn't!" jeered Bill. "Didn't you give 'em the wink? Didn't you tell 'em I was Wild Horse Bill? You damned, greasy Mexican, if you'd had *your* way, they'd be just about hanging me by now! Git up there, dad-blast ye! Now *dance*, you big slob!" Bill shot off the end of his shoe. "Go on and dance!" he ordered as Woolf began to weaken, "because when you quit, d'ye know what we're going to do? We're going to shoot you in the leg, so you can't git away, and then take you out and kill you."

He stood grinning cruelly as the others joined in and splintered the floor at Woolf's feet, but in the midst of the shooting Rose Sheridan appeared, quarreling violently with Brennan, who had left the room, but now came back in her company.

"Stop that!" she commanded, stepping fearlessly in front of Woolf.

But as the cowboys drew back, Butch Brennan whipped out his pistol and shot Woolf through the foot.

"Butch Brennan!" she shrilled as Woolf sank down wailing, "you're a dirty, sneaking coward! And Chris has always been your friend."

"Well, he hain't been *mine!*" broke in Wild Horse Bill truculently, and Brennan welcomed his intervention with a smile.

"No," he said, "and he hain't been mine . . . and now I'm going to kill him, that's all."

"No, you're not!" she contradicted. "You don't know what you're doing. If you kill Chris, you'll lose half your friends . . . they all call you a murderer now!"

"Oh, Chris is it, eh?" sneered Brennan. "That's the second time tonight. You and Chris must be damned good pals."

"No, we're not," she shot back with a look of disdain, "but I won't stand by and see him murdered."

"Well, now, maybe you will," suggested Brennan coldly. "You can't say he hasn't got it coming to him. W'y, if I'd tell what I know . . ."

"You shut up!" she snapped, and, after glaring him down, she turned on Wild Horse Bill. "Take him away!" she ordered, pointing her hand at Woolf, and Bill beckoned hastily to Ab.

"Back to his office," Bill panted, struggling to lift up Woolf, and, while the gang looked on, they dragged him away, leaving Brennan to fight it out with Rose. Woolf's office door was locked, for it was there he kept his money, safely stored in a burglar-proof safe, but he produced the key himself, and, when they were inside, he slammed the spring lock behind them.

"Now, listen, boys," he pleaded, sinking down in a big chair and holding his foot in both hands, "be reasonable . . . gimme a chance! We all make mistakes . . . don't be hard on me, and I'll give you everything I've got!"

"Everything you got, hey?" echoed Bill, suddenly becoming strictly business. "Well, come through, then, open up this safe."

Woolf looked at him a moment, then rose up reluctantly and slumped down before the safe door.

"But I'll tell you, boys," he stipulated, "you'll have to give me a horse. If you don't, Butch Brennan will kill me."

"Open 'er up!" ordered Bill, tapping him on the head with his gun barrel, and Woolf began to turn the knob aimlessly. "I'll call Butch," suggested Bill. "He'll help you remember."

"No, I've got it," stuttered Woolf, and, as he opened the huge door, the moneybags fell out on the floor. "Here it is, boys," he mouthed, making much over the sacks of silver.

But Bill had spied the strongbox within, and he kicked the money aside. "Open that box," he commanded. "What do we care for your dirty dollars? Can we pack all that junk on a horse?" He raised his gun to strike, and very reluctantly Woolf opened the inner door.

"Ah!" exclaimed Bill as he caught the color of greenbacks, and he threw the entire contents on the floor. It lay there in a heap, sheafs of bills and bundles

171

of papers, and, as Bill pawed them over, Woolf grabbed out certain papers and stuffed them into his pockets.

"What's those?" demanded Bill as Woolf with miser cunning sought to hide another package in his shirt, and he snatched them all away, despite Woolf's entreaties, and turned the whole pile over to Meadows. "Look 'em over," he said, "while I give this to Butch. He told me to shake the Jew down!"

He flashed back a grin as he slipped out the door, and Woolf fell on the floor and wept. Red-hot pincers could not have forced him to open his huge safe, except to save his own life, but Bill had tricked him into giving up its treasure and now he was taking it to Brennan. Yet the money that Bill had taken was not a tenth of Woolf's wealth, as Meadows could see at a glance — one bundle of papers consisted entirely of notes and mortgages, paying interest at three percent per month. He had put out his money as fast as it came in, and bills of sale for cattle and sheep and wool showed the outcome of many a rapacious loan. Now he lay there sobbing and begging for them back, so that he could continue to grind the faces of the poor.

"No," answered Meadows, motioning him back to his bed, and Woolf broke into piteous pleadings.

"I'll give you anything, Meadows, if you'll only let me off. Ain't I always been your friend? I'll sign over all them notes . . . they're good as gold . . . and you can look the other way while I go. That's all I ask, just look the other way, and I'll never forget your kindness. You're a gentleman, Meadows, not like these damned outlaws . . ."

172

"What's this?" demanded Meadows, holding up a rumpled paper, and Woolf rose up and clutched at it savagely.

"Say, don't take that!" he cried. "That's my . . ."

"Yes, I know what it is," replied Meadows. "It's your bill of sale for Edwards's cattle. It's the one you won from that poor old man before you followed him up and killed him."

"No, I didn't!" clamored Woolf. "Who told you I did? Butch Brennan killed Edwards himself. I swear to Gawd, Meadows, I'm telling you the truth . . . he killed him for three hundred dollars!"

"Didn't you hire him?" inquired Meadows, suddenly jumping at the truth, and Woolf hung his head in assent.

"What you want me to do?" he quavered at last. "You ain't going to kill me, Meadows?"

"I ought to," Meadows declared, and then he stood thinking while Woolf fell back on the bed. Here was a man as low as any he had known, a creature who had robbed the best friend he ever had and then hired an assassin to kill him. That murderer was swaggering Butch Brennan, who Rose had just called a coward. It was with men such as this that he was dealing with now, but the day of retribution was at hand. He thought of Justina, stripped of all she possessed by this abject brute at his feet, yet staying on and on, hoping against hope that she could avenge her father's death. Her revenge was near now — all he had to do was wait, and Brennan would pay half the score. He would walk in on

173

Woolf and shoot him like a dog — and then somebody else would shoot Brennan.

That was the way it would happen if he turned wolf himself and dealt with these outcasts as they deserved, but there was still something to do, to protect her in her rights when he and these murderers were gone. He sat down at the table and spread out the sale by which her father had lost all his cattle, and then he drew out his roll. It was stolen money, of course, and, unless he guessed wrong, it would never bring any happiness to him, but put in a pile it might buy back the stolen cattle — and the store and land as well. What would be more fitting than to use this stolen money to trim a man who was a murderer and a thief?

"Woolf," he said at last, "I ought to kill you like a dog, but I can't quite bring myself to it. How much do you want for your property?"

"My property!" echoed Woolf, suddenly bobbing up from his bed and then his fat eyes narrowed. "Will you let me go?" he whispered. "Will you look the other way? Ah, *mein Gott*, I never thought this of you!" He hobbled over to the door and set the spring lock against Bill, then turned with a cunning smile. "Now," he said, "how much you got?"

Meadows laid down his roll. "I'll give you that," he said, "for everything you've got . . . the ranch, the cattle, and the store. Just write me out a bill of sale."

Woolf grabbed the money and counted it over swiftly, then caught up a pen and began to write. At every passing footfall he started back nervously, but his stoop and cringe were gone and he signed with a flourish, the result of long years of habit.

"Now look the other way," he suggested softly as Meadows put the paper away. The shifty, weasel look had come back into Woolf's eyes, and he held something hidden in his hand.

"What've you got there?" asked Meadows, reaching quietly for his pistol, and Woolf made a rush for the window. The hidden hand came out and a heavy iron weight smashed a hole in the lower pane, and then with a crash Woolf plunged through after it and fell to the ground below. There was a rush from within, the door burst open, and whooping cowboys took up the pursuit, but Brennan did not join them, and soon they came galloping back. Chris Woolf was gone, but he had left his store behind him and they sent out runners for the musicians.

CHAPTER
THIRTEEN

The celebration at Show Low, from the standpoint of the cowboys, was all that the heart could desire. There was whiskey for the asking, food and raiment for the taking, and no one to say them nay. Butch Brennan was preoccupied with the volatile Rose, who was leading him a devil's chase. They quarreled and made up and quarreled again, and at last at some slight she retired to her rooms and refused to appear again. Some imp of perversity that was closely akin to insanity seemed to prompt her to play on his dark passions, to lash him to madness, and then soothe his wounded pride by smiles and soft words of praise, but Wild Horse Bill, for one, saw whither they were drifting and he beckoned Meadows away.

"Look out, boy," he whispered, "old Butch is on the prod . . . he's liable to shoot, that quick! Keep away . . . it's the nearest man that gits it."

He nodded significantly, with a world of meaning in his shrewd eyes and a muttered curse for Rose. As the evening wore on and Butch took to drinking, Bill slipped off and went to bed. When Brennan began to drink, which was very unusual, he was nerving himself for some blow — and in the morning he was drinking still. It was his boast, when he was sober, that he never let whiskey master him or get away with his judgment, but now, when he needed that judgment the most, he was reduced to a sodden drunkenness. All that day he lay sleeping closely guarded by Bill who had his fears for the money in his clothes, but when the second evening came and the music struck up again, Brennan stumbled out and headed for the bar.

The store was crowded now, for all the neighboring ranches had given up their loot-mad cowboys and the flight of Chris Woolf had been the welcome signal for a descent in force on his store. For years he had drained the community of its wealth — in extortion, in blood money and swollen profits — and now that he had fled and left his stock behind him, the reckless ones swarmed to the spoils. Not a cowboy hat was left, nor a shirt or silk handkerchief, and, as Brennan came in, he saw a crowd behind the counter, still busy with the rest of the stock.

"Here! Git out of that!" he ordered, and, as they tiptoed away, he called for another drink. Wild Horse Bill hovered near, then sighed and slipped away, for Rose was there, and dancing.

She was radiant now, with high color in her cheeks and a wild, excited light in her eyes. When Brennan started toward her, she smiled and danced away as if daring him to follow. It was madness, and she knew it, but the game had stolen her wits — she was determined to outface him still. But Brennan did not follow. He looked at her fixedly and her escort took the hint. At the end of the dance he edged away, and others did the same. Only the daredevils remained, bewitched by her laughter, intoxicated by the madness in her eyes, until Lute Starbuck cut them out and claimed dance after dance, led on by the touch of her hand. He had ridden down early, as had been his habit of late. When Brennan saw them, he thrust out his lip and laughed contemptuously to himself. Then he hooked up with a cowboy and joined in on the revelry, leaving her to flirt as much as she chose. At last he returned to the bar. She soon tired of Lute and of the noisy, jostling crowd, but Brennan had been watching. As she started to leave the store, he stepped over and confronted her at the door.

"Give me a dance, first," he said, but she shook her head willfully, then yielded to the look in his eyes. They whirled about together, Brennan speaking in her ear and she still shaking her head, until suddenly his dark face became distorted with rage and he spoke in a different vein. Then he left her abruptly, and a great quiet fell, for all eyes had been fixed on the pair. It had been a wooing in pantomime, to the music of the dance and the swaying of drunken cowboys, and to Meadows in the corner and Wild Horse Bill beside him the play acting had told its own tale. She had repulsed his advances. He had pleaded, then reproached her. Then, in a flash of devilish anger, he had uttered some threat and left her. But Rose was still defiant, although her eyes were wild and scared, and, when Starbuck came by, she caught him by the hand and drew him down beside her. They whispered a minute, then Starbuck nodded, and they whirled away in a dance. The music stopped abruptly, at the call for the drinks — and then someone missed Rose Sheridan. Yes, Rose was gone and Lute Starbuck with her, although no one had seen them go, but that was no one's business unless it was Brennan's — and he gave no signs of alarm. His lips remained curled in the old cynical sneer as he stood with one elbow against the bar and his dark, handsome eyes seemed to twinkle at some thought that sobered him at last and left him grim. He felt for his gun and started toward the parlor, moving swiftly as if to break in on some scene, but when he came back, the cynical sneer was gone and his lips were peeled back with rage.

"You stay here!" he said, sweeping the room with his eyes as he stopped by the outer door. "I'll kill the first man that follows me." He stepped out swiftly and the clatter of horses' hoofs sprang up suddenly and was lost in the night.

They waited then, an interminable time, each man defending some theory of his own, but all agreed that Lute and Rose had fled, although why and where was a question. Butch's horse had dashed off down the Papalote road, the one way out of his power, and, if the couple had eloped, as many claimed, there were those who predicted the worst. But no man left, for they feared Brennan in his absence more than they had when he was there in the same room. What madness had prompted the pair to take flight? What fate would befall them if they were caught? All these and a hundred other questions were thrashed out — and then there were horses at the door. Butch Brennan stepped in, his face set like a mask, and behind him came Rose, choking back a frightened sob and hurrying straight to her rooms.

"Saddle up, boys," said Brennan, "we'll be starting, right away."

When they were ready, he was waiting. Rose Sheridan stood beside him in her riding suit, her face as expressionless as his, and they rode off in silence, except for boisterous talking where certain maudlin cowpunchers remained oblivious to it all. But as they spurred on toward the north, a chill ran through the company, all the glamour of outlawry was lost, and one by one the faint hearts fell out and turned back while yet there was time. Something had happened to Lute Starbuck — perhaps he had been killed — and the man who led the way, with the frightened woman beside him, was the one they would have to serve. He was a killer, as rabid as a wolf, and the men who stayed with him would live to rue the day, for he would turn and rend them, too. If he had killed Lute Starbuck, old man Starbuck's oldest son, it would be better for them all if they were in the bottom-most pit of hell than that they should live to face the old man. For Lute, although he was wild, was Dave Starbuck's favorite boy and the apple of his worried mother's eye. New Mexico, or the whole world, would not be wide enough to shelter the man that killed him. So they muttered among themselves, falling back as Brennan pressed on, and, when dawn broke at last, Brennan had no more men behind him than he had had when first he had ridden out.

180

They were the same men, in fact, with one or two exceptions: the cowpunchers from Frog Tanks — Harris and McElvey and Willie Johnson and others with rewards on their heads — but the Show Low boys were gone, even those who had joined before, and Brennan's dream of empire was broken. He had ridden out twice to drive the Mexicans before him and make New Mexico a white man's country, but beyond looting Woolf's store and breaking up the dance nothing had come of all his efforts. He had loitered about Show Low, drinking and carousing and making enemies, until at last, glum and beaten, he was riding back to Frog Tanks, there to lose some more of his men.

But all dreams had fled with Butch Brennan, the killer, and he pressed on without sleep, without food, without rest, drinking silently from one bottle after another that he had stored away in his saddlebags. At Frog Tanks, where they changed horses, all the Walking X boys stopped, and several of the others as well, but Brennan did not seem even to notice their absence as he headed for the lava beds on the *chula*. He was riding her yet, the one tireless horse of all that had started from Show Low, and, when they entered the *malpais*, he let her have her head, while he kept his eye on Rose.

She was worn from weeping now and with wringing her hands and glancing mutely back for help, but neither Wild Horse Bill nor Meadows, or any man there, would so much as meet her gaze. To do that would be to court sudden death at Brennan's hands, for Bill had passed the word about Butch, and they rode on in silence, their eyes upon the ground, their hats down

181

over their eyes. Some pity there was for this poor, frightened woman, being led to God knew what fate, but they all remembered, too, her flirtations with Butch. If one were to meet her glance, she might call out his name and beg him to save her from Brennan, and Butch, in his present state of mind, would turn in his saddle and shoot.

It was rough on their nerves after two days and nights of drinking and the long ride across the plains, and of all the men who started there were now only six, besides Brennan and Meadows and Bill. Brennan led the way, and Bill followed him by instinct, like a dog, but if Meadows followed still, it was more from pride than loyalty — unless his was an instinct, too. Since he had learned from Woolf that Brennan's was the hand that had put John Edwards in his grave, he felt a curious prompting to keep him in sight and wait for he knew not what. Perhaps it was revenge — revenge for Justina, since she could not gain it herself, but behind it all was a deep feeling of loathing for the man who could do such a deed. To follow an old man out into the night and kill him for three hundred dollars! No man could be brave who would do such a thing — he was a coward, as his woman had said. And if . . . but there he had stopped, for Meadows had determined that Rose should never embroil him. If it were any other woman, no matter how despicable, he would follow to protect her from Butch, but Rose had shown that she was heartless herself and any glance from her would be wasted on him.

They arrived at the *rincón* just as darkness was falling, and Bill cooked a hasty meal. Then, at a muttered word from Brennan, Meadows picked up his blankets and moved. The others followed suit, taking their cooking outfit with them, and that night they slept out along the edge of the lava, leaving the cabin to Brennan and Rose. In the morning Butch came out, locking the door behind him, and drank a cup of coffee by their fire. Then he turned back, more sphinx-like than ever, to shut himself up for the day. Something was working in his mind, some plot for revenge, some exquisite bit of deviltry, for his face was set in deep thought, but he confided in no one, not even Wild Horse Bill, and they all avoided the cabin scrupulously.

A second day passed, with Butch coming for his meals and taking back coffee for Rose, and except for the dishes that came out to them empty they would not have known she was there. But was she there? The outlaws gathered in little knots behind the horse shed that gave them shelter and debated it under their breaths. Perhaps she was dead, perhaps Butch had killed her and was bringing back the dishes as a blind, or perhaps he was inflicting some inhuman torture to punish her for what she had done. The door of the log cabin seemed to hold every eye with its suggestion of mystery and evil, but no one went near, by day or by night, for Brennan had ears like a cat. Perhaps, too, he was looking out through some chink, trying to read their expressions from afar, and, if he went crazy, as some thought he was already, he might shoot them down from his ambush. Hence their retreat behind the

183

horse shed, which was some two hundred feet away, and the wild look that grew in their eyes.

Butch was out of his mind, they all agreed to that, and he had the woman as his prisoner. What should they do then, if she started to scream, or if it appeared that he was trying to kill her? They were outlaws, every one, yet the thought of what might happen broke down their iron prejudice against Rose. She was a woman in distress, a beautiful woman, and should they stand by and see her murdered? The second day of waiting won over even Wild Horse Bill, and they swore to stand together to protect her. Whichever man Butch picked on was to stand up for the girl and the rest would see him through, and if, by morning, she did not appear, they were to march over in a body and demand to see her.

The third morning dawned and Butch came for his breakfast, and the coffee and plate of food for Rose, but although the time had come, no one dared to speak up, and he returned to the cabin unquestioned. He was their master, after all, and his stern brooding eyes made the hardiest falter and hesitate. While they were debating over what should be done next, he came out and went up to the corral. The horses had come in for water, as was their custom after a long night of grazing on the flat. As they filed through the gate, Brennan set the bars against them and roped out Rose's mount and the *chula*. Then he let down the bars and led the two horses. He went in for the riggings and saddled up deliberately, putting his saddle gun into its sling. Like men numbed or deprived of their will power, the gang looked on in silence. They were waiting to see the woman.

She came out at last at a word from Brennan, pale and haggard but standing erect, and, when her eyes strayed to the huddled group of men, she took a step or two toward them.

"Come back hyer!" snarled Brennan as he sensed her purpose, but she had seen Ab Meadows step out of the crowd and now she was running wildly. Brennan shouted again, and then strode angrily after her while the cowboys looked on aghast.

"He's going to kill me!" she burst out hysterically as she threw herself at Ab's feet. He knew at last why he had come. It was to meet Butch Brennan face to face and prove him a coward or kill him.

"No, he won't!" he yelled, and before he could recover Meadows snatched both guns from his belt.

"Now," he said, "you were going to kill her . . . why shouldn't . . . ?"

"No, I wasn't!" denied Brennan. "For God's sake, what's the matter? I was only going . . ."

"Yes, he was!" cried Rose, rushing up to confront Brennan. "Yes, you were, you murdering brute! You killed Lute Starbuck and you were going to kill me, and hide my body out there in the lava!" She drew away shuddering, and, as Meadows started forward, she leaned over and spoke in his ear.

"Shoot him now," she whispered, but Brennan heard her and he shouted wildly to Bill.

"Take her away!" he cried. "She's crazy, I tell you! And for God's sake, Meadows, don't shoot!"

"I don't know," began Ab, "if I don't kill you now . . ."

"I won't shoot you . . . I won't touch you . . . I give you my word! But don't shoot me down like a dog!"

"What about it, Bill?" asked Meadows. "Do you think I can trust him? Just keep those hands up, Brennan."

"*No!*" screamed Rose. "Don't you trust him! You'll regret it! Oh, kill him, boys, please, for my sake!"

"We'll take care of you," counseled Bill, "but we'll have to tie him up. Will you stand for it, Butch . . . while she goes?"

"Stand for what?" demanded Butch, suddenly lowering his hands, and then he stuck them up higher. "Yes, tie me up," he growled. "I see you're all against me . . . but you'll pay for this yet, old girl!"

"Oh, why won't you kill him?" she burst out in a panic. "Can't you see, boys, what he's intending to do? He'll kill Ab first and then he'll kill me . . ."

"No, he won't," answered Meadows, "because I won't let him . . . but I can't shoot him down in cold blood. We'll settle this . . . now get up on your horse and we'll go."

He led her across the flat to where the two horses were standing, and, as he put the bridle reins over the *chula*'s head, she brushed her soft nose across his cheek.

"Git off that mare!" shouted Brennan in a fury as he came struggling toward him. His head was thrown back and his eyes were rolling as he dragged Wild Horse Bill by the rope. "I knew it!" he cursed. "From the first day

186

you came here, you've had your eye on that horse. You tried to buy her and now you're going to steal her . . . but if you do, by the Lord, I'll kill you."

"No, you won't," retorted Meadows, "because I'll kill you first. Give me twenty-four hours' start, will you, Bill?"

"Are you going to send that horse back?" demanded Brennan pointedly, and Meadows shook his head.

"No," he said, "I'm going to keep her. Isn't that the way you do business?"

Brennan choked and looked at Bill, who was chuckling slyly, and then he fixed his eyes on Ab. "All right," he said, "have your own way, Meadows. You've been framing this up for some time. You can take the horse . . . and you're welcome to Rose . . . but if I live, sure as hell, I'll kill you."

"Any time," returned Meadows, and rode away with a smile, for he had tamed Butch Brennan, the wolf.

A man never knows whether he is a hero or a coward until the moment of danger comes, but if he stands the acid test, then his heart is changed and he seeks for new worlds to conquer. He has proved to himself that his nerve will not crack and it us up to the other fellow to worry. Ab Meadows had matched his nerve against Brennan's and proved him a coward. For a fraction of a second their eyes had met and blazed, and Meadows had whipped out his guns, and in that fraction of a second Brennan had sensed his will to kill and had weakened before the charge. He could have drawn, too,

187

but he knew it was too late, and he chose to save his life — and wait.

That was the system he played, the philosophy he had developed from years of outlawry and killing — never to fight unless he had an even break or better and then to shoot men down ruthlessly. He was one man, an outlaw, against many men organized against him, and, if he fought as they fought, then the end would come soon for the chances were all against him. So his craven heart had weakened and to cover up his shame he had turned a blusterer and a killer. To beat down the just rage of society against him he killed his bravest enemies by stealth, and then, riding forth with his gang at his back, he intimidated the weak and the helpless. Yet all the time a cowardly fear was eating at his heart, and when pursuing a woman he found his courage challenged, his nerve gave way in spite of him. He surrendered before he knew it, but the forces which made him yield had been working for many a day. Ab Meadows, who had stepped out to meet the fleeing woman and to stand between her and Brennan had also responded to forces long at work that had taken the fear of death from his heart. His courage had burst out like a blood-red flame and in the first exultation he had taunted the fallen bully and carried away his *chula* horse for booty. It was more than a robbery, a taking of the prize on which his heart had been set; it was a challenge to Brennan to come and get his horse or own himself a coward before all men.

Meadows rode across the *rincón* at the tireless, rocking trot at which the *chula* ate up the miles, and, as he waved his hand at Bill, he settled down in the saddle for the ordeal that lay before him. Rose was weeping already, her nerves all unstrung and begging him to hurry her away, but the lava lay before them, the last place in the world to hurry, where a wrong turn would spell wandering and slow death. Once lost in that maze of hummocks and shattered fissures they would circle and turn, shut in by the pines, until only a miracle could save them. But Meadows had not forgotten a miracle he had witnessed when he had first entered that monotony of *malpais*, and, as he turned into the trail, he gave the *chula* her head and patted her on the neck.

The horse led off confidently to the south. Meadows sat silently in the saddle, noting her course by the sun, and, when at last they broke out into the open, he stopped and looked back through the trees. This was the fourth time now that he had passed over the lost trail and when he came again he might not have the *chula* to lead him to where Butch Brennan lay hidden. Rose burst out crying when she saw the open plains and turned from the lava with a shudder.

They reached Frog Tanks at noon and found the cowboys all away, for the summer range riding was on, but the cook gave them food, and, still looking behind her, Rose took the long trail for Show Low. She was quieter now, for the broad plains were all about her and the Saw Tooth range rose across their way. As they passed up the wide swale and into the wooded hills, Meadows saw that the reaction had come. She had driven herself mercilessly to escape the haunting thought of Brennan, following hot on their trail.

When they were setting up camp for the night, the time came that Meadows had long dreaded, and which Rose perhaps had looked forward to, since at last they had time to talk. He feared her friendship as much as her enmity, and her gratitude left him silent. She was the type of woman that he instinctively avoided, for he had known one like her before — the kind that is ruled entirely by the head and not at all by the heart. She reminded him of that other woman he had known, who had married the other man, and yet she, and Rose, too, were not without emotions — it was only that they turned them to some purpose. Rose thanked him now, with tears in her eyes, for stepping out and saving her from Brennan, and then she praised him for his manly courage and for his bold defiance of the outlaw, but down in his heart he never forgot that here was Brennan's woman. She was a woman who had sold herself for money and taken stolen gifts, and he answered her diffidently with a slow, uneasy smile until at last she dropped asleep. Then he took a single blanket and went down where he had hobbled the horses and did not return till dawn.

The night's sleep had refreshed her, but the old fear had returned. As they rode on up the trail, she cried out to Meadows and pointed far back down the wash.

"Isn't that Butch?" she exclaimed. "Oh, I knew he would come. They let him get away in the night!"

Meadows reined in his horse and looked long at the moving point that threaded its way up the valley, and then he shook his head.

190

"Don't think so," he said at last, "but there's no use taking chances. You'll be perfectly safe in Show Low."

She started off at a gallop, still looking behind her, and soon they had left the rugged mountains and struck the main road that led down White House Cañon to Show Low. The first *vegas* appeared, then the White House flashed by, and, as the valley opened out, they passed peaceful meadows where Figure 4 cattle lazed and fed. It was home to Ab, the old range he had combed until he knew every ridge and winding trail, but as they drew near Starbuck's ranch, he slowed down to a trot since the horse that he rode was well known. After Brennan had fled, there might be manhunters in the hills, or Starbuck might mistake him for Brennan.

Two of the Starbuck children came down the lane from the ranch house, which was concealed by a point of the hill, and went pelting away to school, and Meadows stopped his horse.

"I'm afraid," he said, "this is about as far as I can go. I might run into somebody I know."

"Oh, the schoolma'am?" inquired Rose, whose spirits were returning, and he answered her in kind.

"No . . . Dave Starbuck," he replied, "but you haven't told me how Lute came to be killed."

"Don't be hateful!" she snapped back. "You might take me to the store . . . I don't want to ride in there alone."

"Very well, then," he returned, and started grimly down the road with one eye on the Starbuck lane. They were almost to the gate when a horse swung around the point and his worst expectations were realized. It was Justina, late for school and coming at a gallop, and she met them almost face to face. Barely two hundred feet intervened when she swung down and opened the gate, and, after one startled look, she left it wide open and disappeared down the dusty road.

"She doesn't like you!" suggested Rose with a peal of brittle laughter, and Meadows shrugged his shoulders in protest.

"No," he said, and dropped down to close the gate, after which he rode on grimly.

Justina had refused to speak to him. No, she had fled him like the plague, but, of course, he could hardly blame her. After all she had done for him he came riding back now with Rose, the woman who had lured Lute to his death, and Rose, harsh and unrepentant, had burst out in strident laughter as her rival had gone galloping off. He should have left her in the road, but his pride was touched and he kept on down the valley. As they came in sight of the store, he saw horses tied to the rack and a lone horseman coming rapidly toward them. Then he looked up sharply, for it was Justina, coming back. She held up her hand and he halted obediently, and then she beckoned him back, but he shook his head and came on. The worst had happened and there was nothing to fear — but he drew away from Rose.

"Go back!" called Justina and then, impatiently, she advanced to meet them in the road. "What's the matter with you!" she burst out, "haven't you got any sense?

Chris Woolf has come back, with Celso Baca and all his deputies . . . they're right down there at the store!"

"Oh, is that so?" returned Meadows, still refusing to be hurried. "Well, thank you very much. Miss Sheridan, can you go on to the store alone? Chris Woolf will take care of you, I'm sure!"

"Why, certainly," replied Rose with a thin-lipped smile, "and thank you very much, Miss Edwards!"

"I wasn't talking to you!" flared back Justina in a passion. "I was talking to Mister Meadows."

"Well, I'll go on, then," said Rose with mock humility, "because I know you want to talk with him. But, oh, *Mister* Meadows, how can I ever thank you for everything that you've done? And if there's anything I can do to repay you for your kindness . . ." She ran on maliciously, talking for Justina to hear, while Meadows writhed under her praise. He had done no more for her than he would have done for any woman, and she knew that he disliked her thanks, yet now, while he waited for a last word with Justina, she took up the time to spite him. No, not to spite him, but to humiliate Justina, who would have left in a moment but for the moral certainty that Rose would join her on the way. But even the worm will turn at last, and he finally broke in on her blarney.

"That's all right, Miss Sheridan . . . glad to have been of some service to you . . . but if you'll excuse me just a minute, I have something very important that I'd like to communicate with Miss Edwards."

"Oh!" echoed Rose, "I suppose my poor thanks . . ."

"I'm sorry," persisted Meadows, "but this is a matter of business . . . and please don't tell those Mexicans who I am."

"No, I won't," she mocked, pretending to smile sweetly as she flashed back a warning glance. "I'll only tell 'em you're Brennan."

She laughed and went galloping off toward the store, and Meadows sat gazing at her blankly. Wild Horse Bill had been right. After all he had done for her, she was lost to all decency and gratitude — and the posse would think he was Brennan! He turned swiftly to Justina and reached into his pocket where he had hidden Woolf's two bills of sale.

"Justina," he began, "I can't stop to explain, but I've got something here I want to give you. I shall never forget . . ."

"You can keep it!" returned Justina, reining her horse away and regarding him with level eye. "Do you think I'd accept anything from a thief? I tried to save you once, but this is the end . . . I hope I never see you again."

"Well, cheer up, if you can," answered Ab, putting the papers away. "Somehow I don't think you ever will."

Their horses wheeled together and galloped away from each other, and, as Justina neared the store, the posse of Mexicans bolted past her and went whipping and yelling up the road.

CHAPTER
FOURTEEN

Next to an Apache, a Mexican will get more speed out of a horse than any rough rider in the West, because he spurs him at every jump. A white man has some mercy when his horse is doing his best, but Mexicans and Indians have none. Ab Meadows was mounted on the best range horse in New Mexico, and he barely led the posse the first mile. Their arms were working rhythmically as they bit the blood at every plunge, but the *chula*, although hard pressed, never broke her even gait, and in the end she drew away. Then they gained the upper cañon where the road twisted and turned and Meadows lost sight of Celso Baca and his posse. But they would ride, he knew that, until the last horse gave out for they thought they were chasing Butch Brennan.

Yet even Butch Brennan had a place to hide, and sworn friends on every ranch, while Ab Meadows had no friends and no hiding place, and every man's hand was against him. As long as he rode the *chula*, the gang would hunt him down to restore his favorite mount to their chief, and so well was the mare known that every officer would pursue him in the hope of catching Brennan, but even if she marked him for envy and pursuit, Meadows patted her heaving side and smiled. As long as he had her, he need fear neither outlaw nor officer, once he gained the open plains. In the mountains it was different for the rough ground killed her speed, and every cañon was by nature a trap. One man at the other end and he was headed off and caught, unless he could get to the rocks.

The cañon up which he rode was beginning to box, to pinch in and grow steep on both sides, and, as the mare began to labor, he pulled her to a trot, looking back with his hand on his gun. Then, as they made a turn, a flying horseman burst upon them, thundering on down the middle of the trail. The *chula* made a quick jump, Meadows clutched at the horn, and the man tore past and stopped short. It was Brennan, by his hat and the black shirt he always wore, and Meadows went for his gun. But the *chula* was in the rocks, and, as he twisted about to shoot, she cat-jumped and leaped back into the trail. Then Brennan's gun barked out, and, as their horses pitched and wheeled, they crowded in and emptied their pistols.

It was hurried, spiteful work, for they were both taken by surprise, and their bullets went wild and high, but as their pistols began to snap, they came to their senses and made a break for cover. Meadows galloped around the point, his heart in his mouth and reloading with feverish haste. Taking pity on the *chula*, he left her behind a rock and went back down the trail at a crouch. This was no quarrel of hers, and, if worst came to worst, Brennan would find her waiting to his hand. His

196

nerves were steady now, and, if he could run in on Butch — he drew back and jumped behind a rock. Then it came, the steady patter, the rush of horses' hoofs, and, just as he took cover, Celso Baca swung around the point and bore down upon their hiding place. He did not know Brennan was there, Brennan did not know what was coming, but as Meadows rose up, he heard two shots from the rocks and Baca pitched out of his saddle. Then both their horses came stampeding past and Meadows ran back to catch the *chula*.

She was there behind her rock, snorting and dragging her reins, for a battle had sprung up behind them, but when Meadows spoke, she halted obediently. He swung up and galloped away. Things were coming so thick and fast that he was stampeded, like the horses, and he fled wildly, without any plan, but at the forks of the cañon he stopped and looked back, smiling grimly at the sound of the shooting. He had put them up together, his pursuers and Butch Brennan, and they were fighting it out among the rocks, while he, who they both sought, was well out of it all and free to make his escape. Some kindly Providence must have watched over him that day or he never would have eluded them all, and now, while they were busy, he could cover up his tracks and take shelter among the cliffs of the Datils.

Where the big cañon forked, there were two narrow trails, cut clean by the hoofs of many cattle, and Meadows turned to the right, then dropped down on the sod and wiped out his tracks behind him. Then he smoothed out his boot prints and rode on up the path — where the cattle, coming to water, would trample out his trail. But unless he was mistaken there would be no further pursuit, for Brennan was surrounded and left afoot and the Mexicans would not know what had happened. They had started out after Brennan and Brennan they had found, and, unless all signs failed, he was putting up a fight that would hold the *paisanos* for some time. Celso Baca was killed, it would be war to the knife, and in the meantime he could escape.

But before he left the country, he must throw his enemies off his trail and hide out till the search had passed, and he must eat and find shelter from the storms that gathered on the peaks every day. No one knew when or where the rains would strike, but every day they swooped down, now wetting bone-dry mesas, now falling in lush valleys where previous rains had brought up the grass, and, when the clouds opened, each stream became a torrent and a man without a slicker was soaked. The great thunder caps were mounting above the high cliffs of the Datils as Meadows rode over the divide, and, as he took the zigzag trail that led up to Kin Savvy Lewis's cave, he felt the first patter of rain.

In all that upper world of roaring pines and open spaces there was only one place where a man could look for shelter and that was with Kin Savvy, the prospector. *¿Quién sabe?* is Spanish for "who knows?" and was the motto by which the prospector lived. All his life was spent in mystery and concealment, and even hospitality, the frontiersman's religion, became a grudging rite in his cave. In a world that, to his mind, was already badly crowded, he had fled to the silence of the heights, and, when some man came to break in upon his solitude, Kin Savvy could but guess the worst. The man must have some motive, and what else could it be but to discover the secret of his mine? Why should he, with his horses to look after and a great treasure waiting to his hand, go out of his way to entertain some young walloper who was doubtless on the dodge, or worse? So he received all with suspicion and to most of their questions he gave the Mexican answer: "Who knows?"

Meadows had no illusions about the welcome he would receive, but in happier times he had done Lewis several favors and he rode boldly up to his cave. It was a low cavern at the base of a sandstone bluff, with cedar timbers set here and there to prevent the roof from falling, and at its mouth in the sunshine sat old Kin Savvy, humped up over an age-yellowed newspaper. He glanced up coldly, then returned to his paper, spelling out the big words with his lips, but at last he put it aside.

"Well, git down, git down," he spoke grudgingly, "what's the news from down below?"

"Oh, nothing much," answered Meadows, and sat down patiently to await an invitation to dine. It was long since he had eaten and the next ranch was miles away — and besides he intended to stay, not only for dinner, but for supper and breakfast, and so on for a couple of weeks. There was one thing about Kin Savvy; he would never ask you to stay, but on the other hand he would never ask you to go. That was against his policy, his gospel of negation, his *quién sabe* attitude toward life. He believed in opposing no one. If the sheriff came by, he was as welcome as the horse thief who had just imposed his society upon Kin Savvy — and not a bit more welcome. He could stay, if he wanted to, but Kin Savvy would not urge him, nor would he tell him a word about the horse thief. It was nothing to Kin Savvy what went on around him as long as they left *him* alone — and the horse thief might come back and kill him. So he took shelter behind a cloak of philosophical calm and let men come and go. Only, of course, they ate lots of grub.

"That's a good horse you've got there," volunteered Kin Savvy at last, "one of them broom tails that runs on the plains."

"Yes," agreed Meadows, and settled down enduringly, whereupon Kin Savvy tried him again.

"Whar you traveling?" he asked.

Meadows shrugged his shoulders. "Over here," he said, jerking his head toward the north. "What's the chance for something to eat?"

"Well . . . ," began Kin Savvy, and then he heaved himself up and looked back into the cave. "Oh, well," he sighed, "ain't eating much mys'f . . . might throw you up a little something. They was a feller come through here a month or so ago and like to eat me out of house and home."

He lit a little fire and cooked some bread in the frying pan, besides warming up some coffee and beans, and then, after their meal, he sat down in the sun and filled his old black pipe.

"Well, what's the news?" he asked, stroking his bald dome reflectively and glancing up out of the corner of one eye. "Lemme see, now, what's that I heard about you?"

"I don't know," responded Meadows, and after a minute's silence Kin Savvy returned to the attack.

"Still working for Starbuck?" he ventured insinuatingly, and Meadows came out with the truth.

"No," he said, "I'm traveling for my health. What's the chance of my staying a while?"

"Well, I don't say you *can't* stay," replied Kin Savvy ungraciously, and then he waited for Meadows to speak.

"It's this way," began Ab, "there's a fellow on my trail that thinks he wants my horse. Get the idea? I'm kind of on the dodge."

"They all are," observed Kin Savvy, "when they come through here. Haven't seen Butch Brennan, have ye?"

"Why, yes," answered Meadows, "but what makes you ask? Is he a friend of yours?"

"I can't tell you that," returned Kin Savvy evasively, "but I'd know that mare of his anywhere . . . he got her from Wild Horse Bill."

"That's right," admitted Meadows, "but she belongs to me now." He gazed long at the *chula*, feeding before the cave.

Kin Savvy's curiosity got the best of him. "How'd you git her?" he demanded, his bearded chin all a-tremble as he leaned over to scrutinize his guest, and Meadows laughed good-naturedly. If he was going to stay with Kin Savvy, he would have to take him into his confidence, and he knew he was perfectly safe. For forty years and more the old prospector had roamed the hills in search of Montezuma's lost treasure house, and he had never informed on anyone yet. That was not his policy — he never told anything — but he dearly loved all the gossip.

"I'll tell you, Mister Lewis," began Meadows at last, "I was over in the lava beds, where Brennan has his hideout . . ."

"You was!" exclaimed Kin Savvy, his eyes lighting up, and then he rubbed his head. "Well, go on," he said, "go on."

"We had a little racket and I got the drop on him and talked him out of his horse. And this morning, while he was chasing me, he ran into a posse of Mexicans and I guess they're shooting it out yet."

"You don't say!" exclaimed Kin Savvy, and, as Meadows described the battle, he drank in every word. But when he had ended, the old man rose up and gazed down the wooded cañon. "I'll tell you something," he said, "this is a bad place to hide out. Do you know what you ought to do? Go back to them lava beds . . . they can't trail you there . . . I can tell you jest the place!"

"No water!" objected Meadows, and after a minute's pensive thought Kin Savvy broke the rule of a lifetime. He told something.

"Yes they is," he said. "I claim to know them lava beds better than any man alive, and I tell you, young

202

man, they is. Did you ever hear of Montezuma's treasure house?"

"Sure," answered Meadows, "that's the gold mine you've been hunting for. Do you think it's over there?"

"No, it ain't," stated Kin Savvy, "and I reckon I ought to know because I put in two summers there, looking for it. But I'll tell you, young man, what they *is* over there . . . they's a cave full of ice and water."

"Is that so?" murmured Meadows, and, as the old man rattled on, he perceived what was on his mind. Kin Savvy was worried lest Butch Brennan should follow and visit his vengeance upon *him*. He was hinting at a better place to hide.

"A great cave!" bragged Kin Savvy, "where the Aztecs used to go to carry out their secret rites. It's a wonderful place, and no white man ever laid eyes on it until I clumb down into it myself. Them Aztecs was the greatest and richest people that ever inhabited the earth, and right here is where they found their gold. They had a big trail that ran down through Chihuahua, plumb to Montezuma's palace in the city of Mexico, where Cortez and his soldiers come, and they took this Montezuma and put him in a room and told the Aztecs they was going to kill him, and the Aztecs, they filled the chamber plumb full of gold if they'd only spare his life. But where, lemme ask you, did them Aztecs git this gold? They got it right here in these hills!"

He nodded his head knowingly, and a wild fire came into his eyes as he pondered the great mystery by which he lived, but after he had expounded the wisdom of the ancients, his talk led him back to the cave.

"They's a trail," he said, "that leads to this cave like it was run by an engineer, but the bloody Apaches have knocked down all the monuments and nobody can find it but me. I took me a compass and two gallons of water and a sack of jerked beef and bread and I criss-crossed that *malpais* from one side to the other on the lookout for Montezuma ruins . . . that's how come I found this trail. And, now listen, boy. I like you . . . you done ketched my mare for me when she pulled out over the summit that time . . . and I tell you what I'll do. I'll make you a map, showing jest where that trail runs, and you go in yander and hide. They's a little *rincón* jest big enough to camp in and to keep your horse in grass, and it's only a short distance to this ice cave of the Aztecs. They ain't a man in the world that can ever foller you, unless I show 'em the way, and I reckon you know old Kin Savvy. I don't blab on nobody, be he friend or be he enemy, as long as they leave *me* alone. Come on now, I'll make you a map."

"Nope," said Meadows, "don't put yourself out. I'm perfectly safe, right here."

"All right," grumbled Kin Savvy, "suit yourself, suit yourself. But if Butch Brennan slips up and pots you from the brush, don't say old Kin Savvy didn't warn ye. And he'll steal that mare as sure as you live . . . Butch Brennan thinks the world of that horse."

"Well, what am I going to eat?" demanded Meadows impatiently. "Even if I did find this lost cave, which don't seem any too likely, what am I going to live on while these fellows are hunting for me? There's nothing

204

in those lava beds but piñon jays and pack rats, and a white man can't stomach them!"

"Well, I'll tell you," began Kin Savvy, and then he glanced at him shrewdly. "How do you happen to be fixed for money?"

"Got lots of it," answered Meadows, "but that don't buy me much here. And I'm safe . . . the rain washed out my tracks."

"Butch Brennan will find ye," croaked the old man ominously. "He thinks the world of that mare. I can give you some grub, if that's all you want, but I'll have to go to the town for some more."

"Don't see much," observed Meadows, looking into the bare cave, and then he bowed his head in thought. It would be taking a long chance to head out into the lava on the word of this half-cracked old man, and yet Kin Savvy was perfectly capable of making the trip he spoke of. No one had ever heard of it, but who heard of anything that Kin Savvy did in his travels? He came and he went and nothing had stopped him yet in his search for the storied treasure. "Can you stake me to a compass?" Meadows asked at last, and Kin Savvy jumped to his feet.

"That's the talk!" he said. "Sure I can stake you to a compass . . . and to grub, and a canteen and everything. I'll do anything for a friend, but if Butch Brennan finds you here, the danged fool will kill *me*, too."

The solicitude of Kin Savvy to speed his parting guest would have been laughable if it had not been so sinister. He scurried about in his dark cave like a chipmunk on a raid, digging up supplies from the most unexpected places, and, as he thrust them upon Meadows, it was as if he said: *Here's your hat, my friend . . . don't hurry*. But Meadows hurried, too, for the sun was getting low and he sensed what was on Kin Savvy's mind. If Butch Brennan did not come, then it would be the Mexican posse, or a bunch of express company detectives, and the only safe place for a man in his plight was out in the middle of the lava beds. If, as Kin Savvy claimed, no one else knew the trail, it would prove a haven of refuge, and after his month of hard riding and fighting Meadows felt the need of a rest. He was soul sick and weary, racked with pains from his half-healed wound and with doubts as to the use of it all, and the thought of the *rincón*, of absolute solitude and security, spurred him on to a last, desperate effort.

Kin Savvy made him a map and gave him his compass and described the route he was to follow, and then he hurried him off, starting down the trail ahead of him the quicker to get him away. Meadows rode off meekly, after paying twice over for the food, convinced at last that he was an outcast and a criminal. Even Kin Savvy refused to house him, when he had been sheltering horse thieves and outlaws since the memory of the oldest inhabitants. If his case was as desperate as that, then he did well to flee the world and hide his head in the silence of the *malpais*. It was bad country, indeed, that great overflow of lava that extended like a blanket from the cindery volcanoes to the north to the Punta de Malpais to the south. It could not be an overflow; it was too extensive, too level; no, rather it was an upheaval, a great rift in the earth's crust, through which the molten rock had boiled up and bubbled and subsided in vent holes and cracks. The place where he was going was the roughest of it all, for a second upheaval had burst through the first, leaving confusion worse confounded.

Yet, according to Kin Savvy's map, there were two great inlets that ran far into the mass, one entering from the northeast and one from the southwest. Connecting these two points, there was an old Indian trail, plainly marked by the skeletons of sheep. In some disastrous moment a Mexican sheepherder had tried to cross his band from east to west, but the trail was rough and dry and many had fallen by the wayside with their heads still pointing west. The blazes on the trees and the monuments had followed, and it was to this trail first that Kin Savvy advised him to go, for it cut across the Aztec trail. Not two hundred yards from the little *rincón* which was to be Meadows's camp, if he found it, the ancient Aztecs had left a graded trail that led on northwest to the ice cave. To find it meant the difference between dying of thirst and of finding a safe refuge from his enemies.

Meadows rode wearily down the trail from Kin Savvy's lofty home and reached the Alamosa at dusk, and, after watering his horse and filling his canteen, he struck out through the hills. Their pace was slow, for he was burdened with provisions and the heavy, two-gallon canteen. As she paced on through the night, the *chula* shook her head and sighed, while Meadows nodded till he swayed in the saddle. Yet he kept doggedly on till he came to the *malpais*, and there in a sheltered inlet he turned the *chula* out to graze while he slept till the first peep of dawn. Then he looked at the country that bounded the lava to the east, the high bluffs of Cebollita and the mesas to the north, and marked the spot on his map. It was ten miles through the *malpais*, traveling solely by the compass, before he would break out into the great inlet, yet the only alternative was a ride of forty miles to circle far around to the north. He saddled up and took the plunge.

The *malpais* through which he passed was of the ancient, moss-grown flow, heavily timbered with pines yet with clear spaces here and there, where no cracks gave a foothold for the trees. The *chula* stepped off confidently, picking her way over the resounding rock, and the brittle slabs of lava *clinked* and rang out like steel as they were displaced by her scrambling hoofs. It was rough climbing at best and soon Meadows dismounted and led her at the end of her rope. He traveled an hour, two hours, three, into the heart of the silent forest, and then he stopped and looked back. Through a gap in the trees he could glimpse the cliffs of Cebollita and the long line of the mesa against the sky, but ahead all was blank, a mystery, perhaps a menace, an endless succession of pines. But to follow a straight line through the fissures and hummocks was impossible, even with a compass, and, as Meadows plodded on and the time slipped by, he knew he had strayed from his course. Either that or the inlet was a figment of the imagination and Kin Savvy Lewis had lied to him. But Meadows had seen those same white limestone hills when he was riding to rob the train with Brennan and he knew they were somewhere to the north, and, where there was limestone, there was open country, too, and escape from the all-embracing lava. He shook up his compass and gauged it by the sun, and then the world seemed to whirl about him. It was high noon now and the sun was at its zenith, but where the compass pointed was not north. And if it was not north, then which way had he been traveling, and where had he brought himself at last?

He pulled himself together and took a drink from his canteen, and at the *slosh* of water the *chula* turned her head and sucked her dry tongue appealingly. But, no, he could not spare a drop of it now if he was to escape from the lava beds alive, and yet — well, she was thirsty, too. Not since the evening before, when they had crossed the Alamosa, had she tasted water at all, and her golden coat was crusted with sweat. He filled the little frying pan that Kin Savvy had given him and she sighed as she supped it dry. Then he stroked her soft nose, and, as he stood there thinking, she turned to where the compass said was north. He swung up in the saddle and threw the reins on her neck and she started off through the trees. Slowly and hesitatingly at first, and then with greater certitude, she laid a course through the forest aisles. As Meadows watched her, he looked at his compass and his sense of direction returned. She was heading northeast, where he had headed northwest — and, far off beneath the trees, there appeared a stretch of sun-brightened yellow. He

209

dropped down to the ground and led the way at a fast walk, and they came out on the edge of a plain.

It extended far to the east — and well to the north, too, where it ended at the base of some hills — but at the west it pinched down to a broad, yellow valley that was lost between the forest and the hills. It was Kin Savvy's inlet and Meadows had been paralleling it for miles, until the *chula* had set him right. He had turned too far west in his journey from Cebollita and had been toiling on through the lava when a mile or two to the north lay this level, grass-grown plain. But he was on the trail, at last. He had found Kin Savvy's entrance, and, as the mare trotted up a broad path, worn deep by wild horses, he passed the bleaching skeleton of a sheep. The head was pointing west, just as Kin Savvy had said, and, as he rode on and on, he passed other gruesome markers, all pointing out the way of death. Yet as the valley entered the hills, it broke up into different forks, and, turning too far south, he found himself in a blind pocket, shut in on all sides by lava. It was rough lava now, rough and rising like a wall up which a man on foot could hardly scramble, and the hill which Kin Savvy had spoken of as marking the entrance to the trail was lost behind the towering trees.

Meadows rode back to the fork and took the other turn, but at last his tireless mount was weakening. She stopped often in the trail, as if questioning the direction, and her head, which she had always held up so proudly, hung low or was tossed impatiently. But she kept on up the long trail, where the skeletons of lost sheep served as markers to blaze the way, and at last, rounding a point, they swung into a round valley where a dry lake shimmered in the sun. Here the trail split again, some tracks leading to the lake and others to cañons in the hills, but Kin Savvy had directed Meadows to pass east of a certain hill, where a vein of quartz running along its slope made a line like a graded road, and for once he caught the pass and, mounting to a higher valley beyond, came to the edge of the *malpais* again.

Some later and less daring sheepherder had ranged his flock through these hills, feeding down the grass when there was water in the lake, and the myriad narrow trails, each leading up some pocket, deceived Meadows again and again. He was off and walking now, for the sun was boiling hot and the poor *chula* had almost ceased to sweat. At last, although it was reckless, he shared his water with her again, after which he continued his search for the trail. The lava flow now lay so close to the hills that it looked like the breakers of a black and angry sea, rising up to strike against the solid land. As the scattered trails came together into one, Meadows pressed on eagerly toward his goal. He was on the trail at last, and it could not escape him now, since there was no place for it to go. It was heading into the *malpais* and far over the treetops he saw the crater that marked the end of the Aztec trail.

This entered the lava beds to the south of Cebollita and led straight to the ice cave he sought, after which it broke up into three smaller trails, the largest of which led to the crater. But all that Meadows thought of was the hidden cave of ice where the Aztecs had come for water, for his canteen was nearly empty, and, if he failed to find more water, he would do well to escape with his life. As for the *chula*, she was hardy, for the wild horses she had run with often went without water for several days and were chased by the horse hunters besides. She would live, and he was foolish to give up his water, but the silence of the forest was getting on his nerves and he conversed with her like a friend. He could not endure to see her suffer, to have her begging for water while he drank and gave her none, so, rather than refuse her, he went without himself and they entered the lost country together.

A great monument of loose rocks and a blaze on a tree trunk marked the entrance to the abandoned sheep trail, and from here on through the trees the path stretched away, although the markers were far between. The trail was leading west, straight into the sun which was swinging dangerously low, and, as Meadows lost the track where the blazes were overgrown, he built him a monument and sat down. Here once more the *chula* came to his aid and led the way, back to the path. She understood at last what he was trying to accomplish, and the sight of the clean trail leading definitely in one direction seemed to raise her spirits and hopes. She stepped off briskly, sucking her lips as she thought of water, and Meadows pressed forward at a trot. If he had followed his instincts, he would have broken into a run, but that way lay insanity and death.

The country was high now, with quaking asps and spruces, and the grass which had been dry on the lower levels was green along the trail — tender and green but

212

absolutely untouched, for no horse had passed this way. The *chula* reached down and cropped the rich crow's-foot grama when it rose up before her in the path, and once in a crack she found a tiny stalk of corn where some wanderer had spilled a few grains, but mostly she sucked her tongue and gazed hopefully ahead for even the green grass made her thirsty. The sun touched the treetops as they toiled up rough ridges and down into gloomy gorges, and then, as a murky darkness began to gather beneath the trees, they clattered down a hill into the *rincón*.

It was a small flat, dotted with pines and surrounded by a black wall of towering disrupted lava, but the Aztec trail which led to the ice cave was somewhere in the rocks behind. Here, indeed, was green grass and level ground to sleep on, but the *chula* could not feed and he could not sleep while they were tortured by an all-day thirst. What they wanted was water and Meadows turned back, dragging the reluctant mare behind him. Not two hundred yards away, as Kin Savvy had described it, lay the Aztec trail to water, a trail so plain that, once it was found, he might follow it even at night. It was graded like a roadway, filling up cracks and plowing through hummocks, but so ancient and unused that great trees had taken root in it and died and made room for others. Only its beginning was concealed from the eye by the work of the cunning Apaches; once he passed the area where they had flattened the monuments, he might yet win to water that night.

He hurried up the path, dragging the mare by her rope, for she held back at every step, and at two hundred yards' distance he turned off to the left, although the dusk was gathering fast. Up rough ridges and along dark ravines he scrambled recklessly, circling back and forth to cut the trail, and then in one black instant the light went out and he found himself hopelessly lost. Time and again Wild Horse Bill had warned him never to get out of sight of a monument, and, if he did, to build another one and circle back, but he had forgotten that warning in his haste to find water and now he was lost for the night. There was no grass there, no water, not even a level place to stand on, and the poor *chula* stood drooping, shuffling her hoofs uneasily as she sought a better foothold among the rocks. Meadows sat down dejectedly and stretched out his wounded leg, which had been aching and throbbing all day, and the old impulse to curse surged up again and all but conquered his will. But he fought it back, still clinging to the one virtue which was left from his blighted past, and buried his face in his hands.

He was whipped at last, broken and battered and brought to destruction, but still he held back the words. They rose to his lips with devilish insistence and he longed to curse God and die, but some instinct toward goodness, newly born from his travails, rushed in and fought them back. He was an outlaw, a murderer, he had broken his faith with Justina, but between him and his God there was still this unspoken pledge and he kept it grimly to the end. He was roused from his reverie by a tugging at the rope — it was the mare, picking her way among the rocks — and, as he gave her slack, she went on down the gorge as if seeking some

214

better place to stop. He followed along, unthinking, his mind far away on things which could never be changed, and, as they clattered down a hill, suddenly he felt the grass beneath his feet — they were back in the black-walled *rincón*.

CHAPTER
FIFTEEN

When a horse finds a lost trail or wins his way home where a man unaided would fail, it is not by the exercise of some superhuman instinct, it is by the use of his eyesight — and brains. A man when he is riding lets his mind stray where it will as he thinks over the problems of his life, but a horse is not given to philosophical reflection and he keeps his mind on the trail. It is his way back to the home from which his master has taken him on business with which he has no concern, and his interest, then and always, is with the home he has left or with the water and feed along the road. He notices it and he remembers it, if he is an intelligent animal, and, when he returns, although it may be years afterward, he will know the way again. His world is a world of material things — of food and water and shelter, and the society of others of his kind — and he knows his way around with the best.

Ab Meadows had been excited when he left the safe *rincón* to seek out the lost Aztec trail, but the *chula* had not; she had followed him unwillingly, and she had remembered the way they had come. And so, when he was lost, she led him back again, by some faculty that to him seemed miraculous, but it was no more miraculous — and no less miraculous — than any other demonstration of intelligence, whether shown by a man or a horse. A fool horse and a careless man will both get lost, even in traveling over a well-worn trail, but the mare was as intelligent as she was observant and careful, and she proved herself wiser than her master. Yet, although they were saved from a night in the sharp lava rocks, their great problem still lay before them, for they had no water to drink.

Meadows camped in the open and turned the *chula* out, close-hobbled. Then, while she was feeding, he tipped up the canteen and drank noiselessly to keep her from begging. He was burning with a fever, racked with pain from his wound that had been injured by the unaccustomed walking, and even in his weariness he was haunted by the fear of what the morrow might bring forth. There was a scant pint of water in the bottom of his canteen, and if, in his search, he missed the hidden cave, it would have to last him two days. Two days of crippled walking, while he retraced his tangled steps and struck out for the railroad to the north, and if, as might happen, he became lost again, it would barely bring him in. But as long as the music of its slosh was in his ears, he could press on and not mind his thirst, while the moment it was gone the fevered madness would return and put his reason in eclipse. He slept uneasily until dawn, then took a final sup and started back to look for the trail.

The *rincón* by daylight proved to be surrounded by huge ridges where the lava of two eruptions had been piled up and rolled closer until nothing but this bare space was left. The ten acres that remained uncovered, out of hundreds of square miles, was just like the plains outside, but the lava here was different, looking like heaps of crumbly asphalt, but ringing like steel under foot. It was the recent flow which, plowing down through the caked lava beds or forcing its way up from below, had mingled its steel gray with the chocolate brown of the ancient flow in a ghastly, writhing mass. All about him as he went on Meadows beheld great fragments set on edge or arrested as they were trembling to fall, and the pine trees that lay storm-wrecked seemed shattered by the forces which had raged there eons ago. Not for a million years had those frozen lava streams moved, but they seemed even then to be jostling and scourging and grinding up the tree trunks like matchsticks.

He rode back up the marked trail, casting about through the chaos for some sign of the Aztec path, and, as his search proved vain, it seemed more and more fantastic that any people should penetrate this place of death. Yet Kin Savvy was right. As he circled to the left, he came upon a trench, a broad ditch through the scattered fragments of lava, which were piled up along the sides in a low wall. The last miracle had happened, for here was the graded trail, each rock thrown out by the hands of the Aztecs or some people equally remote. The trail led on, just as Kin Savvy had stated, seeking its level along hillsides, crossing gorges and natural bridges but holding true to its course. At every turn and high point there was a heap of scattered stones where the Apaches had knocked down the ancient

218

monuments, but by the walls of rock alone Meadows was able to trace the trail which led, if all was true, to water.

So Kin Savvy had said — the trail led to water — but whoever heard of a cave of ice in summer, and where did the water for it come from? At Brennan's *rincón* the water gathered in caves where the lava broke off down to the flat, but here in this new flow only the scrubbiest of trees could live and the old flow was shattered to the depths, yet along the sides of hills and in a tangled gorge the quaking asps showed white and tender green. As Meadows stopped to rest, a pair of turtledoves hurtled by and disappeared in the treetops beyond. Not till then had he believed, for luck had been against him, but at sight of those birds of promise he swung up on the jaded *chula* and spurred her along the overgrown trail. Where spruces and twisted piñons had preempted the way, they turned out and limped through the rocks, and, as they halted again, Meadows saw a second dove fly past and light on a dead cedar stub beyond. He waited and another came winging along behind and joined its mate on the tree. They sat there a moment, then leaped from their perch and disappeared in the bosom of the earth. Meadows hurried over toward them, and, as he came to the cedar tree, he looked off into an abysmal pit.

It was more than a pit, it was a mere peephole through the roof of a giant subterranean passageway. At the mouth of the black cavern which led on beneath the lava cap there was a gleaming patch of water. Meadows grabbed his canteen and ran around the rim, and at the

219

north end he found a stone stairway, descending through a lesser cavern and held in place by the trunks of ancient pines. Great slabs of broken rock had fallen from the roof and half obliterated this path of the Aztecs, but he scrambled on over them and down into the black cave until he came to the hidden pool of water. There he dropped down and drank, despite the startled flock of doves that fluttered out over his head, and just beneath the surface he saw a floor of ice, the source of the precious pool.

The water was freezing cold and as clear as crystal except where, about some pine knots, the charred coals of a fire floated about on the limpid surface. Here it was that old Kin Savvy in his solitary quest had thawed out the water in the spring, but now a gleaming patch of sun lay on the margin of the ice flow and the pool was a foot or more deep. It was forty feet wide, extending clear across the cave, but so shallow and transparent that the ice bed underneath seemed to float on the surface of the water. In the placid depths below, the air bubbles rose up in columns like fantastic, ice-nurtured flowers and the eye was tricked into visions of fairy landscapes and cool vistas of crystal and white. From the roof above, great drops of moisture gathered until at last with a splash they broke the crystal mirror and sent a ripple across the shimmering pool.

Meadows drank again, supping a little at a time and shuddering at the chill in the air, and then he looked beyond at the huge hummock of solid ice that disappeared into the blackness of the cave. A cold wind breathed out over it, laden with moisture from some hidden reservoir, and, as it reached the outer air, it changed precipitately into a mist, which floated away through the dazzling sunlight. But on the opposite side, where it came into contact with the high roof, it was changed back once more into drops of clinging water which fell down and formed a bed of luxuriant moss. Everything was unnatural and difficult to explain, and if, as Kin Savvy claimed, the Aztecs held the cave in reverence, it was not without just cause. Here was ice in the summertime, a pool of water in the lava beds, a cold mist breathing out of a cave, and who, dying of thirst, would not offer some kind of thanks on the margin of this miraculous lake? Filling his canteen with the cool water, Meadows clambered up into the hot sunlight and filled the frying pan for the mare to drink, and then, while she grazed, he went down once more and explored the mysterious cave.

The north cavern was all darkness but the southern cave was illuminated, for another well hole, far away, let down a shaft of light that was reflected on the massive roof above. This was stained in weird colors, reds, yellows and browns, but the floor underneath was so cumbered with huge fragments that Meadows did not go its full length. He turned back to the ice cave and took a fresh drink, and then, sitting in the sunshine, he watched the birds fly in and out and sniffed the damp, frigid wind of the cavern. Old Kin Savvy, for all his name as a prince of liars, had not exaggerated its wonders at all, and even his statements that it was a ceremonial cave of the Aztecs was not altogether lacking in fact.

Along the bank of the pool, but some ten feet above its present level, there was a deposit of ash and charcoal, intermixed with fragments of pottery. This was of the cliff-dweller type, thin and hard and gracefully ornamented, and the women who had come there to fill their *ollas* with ice water had attained to a high degree of culture. Some had pinched down their clay to the thinnest of strips and built up, lap by lap, the symmetrical jars which had been broken at last at the well, and others, further advanced, had smoothed the outer surface and laid on a glaze of white, and then, with a yucca tip, they had painted quaint designs in black and red and brown. But now they were gone, and of all their hopes and fears, their merry laughter and pride in their craft; nothing was left but the fragments of the pottery they had wrought and the coals of their long-dead fires.

Meadows camped by the cave, cooking coffee and bread and recovering from the effects of his hard trip, but as the sun swung low, he filled his canteen and returned to the grass-grown *rincón*. There was something about the ice cave which left him uneasy, as if the spirits of the dead still lingered in the darkness and looked on sadly as he profaned their shrine. At some time and for some good reason a great people had invaded this hiding place, making a trail so straight and level that it could be traveled day and night, and getting their water at this cave. It had been an ice cave even then, perhaps a thousand years before, and the women had carried wood and lit fires on its surface, just as old Kin Savvy had done. But they were gone — death had claimed them as it had claimed everyone else who had taken shelter in the treacherous *malpais* — as it would, perhaps, claim him. It was a lonely place to hide.

As he rode down into the *rincón*, it was still warm with desert sunshine, still carpeted with the grama that the *chula* loved. A family of bee martins quarreled amiably in the treetops and a flock of noisy piñon jays fluttered by, but as the sun went down and darkness settled about them, Meadows felt a sudden thrill of fear. What he feared he did not know, for they were alone in that immensity and no one had passed over that trail, but as he lay on his saddle blankets with his goods close about him, he rose up and looked around. A June bug droned by and butted into the pine tree beneath which he had laid down his bed, and up in the tree-tops there was a deep chorus of sound, like wind making music through the wires. It was as if his tree were a telegraph pole and a storm wind was roaring by above, and, as he stood there listening, the *chula* fed over toward him and then stood with her head held high.

The chorus in the trees was like the hum of a dynamo, and at intervals some huge insect came zooming through the darkness with a *whang* like the bass string of a guitar. Then one fell from the treetops and kicked and struggled in the leaves until Meadows reached out and killed it. He did it vindictively, yet with a feeling of shame that a June bug should so get on his nerves, but just as he lay back down, the *chula* gave a

223

mighty jump and stood staring out into the night. He rose up swiftly now, his pistol clutched in his hand, and he was conscious of some presence in the grim, silent night — of some creature that lay crouching out there, watching him. Every shadow that he observed seemed to hold a darker shadow that moved about and was gone, and, as he dropped back and waited, the *chula* hopped behind him and snorted suspiciously in his ear. Yet nothing appeared to offer a mark for his pistol, and shadows at night are deceiving. The mare dropped her head at last and began a furtive feeding, and he lay down quietly and looked up at the stars. The drone of the questing June bugs died down to a dreamy murmur; the mare fed on with a rhythmic *crunch*. When he awoke, the morning had come, flooding the lava with its cold, thin light.

There are some night-born fears that flee before the dawn, and all of them lose half their terrors, but, when Meadows rose up, he strapped on his pistol and limped off down the trail to the south. It was there that the presence that the *chula* had sensed had appeared under cover of the darkness, but, if it were man or beast, it would leave its tracks in the path, and he would know it was not a devil. But the dust where the trail mounted up over the lava was merely freckled with the footprints of pack rats and he turned away in disgust. All his visions of lurking animals, of prowling Indians, and the pursuing Brennan had been but creatures of his overwrought mind. The mare, like himself, had succumbed to the spell and had seen things that did not exist. It was the silence, the solitude, the

224

consciousness of their isolation, the sense that somehow danger was near, that had roused him and her until their fear-tortured minds had conjured up creatures of the night. But the tracks said differently, and tracks do not lie — he turned back and dismissed the devils from his mind.

Yet, ghosts that have been laid, will walk again when the shadows of night return, and, as the next evening came on, the *chula* raised her head again and stood watching the wall of lava to the south. It was all of the recent flow, gray and flint-like, almost treeless, yet somewhere it housed a presence that she sensed and greatly feared, which she watched for night after night. Meadows's strength was returning, his wounded leg was mending, but as the days passed by and nothing took place, the silence began to get on his nerves. After the rush of his flight and the wild days which went before, when event jostled event in such a mad scramble of excitement that he hardly had time to eat, the endless monotony of his life in the lava left him restless, uneasy, distrait. And this devil of the night, for which the mare was always watching, became a devil, also, for him.

The sheep trail that he had followed did not end at the *rincón;* it led on over clinking lava to some *terra incognita* beyond, which Kin Savvy had not stopped to describe. But it crossed the tangle of *malpais* and came out on the other side, and there, stretching to the horizon, would be the great plains where a man could gallop at will. In the lava every step seemed to encounter some obstruction, a turning stone, a jagged

225

rock point, an ankle-wrenching hole in the rubble, but once on the plains, with a horse like the *chula* — he sighed and looked again at the trail. He was safe, where he was, and not even Butch Brennan would dare follow to his shelter in the *malpais*, but he did not feel safe, and every minute of inaction irked him.

It was too lonely in the *rincón*, he thought too much, and the thoughts that came were not to his liking — they haunted him like the night devil in the lava. Every noise made him start, every movement in the *malpais* made his hand jump back to his gun, and, when he was in camp, he practiced by the hour on the draw that Wild Horse Bill had taught him. One day, when his nerves would not allow him to rest, he had ridden on to the crater to the north, and from there he had beheld the whole area of the lava beds, even to the *rincón* where Brennan hid out. It was not far from his own, not as far as he had thought, and the idea had come to him that a man might ride out and strike through the lava until he found it. There was a blood feud between him and Brennan that could never be settled until one or the other was dead, and why should he, who had outfaced him once, avoid a fight with Butch Brennan now? The sheep trail was open, he had learned the lava and how to travel by compass through the hummocks, why not make a forced march, take his enemy by surprise, and step out and confront him like a man? The time had come to call for a showdown and find out who held the high hand.

CHAPTER
SIXTEEN

The trail to the west led over crunching lava that cut Meadows's boots like glass, and then it mounted a fragile remnant of a natural bridge that spanned a yawning chasm below. When finally it zigzagged out onto the ancient flow beyond, it left him hopelessly lost. In vain he built monuments and circled about for the marked way. He had to make his own trail, leaning dead limbs up against blasted trees, until at last he cut the pathway again. Then the skeletons of dead sheep, strewn thickly along the way, pointed the road to the inlet beyond. The sun was high when he struck the open ground and their journey had just begun. Yet if he turned back at once, the night would overtake him before he could reach the ice cave. If he pressed on, and found no water, and failed to strike Brennan's *rincón* — well, that, of course, was the chance he took, and the open trail beckoned him on.

Down the long, grass-covered inlet he proceeded at a gallop, holding the sloshing canteen in his hand, and the *chula* gamboled off as if she sensed the broad prairie that presently appeared through the trees. But when she had almost gained it, he reined her back and spurred her into the lava. This was where he took his plunge, traveling by compass alone and without even a line of monuments behind him, but now he was not lost for he had looked out the country from the crater and he knew where Brennan's *rincón* must lie. From the point where he had entered it was south and a little east and not more than six miles in. If he missed it entirely and still held true to his course, he would come out on the other side at last. All it called for was nerve, such as Wild Horse Bill had shown when he discovered the *rincón* the first time, and Meadows pressed on boldly while the sun climbed to its zenith and then was lost in a bank of clouds.

There was no north and south now, no long shadows to mark the west or indicate the passage of time, but as he pressed on through the funereal silence, a flight of jays passed overhead, filling the air with their plaintive outcries. Here was a sign that a man could go by, if he wanted to take a chance, for day after day the water hole at Brennan's *rincón* was invaded by flocks of these birds. But they were heading to the east, far out of his course and back into the heart of the *malpais*, and, if he took one more chance on top of all the rest — but what did it matter now? What was one more chance to a man who was taking plenty? He turned and followed the birds. They had flown to the east and east he went, and as he plodded along another flock followed after them — at which his heart leaped up, and stopped. The mass of ashy blue was sifting down through the treetops and the *chula* had raised her head. He dropped down and caught her nose just as she was beginning to neigh — the *rincón* was not two hundred yards ahead.

228

With nervous haste he dragged the *chula* down a slope and tied her up short behind a rampart of lava. Then, building a monument to mark her hiding place, he crept forward with his carbine in his hand. No ground was ever made that was better than this for ambush or for creeping up unawares, but as he drew near the spring, the flock of jays rose up with great clamor. Yet it was not at his approach. As he crouched down and watched them, they came screaming over his head, and a minute afterward a man came up the trail with a water bucket swinging in his hand. It was Wild Horse Bill and he was humming to himself, so Meadows knew that all was well. He hesitated a moment, then called Bill by name, and stepped out from behind his tree.

"Hello, there!" responded Bill after a moment of startled silence, and then he turned and looked back toward the cabin. It was concealed behind the rim and Meadows could not see it, but he knew what Bill had in mind.

"Come over here," beckoned Meadows, and Bill set down his bucket and came hopping out over the rocks.

"What the hell," he burst out, "how did *you* git in here? Ain't the boys out there guarding the trail?"

"Not that I know of," answered Ab. "Who's down at the cabin? And, say, has Brennan got back?"

"Got back and gone," replied Bill sententiously. "Where you been keeping yourself so long?"

"Oh, 'most everywhere," evaded Meadows. "How are you making it, Bill? Has Brennan been on my trail?"

"You're whistling." Bill nodded. "The whole gang is out looking for you. How're you traveling now . . . on foot?"

"Not all the time," said Meadows. "Are you looking for the *chula*, too? Because if you are . . ."

"No . . . heh, heh," — laughed Bill, turning red with embarrassment — "no, I aim to stay out of this, Ab. It's between you and Butch . . . and you're both good friends of mine . . ."

"Well, shake then." Ab smiled, advancing and holding out his hand. "I'm sure glad to see you, Bill." They gripped hands and fell silent, each curious about the other, yet hesitant to ask prying questions, until at last Meadows broke the ice. "Bill, I don't know what's going on, or what's happened to the gang since I left, but you know as well as I do that Brennan has lost out and that sooner or later he's done for. I saw when I left here that the gang was afraid of him . . . that they were afraid he'd kill them, too . . . and a man like that is sure to lose, because even his best friends can't trust him. But you're too good a man, Bill, to be running with these horse thieves and the bunch that's staying with him now . . . why don't you go get your horse and we'll pull out together and . . ."

"Nope, nope," interposed Bill, holding up his hand to stop him, "they's no use talking that, now. I know the bunch is beginning to run out on him, but that ain't the way I'm built. If I throw in with a man, the way I did with Butch, I stay with him till hell's no more. If he was good enough to be my pardner when everything was coming right, he's good enough when everything is

230

wrong. I like you, Ab, and I'd like to go with you, but I'm going to stay right here with Butch."

"Well, all right, Bill," agreed Meadows. "I won't try to talk you out of it, although I do think you're making a mistake. But if Butch and I should happen to have a run-in . . ."

"I'll stay out of it," promised Bill. "I've told Butch I would. That trouble is between you and him."

"And you won't tell him," suggested Ab, "that I came here to look for him?"

"No, I won't tell him nothing," answered Wild Horse Bill doggedly. "But I reckon you better be going."

He held out his hand and Meadows wrung it in silence, then they turned away, and Bill went for his water while Ab disappeared among the rocks. Each man seemed to feel that it was a last farewell, yet neither sought to question the other's right to choose and they parted the best of friends. Only now, when they met again, it would not be as friends but as neutrals in a war to the death. The time had passed when they had built castles in the air and planned a joyous flight into Mexico — but the shadow of Butch Brennan had come between them and death must be the arbiter now. Meadows slipped back through the lava to where the *chula* was fretting, and unloosed the rope from her neck, and then he buried his face in her flowing mane, for he had lost every other friend.

It was sundown when they broke from the somber blackness of the *malpais* and hobbled out onto the open plain. Not for a day and night had the *chula* tasted water and she was sucking her tongue with thirst, yet when Meadows thought of returning to the ice cave, his lonely heart went sick. Not for anything in the world would he go back to that accursed *rincón* and bury himself alive in the lava. No, the broad plains lay before him and the *chula* could take a chance — he poured out half his water and let her drink. Then he ate and watched the sunset, and the dark clouds rushing up, and, as a sudden flash of lightning leaped out and stabbed the earth, he flinched and held his breath for the shock. It came, close upon it, the roar and crash of thunder that shook the solid earth to its foundations, and then there was a patter and a stirring in the grass and the raindrops spattered on his hat.

At such moments as this, when the heavens were unloosed and God's wrath seemed to ride upon the storm, he trembled and bowed his head and all his courage left him, for he felt that his time had come. He stood naked before his Creator while the sins of his past life rose up in judgment against him, and now, as he mounted and turned his back to the storm, his mind went back to Justina. If the unpardonable sin is when man refuses redemption, then with her he deserved the same unhappy fate, for he had refused her helping hand. She had put his feet on the hard road to redemption, but for a rascal like Butch Brennan he had abandoned the rocky path to seek out an easier way. Now he stood convicted and stripped of all his friends, pursued by the just and the unjust alike, a renegade even among his kind. Although he was an outlaw, no outlaw would receive him for fear of Brennan's wrath, and, if he fled from the country, he would be run down like a wolf for the reward that had been placed on his head. The lightning struck again, his horse crouched and fought her head, and at the smash of the thunder he jabbed her with his spurs and committed himself to the elements.

For who can hope to escape the lightning's stroke, if that is to be his death, or who, by taking thought, can escape from his enemies when every man's hand is against him? Meadows rode with the storm, and, when it cleared away, he kept on across the open plain, and by noon the next day he had crossed the Alamosa and climbed up to Kin Savvy's cave.

Kin Savvy Lewis was an easy man to please — since all he asked was to be left strictly alone — and his welcome for the intruder was always the same, blank silence and a strained interest in his newspaper. His tastes were simple and his wants were few, but every few weeks his communings with nature were broken by some visitor like Meadows. He had seen him from afar, for never, if he could help it, did Kin Savvy leave his trail unwatched, and now he was sitting, staring myopically at his paper and muttering angrily under his breath.

"Well, git down . . . git down!" he burst out at last and resumed his mumbled complaint. Meadows dismounted stiffly and unsaddled his horse, but as he was turning her out to graze, Kin Savvy glanced up quickly, and then rose scrambling to his feet. "Eh, eh . . . take that horse away!" he stuttered wrathfully.

"Can't have her here . . . she'll be the death of me. Butch Brennan came in, the very day you left, and give me hell for letting you keep her, and then a posse of detectives come in after Butch and gimme hell fer harboring an outlaw. You'll have to take her away, that's all there is to it. I can't have this happen again!"

"Oh, I don't know," returned Meadows, who had expected something like this, "you seem to be all in one piece. No harm done, I guess, if she stays here a while . . . how're you fixed for something to eat?"

"Say, lookee here, young man . . . ," began Kin Savvy threateningly, and then he stumped in and cooked a grudging dinner, for there was nothing else to be done. To refuse a man food in a place like this was to invite a resort to violence, but, as he watched Meadows eat, Kin Savvy eyed him with a look that was deadly.

"Whar you going?" Kin Savvy demanded. When Meadows shrugged his shoulders, he returned to his own proper grievances. "I suppose you know," he went on, "that Celso Baca was killed . . . and that Dave Starbuck has been appointed in his place? Yep, he's the sheriff, and he's sent out word that he'll kill every outlaw in the country. Bar none . . . them's his words . . . and the express company is behind him . . . they's ten thousand dollars up for you!"

"It's a wonder you don't take me in," suggested Meadows dryly. "That would buy you a whole lot of beans."

"Hell, no!" protested Kin Savvy. "Don't go on talking like that, boy. I jest thought you might be interested."

234

"Yes, I am," admitted Meadows, "go ahead and give me the rest of it. How did the Mexicans ever come to appoint Starbuck?"

"Waal," explained Kin Savvy, "I don't reckon they wanted to, but no Mex would take the job. Butch Brennan killed three of them before he got through with it, and so they give the place to Dave. Express company's behind it, if you want my opinion . . . these damned corporations run everything . . . but the posse came through here, and I'll say this for all of 'em, they're a hard-looking bunch of *hombres*. Regular man killers, every one of 'em, and sworn in for deputies . . . but d'ye think the county is paying for 'em? No more'n it pays Starbuck. He's working for nothing . . . claims he's doing it on account of his son. Brennan killed him, you know . . . they found him dead down the road when he run off with that adventurous woman . . . and now, by grab, Dave is out to get Brennan. They've had one run-in already. Yeah, over by the lava beds, but that *malpais* was too much for 'em. How'd *you* git along . . . find the trail?"

"Yes, I found it," answered Meadows, and went on with his eating while Kin Savvy gazed at him shrewdly.

"You look it," he observed. "Them boots is about gone. Say, Starbuck would like to see you."

"What about?" demanded Ab, suddenly breaking his pose, and Kin Savvy drew into his shell.

"Can't tell ye," he said. "None of my business, you see. But that was the message he sent."

"When was this?" inquired Meadows.

"Oh . . . a while ago," mumbled Lewis, "I don't keep no 'count of time."

"Is he over at the ranch?"

"¿Quién sabe?" The hermit shrugged and with that his flow of small talk ceased. The man never lived that could extract information from Kin Savvy with anything short of a corkscrew, and so far as was known he had never answered a direct question with a direct and unequivocal answer. All his moods went by contraries, and the person who learned the most from him was the one who asked nothing at all. But Meadows was interested in this message from Starbuck — more interested than he was willing to admit — and after he had rested and given his horse a rubdown, he came back and spread down his bed. That was the only way with Kin Savvy, who he knew was on pins and needles for fear that Butch Brennan would return. He was anxious to get rid of him, and, if obstinacy would help, Meadows was willing to go the limit. So he prepared to spend the night.

"What's the matter?" complained Kin Savvy, "ain't you going over to see Starbuck? He asked about you special."

"That was some time ago," responded Ab. "Probably left the ranch by now."

"No, he ain't!" piped up Kin Savvy. "I seen an Injun over at Dog Springs, while I was hunting for my horses, and he told me Dave was home. Said he had lots of white men and horses at the ranch and was sending out runners everywhere. Say, he's looking for a man that knows the trail to Brennan's hide-out . . . maybe that's why he wanted to see you."

"Nope," grumbled Meadows, "I reckon he's just looking for me. That's part of his duties, now."

"Waal, that's all right," admitted Kin Savvy, "like as not that's about the size of it. Old Dave had took his oath and I'll say this much for him . . . he's got a stern sense of duty. No matter if a man was the best friend he'd got, he'd see him in hell before he'd lift a hand to protect him against the law. He's a Yankee, that's the size of it, and them No'therners are all bigotty . . . I never could git to like 'em."

"Even at that, though," said Meadows, "he was the best friend I ever had, until I happened to get mixed up with Brennan. I wouldn't mind seeing him, if it could be pulled off quietly, but if I'd ride into that ranch, there'd be a bunch of Winchesters thrown down on me before I could get up my hands."

"Waal . . . waal, hyer now," burst out Kin Savvy, hopping about in his excitement, "perhaps we can fix this thing up. You're a friend of mine, Ab. I remember right well when you ketched my old mare when she strayed. Now hyer, I'll tell ye, you come along with me and I'll ride on ahead and call him. If we start right now, we can git there by dark and . . ."

"Nope, nope," objected Ab. "I'm all worn out . . . we can talk that over tomorrow."

"Tomorrer!" shrilled Kin Savvy. "You don't seem to realize that this hyar cave is watched! When it ain't Butch Brennan or some of his sidekickers, it's a deputy from over the divide. And do you know who they're looking for? They're looking for *you*, and I don't know which outfit wants you worst!"

"Well, here I am," returned Meadows. "All they have to do is come and get me . . . but they might as well come a-shooting. I'm not going to be taken if there's any way out of it, and I reckon there generally is. I'm here, and I'm going to stay here, but of course . . ."

"Of course what?" clamored Kin Savvy.

"Well, if you want to ride over and tell Starbuck I'm here . . ."

"I'll do it!" snapped Kin Savvy, and ran off down the swale to where his horses were hobbled. He came back at a gallop and, shaking his head at all suggestions, saddled up and started off over the trail. When he was gone, Meadows saddled up as quickly and moved up onto the summits. Not even Kin Savvy knew better than he the danger to which he was exposed, and he camped that night at a little flat where a wild cat could not approach him unawares. But it was not for the manhunters that he watched and listened; it was for Butch Brennan or some of his gang. Butch Brennan knew the country and so did Ben Cady, the champion horse thief of the gang, and in order to make certain that the *chula* was not stolen Meadows slept within the circle of her picket rope. For the *chula* was the lure to which Brennan would come when all other temptations failed, and, if Starbuck would talk business, Meadows could practically guarantee to bring Butch out of his stronghold.

Meadows's mind had not been idle while he was waiting for Kin Savvy, and he had recognized in a flash

238

his value to Dave Starbuck and the chance that it gave him to win immunity. To be sure he had robbed the train, but the express company would overlook it if he brought the master outlaw to their hand, and, if Starbuck was the sheriff, even Ab's battle with the Mexican deputy might appear in a different light. The times were awry, stern men were in the saddle, and desperate measures perforce must prevail. Since Brennan was on his trail, what course was more logical than to throw in his fortunes with the enemy? No man can survive when he is ground between two millstones, but once he was aligned with the forces of law and order, he could carry the war clear into the *malpais*. Only they must promise him immunity.

He slept little that night for his brain was seething with alternate hopes and fears, and now he imagined himself received like a hero, and then dreamed of being pursued as an outlaw. If they gave him what he asked for and overlooked his mistakes, he would take Butch Brennan or die, but if they refused his request and held him strictly to his record, he would fight even Starbuck to escape. Not for any man that lived would he lay down his gun and consent to be a prisoner for life, and no Mexican jury would ever sentence him as long as he had his pistol and the *chula*. She made him a marked man, but she could carry him in one night halfway to the border of old Mexico, and once he crossed the line, he could head for the Sierra Madres and lose himself in their fastnesses. There was always a chance, if one had the nerve to take it, and a man was never whipped till he quit.

The dawn found him out on the point of a high cliff, overlooking the trail from the ranch, and early in the day he saw Starbuck and Kin Savvy coming, and nobody else behind. Starbuck was a man he thought he could trust, and he rode ahead and met them at the cave. The new sheriff looked just the same, only he wore one more six-shooter, and he gazed grimly at Meadows as if expecting him to speak, but Ab merely nodded and stood silently.

"Well, what is it . . . what is it?" boomed out Starbuck impatiently. "What do you want to see me about?"

"Why, you wanted to see me," replied Meadows, staring blankly, and Starbuck whirled on Kin Savvy.

"You old walloper!" he began, and then he laughed shortly as Kin Savvy ducked into his cave. "Well, well," he went on, "let it go . . . what's the difference? But I knowed danged well he was up to something funny, the minute I see him coming. Told us both the same story, I guess."

"Very likely," agreed Meadows.

"Suppose you want to give yourself up?" suggested Starbuck, but Meadows shrugged his shoulders.

"That depends," he said, "but I'll tell you right now I'll never go to prison."

"You won't!" challenged Starbuck, and then he settled back and eyed his former broncho buster attentively. "That's a pretty strong statement," he said at last. "Don't you know I'm the sheriff now?"

"Yes, I know all that," answered Meadows doggedly, "but I'd rather be killed, that's all."

"Don't you think you've got it coming to you?" inquired Starbuck bluntly. "You've killed a deputy sheriff and helped rob a train . . . don't you figure on even standing trial?"

"Not if I can help it," replied Meadows, "because those Papalote Mexicans . . ."

"You're dealing with me!" cut in Starbuck austerely. "I'll see that you get a fair trial."

"Well, that's kind of you, Mister Starbuck, and I sure appreciate it, but . . . didn't you have some proposition to make?"

"Proposition?" echoed the sheriff, and then he drew himself up proudly. "Yes," he said, "I've got just one proposition for you, and that is that you submit to the law. You must know by this time that I won't compromise a felony . . . I'm here to enforce the law." He stopped and Meadows faced him, his lips grimly set, his eyes watching for the first move toward his gun. "But I'd tell you," went on Starbuck after a thoughtful silence, "I might square you for that train robbery with the express company. They might agree not to prosecute."

"They wouldn't need to prosecute," returned Meadows, "if I was tried for that killing. But I believe I can take you to Brennan."

"You can?" exclaimed Starbuck, and suddenly the office fell away from him and he became Dave Starbuck, the man. "Well, you do it," he said, "and I'll spend my last dollar to keep you out of the pen. I'm sorry for you, Ab . . . sorry you came to get into this . . . but it warn't your fault, back there where it started, and I'm going to strain a point. All I ask is that you take me to Brennan."

"I can do it," asserted Meadows, "and I'll do more than that . . . I'll go in and get him myself."

"You show him to me!" burst out Starbuck hoarsely. "I guess you know, Ab, he killed my boy . . . Lute."

"Yes, I know it, and I'm sorry, but I've had trouble with Brennan . . ."

"Leave him to me, boy," pleaded Starbuck, "and, if there's anything in the world that . . ."

"No, that's all right," broke in Meadows. "I know how you feel. But if it comes to a showdown, I'm not going to wait on anybody . . . it's him or me, that's all."

"How'll you work it?" demanded Starbuck. "That's all I want to know . . . how'll you get him out of that *malpais?*"

"Just show myself," said Meadows, "and ride this mare. He'll come, or I miss my guess. But if he don't . . . well, you wait. I know those lava beds. I'll take you to his hide-out from behind."

"You're deputized!" declared Starbuck, laying a hand on his shoulder, "and we'll start for the North Plains tonight."

CHAPTER
SEVENTEEN

The wheel of fortune had turned with dizzying swiftness for the man who had been a fugitive and an outcast. Ab Meadows rode back to the ranch from which he had fled with a deputy sheriff's star on his breast. Although he was an officer, his crimes were not condoned. To do that was beyond Dave Starbuck's power. The star was there to protect him from arrest at the hands of the express company detectives. There was a reward on his head and the detectives were hard men, especially when they had been balked in their quest, and the opportunity to make an important and spectacular arrest might be more than some of them could resist. Kin Savvy had guessed right when he ventured the opinion that the express company was behind Starbuck's appointment, and he could have gone still further and stated as well that its detectives made very poor deputies.

They were men from many different walks of life, but they had this in common: they were more accustomed to command than they were to take orders from a stranger. Dave Starbuck knew this well, for on his previous trip to the lava beds they had shown so much initiative as completely to thwart his purpose, and now that as a last resort he had enlisted the services of Ab he looked, and rightly, for trouble. Ten thousand dollars is no mean reward to a man who is working for a salary, and the question might arise as to whether the sheriff of a county had the authority to deputize a criminal, also whether a detective, if he had the nerve, could not step in and claim the prisoner. So, to allay doubts in the minds of his assistants, Starbuck made it a personal matter, and, when he rode in, he announced to all and sundry that Meadows was his friend. To make everything perfectly clear he announced still further that Meadows had not been promised immunity and that, after Brennan's gang had been wiped off the earth, he would have to stand trial for his delinquencies. But until that time he was a deputy sheriff and the equal of any gentleman present.

This ended the speech making, and the deputies saddled hurriedly and prepared for their trip to the North Plains. When they rode out, they glanced at Meadows sourly, as at one who had horned in on their game. There was a reward for Brennan, and for Wild Horse Bill, and for certain other members of the gang, and, if this man who had turned informer should actually deliver the goods, he would naturally expect his cut. He might even demand a big cut or, by putting something over, hop in and take Brennan himself, in which case, of course, they would lose out entirely and have nothing but their work for their pains. So they looked at him grimly as he rode ahead with Starbuck, explaining his great plans in his ear, and several of them remarked that, if he was as smart as he acted, he could take the whole job off their hands.

They rode on up White House Cañon and out over the north trail, past the battleground where Brennan had killed the Mexicans, but when they swung down into the Frog Tanks trail they found a fresh horse track ahead of them. Butch Brennan was by no means whipped, nor had he lost all his friends, for this horseman was a lookout, or some spy from Show Low, riding ahead with news of the posse. At Frog Tanks, when they rode in there in the dead of night, the ranch house was practically deserted, and those who came out gave them only a grim welcome and glared at Meadows with the malignity of a rattlesnake. No, Butch Brennan was far from whipped, his gang was still intact, and on the North Plains his word was law, and not even before the sheriff of Papalote County would the stiff-necked Walking X boys unbend.

The Walking X crew was from Texas, wearing tremendous big white hats and winged chaps as broad as a blacksmith's apron, but so far as was known there was nothing against them which would warrant an arrest on suspicion. Yet they were surly and inhospitable, and at the first peep of day they loaded their chuck wagon and started off to the south. The fall roundup was on and for a month or more now they would be branding and gathering beef steers on the plains, but their real object in moving was to leave the posse flat and force them to depart from the country. But the sheriff of a county has the power to commandeer supplies when engaged in the pursuit of a criminal and at the grudging invitation to make themselves at home Starbuck replied that they certainly would. He moved into the house, helped himself to provisions and horse feed, and set to work on his plans.

It was not so simple, now that they were on the ground, but the plan was to put the *chula*, along with the other night horses, in the pole corral down by the tanks, and, when Brennan ventured out to steal her back, men in hiding could rise up and shoot him. Dave Starbuck had no other intention than to kill the outlaw on sight. That was the way they had done it when they cleared the country of Apaches, and it was the only way he knew. Butch Brennan and his gang had become the same menace that the Apaches had been before, and he felt it his duty as sheriff and as a citizen to burn them off the earth.

There was no great necessity of riding the *chula* about or of flaunting the bait before Brennan — if the runner who preceded them had not already given Butch notice, the boys from the Walking X had. It was a scant five miles to the Punta de Malpais, and from the beginning of Brennan's trail, where he would have a lookout with powerful glasses, it was certainly not more than ten. No, already Brennan knew that Ab Meadows had come to Frog Tanks and that the *chula* was in the round corral, and it would defeat their own object if they showed her off too ostentatiously or did more than keep her corralled. As soon as dusk came on, they dug two trenches by the gate and another one behind the corral, and all that night Meadows and Starbuck lay in wait, but no one approached the enclosure. On the second night it was the same and the deputies began to grumble and to ride restlessly out toward the lava, and in order to placate them Starbuck gave up his place and put a new guard over the horses.

Yet Starbuck was the sheriff, and nominally they were his deputies. Since he requested it, three men went out at sundown and camped down in the manholes by the corral. The night passed uneventfully, but when Meadows came out at dawn his horse had disappeared. The gate was still lashed, all the other horses were there, but the glorious *chula* was gone. She had been stolen in the night, spirited away from the pole corral while two men lay not ten feet from the gate, and in the recriminations that followed Starbuck for one was convinced that the guards had not even tried to keep awake. They had stretched out comfortably in the bottom of their holes while some man with high-heeled boots had slipped into the corral and led Meadows's horse out the gate. Her hoofs had been muffled by four of their own grain sacks, which had been cast aside later on the flat — the wolf from the lava beds had stolen the bait from their trap without losing so much as a hair.

Starbuck cursed the guards roundly and sent all three of them back to Albuquerque to report for a job in town, and then he asked Meadows if he could lead what was left of them to the trail that led to Brennan's back door. They started that same morning, the detectives quite subdued, and all day they rode north along the east edge of the lava flow, as if they were returning to the railroad. A great finger of the *malpais*, thrust out north from the main body, warded them off from the limestone hills to the west, but when darkness had fallen, Meadows crossed over by a dim road and swung back to the inlet to the sheep trail. They made a dry camp and started on at sunup, and at noon they gained the ice cave and watered their gaunted horses at the end of the Aztec trail. Then they camped in the *rincón* and the murmur of protest ceased, for Meadows had brought them through.

It had been a hard trip, and not without its bad moments, for no man could follow the trail unerringly, but after they had rested and boiled a pot of coffee, the spirits of the posse revived. They were stern and hardy men, accustomed to rough trips, and the prospect of taking Brennan and his gang by surprise more than reconciled them to the perils ahead. Several of them declared for an immediate start, for fear they might be too late, but Starbuck overruled them and they left the next morning, after a second trip to the ice cave. There the canteens were all filled and the horses well watered, and by ten o'clock they were back at the *rincón* and ready for the final dash. They were enthusiastic now and the hotheads took the lead, but the best of them were lost, and Meadows himself was lost, before they won out to the other side.

It is part of the psychology of being lost that the will to press on and to overcome all obstructions rises up until it becomes a sort of mania. This it is that urges the lone man to break into a run, to rush ahead and scramble over obstacles, but in a party of men the madness is vented in mutual recrimination and

248

opposition. Those who follow blame their leaders for every mistake, and the leaders in turn see the cause of their blunders in the unreasoning clamor of their followers. An atmosphere of confusion and nervous tension springs up, and, unless a strong character takes the situation in hand, it speedily passes all bounds. Starbuck's posse was not lost, since they knew their way back and were furthermore on the edge of the plains, but the sinister influence of the lava beds had begun to take effect and they were rapidly becoming rebellious. Each time they had been lost on the trip from the *rincón*, the waste of lava had seemed to whirl before them — the sun had lost its place in its orderly course from east to west and become suddenly a spot in the sky, the compass had seemed wrong, north and south had lost their meaning, even their back trail had whirled, and, when the trail was found, they went on with the feeling that everything was wrong.

Such brainstorms are dangerous, and Dave Starbuck knew it or he would not have spoken the way he did. He whirled on the leader, a big Texan named Reavis, with narrow eyes and thick, petulant lips, and cursed him until he cringed, and then he told his deputies that they could do as he ordered or take the back trail to Albuquerque. They capitulated, but grudgingly, for they had been put under his command because their own efforts, as individuals, had failed, and each man in his heart would almost have preferred to fail again rather than to bring any glory to their chief. A sheriff, as they regarded him, was primarily a politician and always a local county officer, whereas they, from a wider experience, were citizens of the world and officers wherever they went. They were chosen for their nerve and proven ability as manhunters, and to be placed under the command of a ranchman turned sheriff was more than they could lightly endure. Yet they submitted to him now, for Brennan's *rincón* was close at hand and they were anxious to be in at the finish.

Each man was loaded down with his guns and ammunition, his canteen, and a package of food, and, as they clumped forward in their high-heeled riding boots and no *rincón* appeared, they began to grumble once more. It was an eerie place, in the midst of a great forest which cut off all landmarks from their view, and their trail, such as it was, wound back and forth over cracks and fissures, around hummocks and enormous blowholes full of trees. The sun was sinking low — there could be no return that night — and, if they did not find the *rincón* and make a clean up before dark, they were due to sleep in the rocks. If they missed it altogether, which seemed to most of them certain, they would have a long walk back and a long ride after that, before they got their first drink of water. Yet Meadows pressed on steadily, heading well east of south, looking expectantly every minute for the *rincón*.

An hour passed, and two hours, and Meadows began to watch for the jays to lead him by their flight to the spring, but the forest aisles were silent, not a bird passed but the vagrant flycatchers, and at last in sudden doubt he stopped. Then it broke loose, the torrent of pent-up wrath which had been gathering behind his back. They all talked at once, giving vent to their vexation in words none too nicely chosen. Some pressed forward with advice, some crowded in to ask him if he had any notion where he was, but Dave Starbuck stood silently, taking it all in grimly, until at last he set down his pack.

"We'll camp, boys," he said, seeking a soft place among the pine needles, and the posse saw the point. They were lost and he knew it. His pet train robber had led them astray — they must spend a night in the lava.

CHAPTER
EIGHTEEN

A night in the rocks did not add to the *entente cordiale* between Starbuck and his deputies. They were insolent and mutinous, and he expressed himself frankly regarding their qualifications as manhunters. A proper officer, as he looked at it, expected to sleep out a few nights, and, as long as they achieved the object of their errand, he saw no reason to kick. But right there the discussion took a personal turn, for Reavis, the big Texan, ventured an opinion of Ab Meadows that would not look well in print. The point of it was that their guide was a wart head, without the sense that God gave a rabbit, and it was his private opinion, publicly expressed, that Meadows had never even been to the *rincón*, or, if he had, he had not put them within forty miles of it now and didn't know anything straight up from a hole in the ground. Meadows left about then and stepped out into the open, for he had seen a dove whiff past.

The dove was going in just the opposite direction from where he believed the *rincón* must be, but, as he stood there watching, he heard a distant and heartening clamor and a flock of piñon jays flew past. They were off to one side, but their flight had been in line with that of the passing dove, and, while he was marking the direction with his compass, Dave Starbuck strode over and looked at him questioningly.

"Well," he said, "where do you think they are?"

Meadows pointed out through the trees.

"What makes you think so?" inquired Starbuck. When Ab told him, he nodded and patted him on the back. "We'll wait a minute," he said, and stood watching the sky till they sighted another flock of jays. They were flying high, in a long, undulating line, and it seemed at the end as if they settled among the pines instead of keeping on their way to the north. "Come on!" exclaimed Starbuck, starting back to get his pack. After a sup of water from his half-empty canteen, he led off through the lava, with Meadows making monuments behind him.

The posse stood and stared, then followed along behind, for they sensed a sudden purpose in it all. Starbuck was not groping at random, he was heading for one place, and that not so far ahead, if they could judge by his circumspect approach. So it turned out, for, as Meadows looked ahead, he saw a waterfall of blue through the trees, then the piñon jays came past, flitting back to their feeding grounds on the edge of the distant plains. It was the *rincón* once more, the flight of the birds had revealed it where his compass had failed again, and now the idea was to slip up unobserved, before the gang left the *rincón*, and surround them in the cabin. He ran up ahead, and, as he was consulting with Starbuck, the posse came hurrying to join them.

"Well, boys," said Starbuck, "here's the place, right ahead. Now, listen to what I say. The cabin where they live is on the south slope of a hill, and there's only one door, in front. We'll move up from this side to the edge of the lava, and then we'll spread out along the rim. When we're all set, I'll fire one shot and call on the bunch to surrender. If they don't, we'll kill every one of them. Meadows will go in the lead, because he knows the ground, and I've got just one more thing to say. I want every man to keep in the rocks until I give the word to step out. Don't take no chances with a man like Butch Brennan, and shoot at the first crooked move."

He motioned Meadows ahead, and they advanced at a crouch, all their bickerings and dissensions forgotten. At last they came within sight of the *rincón* and of the cabin across the flat. It was broad and low and sunk into the hillside, and from the stone chimney behind a wisp of smoke was curling up, while the door stood carelessly open. The gang was caught napping, absolutely unprepared, probably gathered about the fireplace cooking breakfast, and Meadows's heart leaped as he saw a tall form pass by and look out the doorway. It was Brennan, come in from his night's rest in the lava, but now he was trapped, for the cabin had but one door and their guns had it covered already. But as they crept up closer, they heard a whoop of laughter, and Meadows's heart sank again. It was Wild Horse Bill, unsuspecting of his fate, whooping and laughing at some rough joke that was likely to be his last. Yet the surround was started and now it must go on, no matter who fell into the net. They crawled up to the very edge, not a hundred yards from the log cabin, and spread out to the right and the left. The trap was set and there was no escape, except under the fire of their guns — Starbuck motioned his men down and fired.

There was a moment of startled silence, a scuttling of men within the cabin, and then the door was kicked to. Then silence again, and waiting.

"Hey, there!" hailed Starbuck, his voice rumbling like a great bull's. "Come out! We've got you surrounded!" He waited, and, as no answer was returned from the cabin, he glanced up and down his line. It was thrown in a quarter circle, commanding the doorway from every angle and the sloping hillside behind — no man could escape them alive. Yet his own men were overeager, they were up behind trees when he had ordered them to stay in the rocks, and he knew what was in their minds. They were anxious to be the first to lay a hand on Brennan and make sure of their share of the reward.

"Get down there!" ordered Starbuck, motioning one back into the lava, and then he spoke again. "This is Starbuck!" he said. "I've got men all around you. Come out or the place gets shot up."

He waited, long enough, but there was only the grim silence as the outlaws awaited the attack, punching out loop-holes between the logs.

"Give 'em hell, boys!" shouted Starbuck, and the posse opened up, knocking the mud in showers from the chinks. The board door was splintered, the wall itself was riddled, and, as they stopped to reload, a

255

voice from the cabin announced that they would come out. There was nothing else to do, for the high-powered rifles could shoot through two feet of solid oak. Yet, although they had surrendered, the outlaws still lay hidden, engaged in some mysterious preparations. Starbuck shouted again, warning them to come out at once or he would shoot until the last man was killed. Then, reluctantly, Brennan and Wild Horse Bill stepped forth, their hands held high above their heads. The others, if there were any, still kept under cover, and Starbuck spoke sharply to his men.

"Look out now!" he warned. "There's more of 'em inside. Keep down or they'll fill you full of lead."

Brennan and Bill advanced slowly, dragging their feet through the grass and rabbit bushes as if they could hardly walk. As they came nearer, Meadows noticed that they both had on their chaps that were of the heavy, leather-winged kind. This struck him as unusual, for it was early in the morning and their horses had not even come up, but, before he could discover any signs of concealed weapons, they stopped and looked up at the lava. It rose before them like a wall, full of deep cracks and fissures where the hardened crust had caved off onto the flat, and here and there along the edge there stood solitary pines, behind each of which a deputy was hiding.

"Well, here we are," said Brennan, and the moment he spoke a deputy stepped out into the open. That was his cue, and he took it, but before he had gone two steps a shot rang out from the cabin. The deputy stumbled and fell, the posse was thrown into confusion,

256

and in the scramble that followed both Brennan and Wild Horse Bill suddenly dropped down behind a low reef of lava. Then as if by magic two rifles came over the top and a deputy behind a tree was shot through and through before he could leap back among the rocks. The steel-jacketed bullet bored its way through the tree trunk as if it were nothing but paper, and in the fusillade that followed a third man was hit as he rose up to shoot down on the outlaws. It all happened in a few seconds, and then from the log cabin three more outlaws burst out, taking advantage of the diversion, and went scampering over the hill. Instantly every gun was trained on them, and, as they emptied their magazines Wild Horse Bill and Brennan made a bolt for the lava and were lost in its caverns like weasels.

The battle was lost, the surround had come to nothing, every outlaw had made his escape, and in Starbuck's posse two men were dead and another was shot through the arm. Nor was the danger past, for Brennan and Bill might easily attack them from the rear. Starbuck saw he was beaten, and without waiting for fresh disaster he ordered a hasty retreat. All the outlaws were in the rocks and to try to reach them there would be to invite further losses. So the posse crept away, taking the wounded man with them and leaving the dead where they lay. It was all over in a minute, and their defeat was made doubly bitter by the ruse that Brennan had employed. Behind their flapping chaps he and Bill had dragged their rifles, attached to their feet with ropes. When the lava reef had been reached, they had dropped down behind it and risen up the next moment, shooting. The posse had been outwitted at every turn — there was nothing to do now but retreat.

Starbuck led the way grimly along the trail marked by monuments they had made during their approach. If there had been bad blood before, when they had advanced full of hopes, it was nothing to the hard feelings now. Two of the deputies had been killed and one shot through the arm in Ab Meadows's ill-fated attempt, and, although he was not even indirectly to blame for it, there were black looks and mutterings against him. The whole party was out of water, and there was a long ride ahead of them before they would get any more, but their misery held them together until they rode in to Frog Tanks and drank their fill at the troughs. Then Reavis, the Texan, glanced about at the rest and hitched up his belt significantly.

"Well, boys," he said, "we got one of 'em anyway!" And he jerked his thumb toward Meadows.

"One of what?" demanded Starbuck, immediately sensing his meaning and bristling with indignation, but the Texan only laughed.

"You know," he replied, "we was sent out to git 'em, so I reckon we'd better take him in."

"You'd better take yourselves in," retorted Starbuck fiercely. "You're fired, the whole damned outfit. And now if you think you can take him away from me, I'm just waiting for the first man to try."

There was a pause, in which the ex-deputies were very particular not to move their hands toward their guns, and then Starbuck addressed them again.

"You can turn in them badges, every damned one of you, and report to the head office at Albuquerque. I don't need any detectives to show me how to run my business . . . what I want is a few extra men to obey orders. And as I say . . . if you want him, come and get him."

He stepped over beside Meadows and the two stood together while the detectives glared back at them hatefully. Then Reavis burst out into a guffaw of mirthless laughter and led the posse up to the house. A few Walking X boys, who had heard about the battle and had returned to stare at the vanquished, joined in on the hectoring laughter, at which Starbuck went suddenly grim.

"Come on, Ab," he said, "we don't class up very high in this aggregation of Texas horse thieves and detectives. But if I don't come back," he muttered, "and put the fear of God into them Walking Xs, then I'm a hound and you can call me Sickem."

They rode off together and the Walking X boys smirked — this would be a good one to report to Brennan. He was their hero and chief, their uncrowned king; and, as Meadows glanced back and saw the laughter in their eyes, it struck him suddenly that even they might be used. They were loyal to Brennan and ran to him with all the news. The battle was over, Brennan had emerged victorious, and presently he would rally forth. Was not this the time, when pursuit was least expected, to make yet another bold stroke? The battle could never be over for him till Brennan was dead, or he was. Otherwise Reavis would have his wish and Ab Meadows would be taken to jail. Others might pause, but not he, for his life itself was the forfeit if he failed to bring Brennan to book.

What Starbuck really needed was men who were *not* detectives, men who would obey him unquestioningly and follow his lead without trying to do anything spectacular. Both the deputies who had been killed had come to their death by disobeying orders, for Starbuck had warned them repeatedly not to take shelter behind the pine trees but to remain under cover of the lava. Butch Brennan knew well the driving power of his new rifle, having shot at pine trees before, and, when he saw the deputy leap behind the tree, he had bored him through and through. The other man had done exactly what he was ordered not to do, stepped out into the open to claim the prisoners. From that moment, thick and fast, the disasters had piled up until they had had to flee in defeat. It was a bitter pill to swallow for a man like Dave Starbuck, for his honor as a fighting man was at stake, and, as Meadows began to speak what had come into his mind, the old man straightened up in his saddle.

"You're right," he said, "you've got the right idea, but I've got a better one still. I aim to show them Walking X boys who's the sheriff in this country. I ain't even started . . . yet."

260

CHAPTER
NINETEEN

For a man who had fought a grizzly with his fists and still carried a butcher knife in his boot, Dave Starbuck was more subdued than the wise ones had expected, after his defeat at the hands of Brennan. He returned to his ranch and remained there for some days, taking on cowboys for his fall work on the North Plains. Then, with over twenty hands, including the stray men, the chuck wagon was pulled over to the Trincheros. The hands camped by the lake for several days, branding calves and gathering steers for shipping, and then they moved down on the edge of their range, on the road to the Walking X headquarters. There was no love lost in the best of times between the Figure 4 outfit and the Xs, and Starbuck's appointment as sheriff along with his aggressive campaign against Brennan had not served to allay the hard feeling. Some of the men at Frog Tanks had been eating Figure 4 beef, and the least they expected to happen was to be arrested for stealing cows.

But Dave Starbuck was not the man to turn his office to his own advantage — his invasion of the North Plains was but a part of a bold plan that was about to be put to the test. They left Trinchero Lake at noon and camped again at sundown. Directly after supper Starbuck called his men together and made them a little talk.

"Boys," he said, "you know why I'm sheriff . . . it's because my boy Lute was killed. I took the job to rid the county of Butch Brennan and keep other boys, like you, from going wrong. There are some men of you here that used to run with Brennan, and maybe you stand with him yet, but I want to tell you, boys, that wild work don't pay, and I'm asking you to give it up. I'm asking you and I'm warning you, because as sure as God lives I'm going to kill every outlaw in this county. I lost Butch Brennan last week by being too easy . . . and Wild Horse Bill and three others . . . but the next time I run up against them I'm going to begin shooting, and I won't stop till the last man's down. Now, if there's any man here that wants to pull out, I'm giving him a chance to go, but every man that stays is going to be my deputy and he's going to do what I say. That's all now . . . who'll volunteer?"

He did not have to wait for each man stepped forward, and he looked them over grimly.

"I knowed it," he said. "I picked ye for this work and you're going to do me proud. All I ask of you, boys, is to do what you're told to and don't let a man escape. Were going down to Frog Tanks and arrest every man there, for standing in with Brennan, and I'll leave part of you there for three or four days to hold every man that comes in. Then Ab and some more of us will go out with the wagon and see if we can't get Brennan.

262

But don't forget, day or night, that, if just one man gets loose, we might as well quit and go home."

Dave Starbuck had indeed picked his cowboys well, although several of them had once run with the Wild Bunch, and the prospect of arresting the arrogant Walking X boys sent them running to catch up their horses. They were good boys at heart and the death of Lute Starbuck had lost Brennan many a friend. He had been stripped of his glamour and they knew him for what he was — a cold-blooded, treacherous murderer. So they held up their hands and were sworn in by Starbuck, and that evening about midnight they threw a circle about Frog Tanks and closed in silently on the ranch house.

It stood on a low hill, a huge, adobe building, halfway between a fort and a stockade, and a chuck wagon by the corral at the foot of the hill gave notice that the outfit was at home. The cowboys rode in slowly, stopping just outside the settlement, and then Starbuck, with three cowboys, advanced to the wagon and routed the cook from his blankets. He rose up ready to fight, but a word from Starbuck tamed him down and he led the way to the house. There in the big room that served as a bunkhouse they found the Walking X outfit, sleeping. A cowboy's days are long and his nights are short and broken by many alarms. They were taken by surprise, and, when the cook tried to rouse them, they still thought it was the call for horse wranglers. So they grumbled and resisted, waking up one at a time to find their six-shooters gone. Before they were aware of what was going on, they were disarmed and put under guard.

The great stockade behind, made with walls ten feet high to protect the horse herd against marauding Apaches, was turned into a prison yard. When the night herders came in to wake up the next guard, they, too, were taken into custody. When day dawned at last, Frog Tanks was outwardly the same, but within all was changed and every man who entered was held up at the point of a gun. This time the mantrap worked, for at ten in the morning Ben Cady rode in from the lava beds. He came ambling across the plains and entered the open portals without so much as a look around. When Starbuck threw down on him, he put up his hands quickly for he saw what was in the air. Dave Starbuck had no desire to take any man prisoner, and especially a man like Cady who had a name as an expert horse thief and jail breaker. He it was who had stolen the *chula* from the guarded corral, and he had participated in the battle at the *rincón*, but he weakened at once when Starbuck took him aside and questioned him regarding Brennan and Wild Horse Bill. They were both in the *malpais*, with Curly Harris and Jack McElvey, and they had sent him out for more whiskey, but whether they would follow or remain hidden in the *malpais* was more than he could answer. One thing he did know — they were nearly out of whiskey — and they would have to come to Frog Tanks for more.

"Good enough," said Starbuck, and locked him up in a storeroom, the door of which opened on the court. After that, he called Meadows, and with six cowboys

264

they prepared to take out the wagon. The Walking X chuck wagon, like most of its kind, served as bed wagon and water wagon as well. The high chuck box stood in the rear, the bedrolls were loaded in front of it, and the water barrels were hung on the sides. By driving the horses to water in the shallow lakes formed by the rain, the drinking water would last three or four days. With the Walking X cook to help them, the cowboys hooked up the wagon, and they started out across the rolling plains. Keen eyes might be watching them from the edge of the lava, where Brennan's lookouts were hidden, and every cowboy now wore a Texas hat and a pair of broad, apron chaps. These they had borrowed without protest from the captured Walking X cowpunchers, who were kept herded like convicts in the stockade, and to make the verisimilitude complete each man wore the rigging of some cowpuncher that was nearest his size. They even rode the same mounts, which were pointed out by the cook, and halfway to the lava beds they camped by a tank and proceeded with the routine work.

All the posse except Starbuck, who would be recognized by his beard, threw a circle and brought in the bawling herds. As the branding went on, two horsemen left the lava and came galloping out to join them. They were the guards, Harris and McElvey, who had been looking on from a rough butte not far from the entrance to the rincón, but the loneliness of their task and its apparent futility had tempted them to desert their post. They came on suspecting nothing, while the Figure 4 cowboys kept on dragging up calves to the fire. It was only when Dave Starbuck rose up from behind the wagon that they realized their mistake. It was too late then even to think of resistance for he would have killed them before they could draw. They surrendered without a murmur and were taken to the ranch where they were thrown in with the horse-stealing Ben Cady.

Then came the long wait, a heart-breaking two days during which no man came to their lure, and it was generally believed that Brennan and Bill had smelled a rat or had been warned by some unseen spy. Yet the roundup went on the same as before, moving nearer to the *malpais* each day. On the morning of the third day, as they were camped under a rocky hill, Butch Brennan suddenly appeared on the ridge. He was riding the *chula* and coming down at a trot, and, as the outfit who were at breakfast glanced up from under their hat brims, they saw her shy and leap snorting from the trail. Brennan grabbed at the horn to save himself from a fall. As he came up cursing, there was a whoop from behind and Wild Horse Bill racked over the hill.

"What's the matter, Butch?" he laughed, as Brennan lashed his frightened horse, and then his own mount shied. A thin, searching sound, like the hiss of escaping steam, rose up above the *clatter* of scrambling hoofs, and even the Figure 4 horses drew back — it was the warning note of a rattlesnake.

"Let's kill the bastard!" exclaimed Bill, fighting his horse to a stop and dropping his reins as he dismounted. He stumbled about on the hillside, searching for a rock small enough to throw, and, while the posse looked on with their hearts in their mouths, Butch Brennan made his fatal decision.

"Aw, let 'im go to hell!" he answered impatiently, and spurred on down the hill. In the excitement of the moment he had barely glanced at the posse — the wagon and cook he knew, and the broad hats of the cowboys were the same that the Walking X boys wore — and he had dropped down to get a drink before the intense stillness of the men suddenly warned him that something was wrong. He had been fighting his mare, and the rattlesnake had diverted him, but now he came back to earth. He glanced about quickly, alarmed at the strange faces, and then his eyes fell on Meadows. He was sitting like the rest, with a tin plate across his knees — and Dave Starbuck stood behind him, near the wagon. Brennan saw it all then and he knew he was trapped, but his nerve did not fail him in the pinch. Once before he had weakened, but this time he was game — he turned swiftly and started toward his horse.

"Well," he said, addressing his remarks to the cook. "I see this is no place for me." Then he made the break.

It had to be done or his doom was sealed, for the law would hang him surely — he made a run for his horse. But the *chula* was frightened and excited by her beating, and she flew back and made a swift plunge. Brennan saw his last hope gone and he swung about cursing, just as Meadows rose up to shoot. Meadows had withheld his fire before, for fear of hitting the *chula*, but now they both drew at once Meadows was standing at a crouch with Starbuck close beside him, and in the fraction of a second that preceded his shot

267

he heard Starbuck's rifle *bang*. Brennan rocked before the blast and the dust rose from his coat where Starbuck's bullet had struck, and then Meadows shot him twice. Brennan's bullets passed over him, for he was shooting wildly, and, as he turned to run, his legs crumpled under him and he fell face down in the dirt. The firing suddenly ceased, the *chula* snorted and backed off farther, still staring at the body of her master, and then the crowd of cowboys were scattered like rabbits by a plunging fire of bullets from the hill.

In their rage to shoot down Brennan they had forgotten Wild Horse Bill, still standing where he had stopped to kill the rattlesnake, but Bill, after the first shot, had run to his horse and snatched his repeater from the saddle. Now, when they looked up, he was pumping the bullets down at them, standing boldly in the middle of the trail. Every man but Starbuck made a rush to escape them — he stepped out and answered back. Three times he shot and Bill did not flinch, but as he was turning to run, a heavy bullet seemed to lift him and throw him on his face among the rocks. His gun clattered and fell, and Bill lay sprawling for a moment, clutching feebly at the jagged lava. Then, while they looked on in horror, for he was well liked by all of them, he squirmed swiftly away behind a rock. A minute later they saw his hat bob up from a deep crack that led into the shattered lava. When it was too late, Starbuck saw his mistake, for he had allowed his man to escape. Not that he regretted it overly much, for he bore no grudge against Bill, but by that much he had neglected his duty. He had steeled his heart to kill without mercy, but pity had held his hand. Yet Wild Horse Bill was badly hit and the hill on which he hid was a single, jagged outcropping of lava. Starbuck rushed for the rocks. As his posse followed after him, they cut off all chance of retreat. Wild Horse Bill was surrounded and Starbuck's voice was almost gentle as he called on the outlaw to surrender.

"Go to hell!" shrilled Bill, his voice savage with pain. "I'll kill the first bastard that shows." He lay groaning and muttering, then rose up in a frenzy and emptied his pistol among the rocks. "You got me," he moaned as they called to him again, "but I ain't whipped yet . . . I'll fight back till I die." He stood them off while the posse crept slowly closer. It was agonizing for all of them, but he held firmly to his purpose and at last they called for Meadows.

He alone of the posse had remained at the wagon, looking on in heartsick silence, but when they called him, he came up quickly and added his voice to the rest.

"Oh, Bill," he called, "this is Ab Meadows speaking . . ."

"Well, you can shut up, then," retorted Bill. "I ain't got no use for you. You framed this all up, to git Butch."

"Yes, and I got him," answered Meadows, stung to the quick by his tone, but Wild Horse Bill hooted derisively.

"Yes, you did!" he mocked, "same as you got that Mexican deputy. You let Starbuck shoot him first and then you chipped in on it . . . I killed that damned deputy myself."

"No, you didn't," returned Meadows. "I know what I did. But say, Bill, be reasonable. We all want to help you. Give up and we'll get you a doctor."

"Yes, and, when I git well, they'll take me out and hang me. I know what you boys are all fishing for . . . you want to take me alive, so you can put in your claim for the reward. You're a bunch of dirty dogs, if you want to know what I think. You killed me, by grab, for the blood money."

"No, we didn't," protested Starbuck, "we don't want a dollar of it. You just surrender now, Bill, and I'll do everything I can for you . . . I'm sorry I had to shoot you."

"Well, you ain't half as sorry as I am," cursed Bill. "I wish I'd killed every one of you. I'd 'a' done it, too, if I'd knowed who you was . . . I thought you was the Walking X outfit."

He rose up from his hiding place and glared about with pain-mad eyes, and then he began shooting again. So it went until Meadows sickened of the scene and went down to wait for the end. His cup of bitterness was full to the brim — Wild Horse Bill had cursed him for a traitor. All their friendship in the past, their farewell in the lava beds, all the bonds which had bound them as partners were gone and forgotten now, and, as he lay there dying, Bill boasted of his killings, naming all the officers he had shot. But of one thing Meadows was sure, Bill had not killed both the deputies. He remembered the scene perfectly, the big Mexican up there shooting at him while he stopped to take careful aim. Of course, he and Bill might both have shot at the same time, or perhaps — but no, if Bill was doing it to protect him, he would never have cursed him like that. He had never cursed him before, there had been nothing but friendship between them, and now — he shuddered and turned his head, and at last they brought him down, all that was left of light-hearted Bill, the partner that he had loved to the end.

CHAPTER
TWENTY

The return to Show Low was a long agony for Abner Meadows, for the death of Wild Horse Bill had poisoned his triumph over Brennan and left him broken with grief. He had vanquished Brennan, yes, and won back the *chula*, but Bill was gone and he had cursed him and haunted him now with his hoarse, cackling laughter. It was not like Bill. They had always been friends, but the pain had driven him mad. If he had known what he meant, he would never have spoken the way he did, but he had cursed them all and died unrepentant, an outlaw to the end. Now he lay silently, wrapped up in a blanket, beyond the reach of prayers or tears.

They buried him on the hillside just above Show Low, and, as the crowd went away, Meadows made a rough cross and placed it at the head of his grave. It was said at the burial that the sight of those two graves — one for Bill and one for Brennan — would be a warning for all young men, but for Meadows one held all that he had loved in the world and the other all that he had hated. They had buried them side-by-side and gone down to the store, where the cowboys were buying the drinks, and no man or woman had lingered but him, unless Justina was waiting. She had ridden by twice, going to and from the schoolhouse, which was closed now until the fall term, but she of them all had been the hardest on poor Bill and he would find no sympathy there. Not since the day when she had called him a thief had he spoken to or looked at Justina. She had hoped she would never see him again, and now she never would. At noon he and Starbuck were to start into town, where he must stand trial for killing the Mexican deputy, and then, if he came clear, he would mount up on the *chula* and ride till he found a new range. If he did not come clear, then he must lie there in jail while Dave Starbuck tried to square him with the law. But with Justina, who had tried to save him, he would never speak again. She was one more regret, another millstone in his life, something more to try to forget.

He took the bridle off the *chula* and hung it on her saddle. While she nibbled the short grass, he gazed at her sadly, for she was all he had now to love. Bill was gone, and Justina — and with a horse like the *chula* the time would soon come when some Mexican would steal her, too. But Justina had not forgotten him because, as he sat there thinking and looking down at the store, the rocks rattled behind him and she came along the hillside on Nipper.

"I just wanted to tell you . . . ," she burst out eagerly, and then she glanced at the graves. "Why do you stay here, by them?" she asked with a shudder, and Meadows shrugged his shoulders.

"Bill was my friend," he said, and looked away at which she dropped down and came over closer.

"Well, what I wanted to say," she went on hastily, "is that I'm glad he told what he did, and, if it will do you any good, when it comes to the trial, I'll come down and testify, too."

"Testify to what?" inquired Meadows, glancing up almost sullenly.

She went on undeterred. "Why, to what he said when I found you in my cabin. Don't you remember . . . when I charged you with killing the Mexican deputy he assured me you didn't do it?"

"He'd say anything," returned Meadows, "to accommodate a friend. I guess I'll get along all right."

"Oh, of course," she began angrily, "if you don't want my evidence . . . but don't you think he did it? The boys all say that they *know* he did it now, they'd swear to it on a stack of Bibles because, if you and he had been friends, he might have confessed to it to protect you, but he cursed you out worse than any of them."

"Yes, that's right," admitted Meadows. "I can't hardly get over it . . . but I know who killed that Mexican. Bill might have killed one, but I killed the other and . . ."

"Then he did it to save you!" she burst out impulsively. "I'm sorry I was always so hateful to him. Isn't it wonderful that he should do it . . . and he knew if he cursed you . . ."

"I believe he did!" exclaimed Meadows, his face lighting up. "I believe he did it on purpose. He knew

274

they'd believe it, then." He turned to Bill's grave and stood there in silence. "Well, thanks," he said at last, "you've taken a load off my mind. But I don't think we'll need you to testify."

"But why?" she demanded. "After he's done all this . . ."

"He meant well," answered Meadows, "and that's the main thing . . . but I killed that Mexican myself."

"And are you going to go down there, after all he has done, and let it come to nothing? Why, that wouldn't be honest, it wouldn't be right . . . can't you see that you owe it to him . . . now?"

Meadows turned away again and gazed down at Bill's grave, and at last he bowed his head. "You're right," he said. "He was a good friend, after all, the best friend I ever had."

"Yes, he was," she murmured, "I . . . I tried to be your friend, but I guess I didn't know how. I disliked him because he was a thief."

"Yes, and I'm a thief, too," answered Meadows, flushing. "I believe you mentioned it once. But all the same, Justina," he went on hastily, "I'll never forget what you did for me. I was going to give you something that would help your case against Woolf . . ."

"Oh, what is it?" she cried. "You know that woman has come back and she's frightened him nearly to death . . . he's giving her money and everything. Did she tell you what it was she had on him?"

"Yes, she did," admitted Meadows, "and, when I helped Bill rob his store, Woolf told me what it was himself. But what I wanted to give you was this bill of sale . . ."

"What about Chris Woolf?" she clamored, her face going white. "Did he kill my father?"

"No, he didn't . . . he was too cowardly for that . . . he hired that man to do it for three hundred dollars." He pointed to Brennan's grave, and she caught her breath angrily, then turned and seized him by the arm.

"You come along with me," she commanded resolutely. "I'm going to tell Mister Starbuck."

She started off afoot, oblivious to everything but the stunning news she had heard, but Meadows drew her back and helped her on her horse, and they rode away at a gallop. She was all aflame now, raging and inveighing against Woolf for his part in the horrible crime. When they met up with the sheriff near the store, Starbuck shook his grizzled head, and Justina relapsed into brooding silence. The fox was not trapped, and many times before he had eluded the carefully spread net. It was necessary, if they would entangle him, to proceed by degrees, beginning with his title to the ranch. But if they would do as he said, Starbuck promised them both that he would land the rascal in jail.

He led the way into the store, with Meadows beside him and Justina following closely behind. When Woolf saw them coming, he bustled out from behind the bar, while the cowboys evaded Justina's eye. The store was not a store, it was a barroom now, and the cowpunchers who had ridden with Starbuck after Brennan were ringing their money on the counter.

276

"Good morning," greeted Woolf, looking his visitors over swiftly. Then his eyes rested on Meadows. After that night in his office, when he had sold Ab his ranch and then treacherously wanted to murder him, he had never ceased to egg on his pursuers in the hope that he would yet be killed. Now at last he beheld him with the sheriff on his way to stand trial for his crimes.

"Vell, vell," he said, smiling ingratiatingly at Starbuck, "so you are taking him down to town. The last of the gang, and I'm glad for that . . . he helped them rob my store. Was there anything else I could do for you?"

He stood wiping his hands, the typical shopkeeper, but his piggish eyes roved restlessly about, for he knew he was handling dynamite.

"There is a little matter of business," began Starbuck ponderously, "before I take Ab to town. Can I see you in private a moment?"

He started back toward the office, and Woolf ran before him cringing for he guessed what was in the air. He had given a bill of sale for sixteen thousand stolen dollars, and they had come to call for an accounting. But Woolf was no craven except before a gun. In matters of business and in everything but sheer fighting he was as brazenly aggressive as the boldest.

"Vell, what is it, what is it?" he asked, tittering nervously, and Starbuck handed him the bill of sale.

"Is that your signature?" he asked, and Woolf nodded and leered at them slyly.

"That's my name," he said. "I don't deny that, but this bill of sale is no good. It was obtained by duress and violence. I have consulted with my lawyer and he tells me it is valueless . . . and besides, the purchase money was stolen."

"From the express company, you mean? Well, if that is the case, I'll have to ask you to return it. I'm sheriff, you know, and, of course, if it's stolen . . ."

"But I don't know it then!" protested Woolf in a panic. "I accepted the cash in good faith. And my lawyer has told me that . . ."

"Well, in that case," put in Starbuck, "I guess the bill of sale is good. That's what we wanted to know."

"Good!" echoed Woolf. "Don't I told you it was illegal, that it was obtained by duress and violence?"

"So you say," returned Starbuck, fetching out another paper. "But how was this bill of sale obtained?"

Woolf stared at him a moment, his lips worked noiselessly, his ferret-like eyes on the move, and then his gaze shifted to Justina. She had been watching him from the first with a sort of hateful fascination, a world of loathing in her eyes, and now her anger burst forth.

"You know as well as I do," she exclaimed in a passion, "that paper was obtained by fraud! It was signed in a barroom and won in a gambling game . . . and what's more, you had my father killed! You hired Butch Brennan to kill him!"

"I did not!" denied Woolf, suddenly shrinking away from her. "I assure you, Miss Edwards, upon my word of honor as a gentleman . . ."

"Didn't you tell Meadows," demanded the sheriff sternly, "that Butch Brennan had killed John Edwards?"

278

"That's another thing," asserted Woolf suddenly, finding firm ground again. "I'm satisfied myself that he did. But what I told Meadows would not stand in court because it was obtained by threats of violence. He stood with a loaded pistol at my head, and I said that to keep him from killing me."

"Oh, he threatened you, eh?" observed Starbuck shrewdly. "Well, what about this woman, Rose Sheridan? Did she resort to violence?"

Woolf's face turned dead white, then flushed an angry red. "That woman!" he screamed. "Would you believe what she says? She's a criminal, a blackmailer . . . I've paid her thousands of dollars, and, listen, I tell you something more!"

He stepped closer, as if to reveal some great secret, but as he was about to speak his jaw dropped on his breast, for a dark form had glided in through the door. It was Rose herself — she had been listening outside — and, as she stepped in, she fixed him with her eyes. They were big and black, with a flicker of venom that was more fearful than the hot flames of hate, and she smiled at Woolf disdainfully.

"You pig," she began in a voice that cut like a whip, "I've heard what you've had to say. Go ahead now, if you like, and tell him the rest of it. Never mind about the truth . . . speak out!" She curled her lips again and drew out a bundle of letters, and, as Woolf divined her purpose, he made a savage rush, only to be struck to the floor by Starbuck.

"Oh!" she mocked as she drew her skirt away from him, "you thought I was afraid of you, didn't you? Well,

279

I'm not, and, if those letters don't do the business, I'll come down and testify myself." She glanced at him again, and then swept out of the room, handing the letters to Starbuck as she passed.

He pawed them over slowly, examining the addresses through his glasses, and then he began to read one through, while Woolf fawned and sobbed at his feet.

"How's this?" frowned Starbuck, his eyes beginning to blaze, and then he looked down at Woolf. "Oho!" he said, "so that was your little game? You're the man that sent the tips to Brennan. Well, that explains a lot of things, and, incidentally, it gives me the goods on you. So git up, Woolf. If I wasn't an officer, I'd wring your neck like a rabbit." He fetched him up with a bone-wrenching jerk and shook him like a rug. "You scoundrel!" he burst out. "It was you killed my son by selling him your cursed whiskey. You and Brennan and that woman . . . but I believe in respecting the law." He paused and stood panting, his great hand closed down on Woolf like a pitiless, crushing mechanism, and then he turned to go. "You're arrested," he said. "I'll do my duty, like an officer. But if the court don't do *its* duty, I'll resign my position and make you answerable to me . . . personally." He rushed him out the door, dragging him clattering through the barroom, but as Meadows started to follow, he suddenly remembered Justina.

She had sunk down in a chair — one that her father had owned when this house had been her home — and buried her face in her hands. When Meadows came back, she looked up. Never before had he seen tears in the clear gray eyes which made her look like Botticelli's

"Queen of Spring". They had always been laughing, or full of the divine discontent that somehow added to their charm. But now there were tears on the misty lashes and a glance of appeal in the gray eyes, and he stopped in the midst of his stammered farewell to take her outstretched hand. An impulse swept over him to take her in his arms and speak as they had spoken long before, but nothing but sorrow had come from those words and he stood silently amid the ashes of the past. He drew his hand away and sat down with paper and pen, and, as he wrote, she looked over at him inquiringly.

"I hope you didn't think," he said at last, "that I intended to keep your property. You probably won't need this, because Woolf's title was obtained by fraud, but I'm writing you out a bill of sale."

"But the money!" she protested. "You paid him sixteen thousand dollars. And, besides, I can't take it, anyway."

"I think you can," he said, "when you understand the circumstances. Otherwise you would place me in the unenviable position of trying to steal your property. I admit, in advance, that the ethics are badly mixed, but because one thief robs another thief of something he stole from you is no reason for not taking it back."

"I don't know what you're talking about," she answered impatiently, "but I'm not going to accept that bill of sale."

"All right," he said, rising abruptly from the table. "You'll get back your property, anyway. Only this will give you possession at once, and you can go out and close down that bar. Wasn't that what you wanted to do most?"

"No, it wasn't," she replied, more resolutely than ever, and he noticed a strange look in her eyes.

"Well, you can pay me back the money," he went on at a venture, "and you don't need to worry about its having been stolen, because I've squared that all up with the company. My reward for getting Brennan more than makes up the loss . . . and they agreed not to prosecute, anyway."

"Oh, did they?" she cried, suddenly sitting bolt upright. "Then you're free, except for this case of the deputy. Oh, Ab, I didn't realize that! And all the time, when I wouldn't even speak to you, you've been trying to give me . . . this!"

She reached over and caught up the bill of sale and clasped it to her breast, and then she looked at him again. There was something in her eyes more disquieting than ever, and he looked about dumbly for his hat.

"Well, I'm sorry," he began, "but before I go . . ."

"Oh, but I'm going, too!" she cried, bounding up. "Well, I just guess I am! You don't think I'm going to sit here while you're tried for your life . . ."

"Oh, that'll be all right," he protested with a shrug. "But Justina, if you wouldn't mind riding down the road . . ."

"Well . . . what?" she challenged, and he looked down at her smiling.

"There's something I'd like to tell you."

"What is it?" she smiled back, and, when his eyes answered, she sighed and sought forgiveness in his arms. "Do you love me?" she asked, "do you love me still? Then nothing matters . . . and we'll begin all over again."